Praise for Lauren Dane's
Revelation

"REVELATION totally caught me by surprise and turned out to be an awesome read! The plot and its twists and turns, the characters and their development, the beautiful and at times surprising romance rife with intensity and some very hot sexing, it all came together to create a perfect read and have me desperate for more in the world of the De La Vega cats."

~ *Pearl's World of Romance*

"Once again Lauren Dane delivers another awe-inspiring tale that captivates the imagination and leaves readers questioning when the next DE LA VEGA CATS story will be released."

~ *Romance Junkies*

"The book has laughter and excitement with alpha males being brought to their knees by their alpha mates, and bigotry and conflict as Max and Kendra battle the mages and others who want to stop the mating of witches and shifters."

~ *The Romance Studio*

"I loved getting lost in the enchanted world created by Lauren Dane! Revelation is another perfect example of her astonishing writing skills. This book has it all - thrilling suspense, super-hot passion and a mystery that kept me glued to my seat. Kendra was a protective, compassionate, smart and strong heroine, while, Max was a very strong-willed, powerful, drop-dead gorgeous alpha that demanded respect with just his presence. Oh what a perfect match! As you can imagine the passion between the couple was intense and lusciously hot. I highly recommended Revelation to all!"

~ *Fallen Angel Reviews*

Look for these titles by
Lauren Dane

Revelation

Lauren Dane

Samhain Publishing, Ltd.
577 Mulberry Street, Suite 1520
Macon, GA 31201
www.samhainpublishing.com

Revelation
Copyright © 2010 by Lauren Dane
Print ISBN: 978-1-60928-132-8
Digital ISBN: 978-1-60928-110-6

Editing by Anne Scott
Cover by Mandy M. Roth

First Samhain Publishing, Ltd. electronic publication: July 2010
First Samhain Publishing, Ltd. print publication: July 2011

Dedication

Thanks go to Vivian Arend, who gave me this title after I'd been searching for some time.

Anne Scott who took me on when I needed a new editor—thank you for your endless patience and your fabulous edits (even if you won't let me say "just" every three sentences).

Various people who make my life better simply by existing—my dude, Ray, who fills me with happy, my kids who make my hair gray but keep me on my toes, my parents and friends.

And as always thank you to all my readers!

Chapter One

Kendra sat up in her bed on a strangled gasp, her hand outflung to ward off the danger she'd dreamed of. Before she could shake off sleep enough to call Renee to check on her sister, her phone rang.

She scrambled to grab it as the dream wore off and set her free.

"Yes? What's happening?"

"Kendra, can you come over please?"

Kendra shoved her hair from her eyes, getting out of bed and yanking pants on. "Jack?" she asked, recognizing her brother-in-law's voice. "What's going on?"

"Renee's had a dream. She's upset and she won't talk about it without you."

"Give me a few minutes. I'm on my way."

"Max is on his way to your apartment right now. I'd send one of my men, but he's closer and obviously capable of protecting you. Don't leave until you know it's him."

"I don't need an escort," she managed to say as she pulled on her bra and then a shirt. *Max.* A delicious warmth pushed away some of her panic. Still, it wasn't time for adolescent mooning over a boy she could never have. "I'll be there in five minutes."

"Kendra, your sister will kill me if something happens to you because you were attacked." Jack's voice lost some of its bite. "She's safe now. I know you're worried. Just sit tight. Please?"

She smiled, knowing he couldn't see her and also that he loved her sister with a ferocity she'd only ever seen in a shifter. For such an alpha male to break down and plead only made her more worried about her sister even as it pleased her that he clearly adored Renee.

She sighed. "Fine. Just keep her awake and don't let anyone inside until I arrive. If he's not here in five minutes, I'm going without him."

His sigh was way less tired and more agitated.

"What? Come on, Jack, I'm worried about her and she's there and I'm here. I can't wait all night. I'm worried. All right?"

"All right. And Kendra?"

"Yeah?"

"Thank you."

"I love my sister. It's not a thing."

She hung up and put on shoes while she brushed her teeth quickly. Max de La Vega was one of the hottest men she'd ever laid eyes on, the least she could do was not look like a hag when he arrived. They'd exchanged some looks. Mild flirting. Renee had told her he was dating a woman, another jaguar shifter, but had broken things off a few months back. Renee seemed to think it was about Kendra. She'd love to believe that, but he was not her normal fare. Like a five-star restaurant with all the dollar signs and she was that little pho shop down the hill that everyone loved because it was good and fit a budget.

Hm. That didn't necessarily sound right. But whatever, it was an argument she was having in her head, who would judge?

She heard the purr of an engine and looked out to the street where Max had just pulled up. Not bad. Four of the five minutes she'd given Jack. He probably drove like a crazy person, which given the situation, she appreciated as she jogged down the inner stairs and outside to meet him.

He—*good sweet heavens*—looked soooo good standing there on her stoop she nearly forgot her sister was in trouble.

"Did you look through the peephole before you came barreling out here?" he asked her in that voice, the voice she'd been thinking about since she'd first heard it nearly four months before. A rumble, a growl and sometimes if she was very lucky, nearly a purr.

Still, *hello*, she wasn't a five-year-old.

"Nope. I rushed out here with dollar bills pinned to my shirt."

He snorted, a smile hinting at the corners of his mouth. "Come on then, car's right there."

If by car, one meant a sleek, black jaguar. Which, okay, she laughed and he looked at her sideways.

"What?" He hustled her inside the still-running car, and he lectured her about opening her door? "You're a black jaguar, am I not supposed to notice your car is too?"

Without asking, he reached over and belted her in before squealing away. "Watch the upholstery, you're going to rip it to shreds."

"If you didn't drive like a maniac I wouldn't have to hold on so tight. Also, you left your car running! You lectured me on opening my door, which yes, I did look out first, I'm not a moron, and your car was unlocked and running on a city street in Boston at three in the morning."

"Who's going to steal from me, Kendra? Hmm?"

He had a point she supposed. "It's not like a thief is going to know you're some super-dooper alpha jaguar shifter."

He laughed then. "Oh little witch, you're so smart and powerful and yet, naïve sometimes. Predators always know other predators. Or they become prey."

Oh.

"I'm nearly five nine, I'm not little."

"You are compared to me."

Hmpf. If he wasn't eleven feet tall that wouldn't be true. Then again, if he wasn't six and a half feet tall of delicious chocolate skin, he wouldn't be as ridiculously sexy as he was. Which would be a shame because he was the fodder for many of her best masturbatory fantasies.

"Why are *you* on guard duty anyway?" She pretended to ignore the way he drove all while fervently thanking the universe for airbags.

"Galen asked. It was you. I came."

It was her? Really? What did he mean? That she was Renee's sister and so his relation? Or her specifically because he had fantasy wankfests about her? Gah, okay, she didn't need to go down that road just then. They turned onto Renee's street, and she tensed, holding her bag ready.

"Hold on, babe. No need to hurt yourself jumping from a moving car," he said, screeching to a stop.

"Babe?"

"I could call you sexy if you prefer."

She huffed an annoyed breath, swinging her door open and jumping out. "I'm not that girl, Max de La Vega."

"Dream on, Kendra. You are and more," he murmured as he got out on his side, making her all flustered. Several times over the last few weeks he'd turned her into goo with silly things. The way he looked at her, or some tossed-out comment.

At first he'd sort of been wary, but friendly. Slowly though, it had felt as if he'd begun to focus on her in an altogether new and non-related sort of way. His attention wasn't so much off-putting as intense. He had a way of looking at her, intimate, as if he brushed her skin with his lips as he stared.

They were all that way, the shifter males, no matter the rank, they were intense beings. They paid attention on a level she hadn't thought existed.

This one in particular also had a way of moving like there wasn't a damned thing in the universe capable of scaring him. He owned every single step he took. Simply expected everyone to pay attention and be there when he needed it. Like the way he handed his keys off to Gibson, Max and Galen's brother and the Bringer of the jamboree, who tossed them to another guy who drove off without a word.

Cripes, there were at least six shifters out in front of the house, all on guard. Their magick filled the area with loam and fur. Her magick always rose in the presence of Weres, it flowed around her like a warm breeze.

Gibson cleared people from the base of the steps and nodded at Kendra. "They're inside waiting." Gibson rarely said much, but damn he was pretty to look at.

Two extra-large males flanked them, leading them into the house. She really had no idea how Renee could take all this coddling and manhandling. It drove her nuts.

"Come on up. Renee is waiting for you." Galen motioned to her and she pushed past the guards to jog up the stairs to her sister.

"She's in the bedroom," Jack stood at the door, directing her inside.

13

Renee was there, sitting in the bed, her eyes wide, glossy from unshed tears. Kendra went to her, hugging her tight. Their connection snapped into place, filling Kendra with the warmth of their like magick.

"Shhh. I'm here. You're here." Kendra pushed the hair from Renee's face. "No one else is." She knew her sister would always carry the fear that something or someone had gotten inside her. Who wouldn't be after her experiences in the last several months?

"You sure?"

She nodded. "Would you like me to scan you again? And the room too?" She could simply barge in and see herself, but Kendra believed very strongly that it was a violation of her gifts to not seek permission to use her magick on another person in anything other than self-defense.

"You can do that?"

"We have something called othersight. Some of us have more than others. It's like you with healing, right? Each of us has a unique set of gifts. We talked about this before, and I think you're coming along so well I can teach you."

"Then yes, please."

She stood and went to where Jack guarded the open door. The place had filled up with so much alpha shifter it stirred her blood and messed with her concentration.

"I need to close the door. There's a lot of energy out there. It's like white noise. You can stay in here, or just on the other side. All right?"

He nodded once, his gaze returning to Renee, who smiled at him, relaxing the rigidity of his spine a bit.

"Whatever you need."

She closed the door after squeezing his hand.

"Okay then." Kendra reached inside herself, unlocking the door to the well of her magick, letting it flow outward to fill the room. Through the eyes of her magick, she saw nothing but Renee's energy, green and vibrant, connected in a thousand ways with Galen and Jack. Their bond was written all over her, all over the space. That protected her.

There was nothing else inside her sister, but her sister. Though she could see the marks made by Renee's past and whoever had manipulated her memories. It had scarred her, but Renee would heal.

She opened her eyes, letting the energy swirl back to where it belonged. "It's just you inside. There's something outside. A shadow of something. I can't tell yet if it's old or new. But what's in here, it's not dark like before. The wards will hold." A shadow was a whisper beyond the wards and Kendra had a feeling that's what had awoken her from a dead sleep just a few minutes before.

"Thank goodness. I dreamed she knew. I dreamed, no, not dreamed. Kendra, she, Susan, had something to do with Mom's murder. She knew and they did something to me. They put something in me to make me forget."

Kendra's breath gusted from her lips. "Your memory came back?"

"Not all. But parts. I was on the swing set in the backyard and they were talking about Mom being dead. Talking about what to do with me. He knew. He was in on it. Our father had something to do with her murder." Renee's gaze had been on the past, but it sharpened, focusing on Kendra's face. "You knew it."

"Not for certain, no. But it felt logical. Logical that the way he'd acted pointed to his guilt on some level." She hadn't mentioned it because her sister hadn't been ready to hear it.

But the man had abandoned an infant and then had disowned another for daring to ask questions about her own past. That had guilt stamped all over it as far as Kendra was concerned.

"We need to call the police." Renee sat up, stronger now that she'd been given the all clear.

"The police can't help us and you know it. You need to drink that tea and go back to sleep. We don't know where he is yet. Rosemary and Mary have been working on finding accurate locator spells. We've tried a few, but they haven't worked so far. There's nothing we can do right now but be patient."

Jack tapped on the door, poking his head in. "Is she all right?"

"Some of our aunt's spell is working. Her memories are unknotting, rising to the surface. This happens while we sleep a lot because our consciousness is at rest. She's all right. The house is clear, the wards are holding."

"What can we do?" Galen came in, pressing a mug into Kendra's hands before moving to Renee and giving another to her. "Drink it."

"He was part of her murder," Renee said softly. Kendra didn't have to ask who *he* was. Renee had just told her their father had a part in their mother's murder. A fact Kendra had long suspected.

Kendra settled in and tried to stay patient.

"The memory... I was on the swings in the backyard. She came out, Susan, and they talked about Mom, how she was dead. They started talking about me. She said Mom had written spells into my skin, into muscle and bone, and they couldn't kill me. He-he said she should put a pillow over my face." Renee's voice broke and Kendra wanted to hurt their father very much.

"He'll get what's due him. I promise you that." Kendra meant every word. What had happened to their mother needed

16

to be avenged. What they'd done to Renee, and to Kendra. They needed to pay and they would.

"Susan told him they could drain me for years. They broke my memories."

And Susan had been drawing from her since. A chill passed through Kendra at that. "It's what kept you alive. That and the wards Mom made for you. It also means we know for sure Susan is a mage. She's stealing magic."

"We have laws for dealing with thieves and murderers." Jack took a deep breath as he drew his fingertips along Renee's temple. "And anyone who dares to hurt those weaker, like women and children, have a special place in hell. I'm going to kill them both to underline that point."

Kendra patted his arm. "We have to find them first. I'm working on it with Mary, my teacher. It's a matter of finding the right, um..." she paused, searching for the right word, "...frequency. That's not it exactly, but it's close enough." Her head began to hurt, and she remembered she had to be up in a few hours to get ready for her third day of work. She had been building a normal life and it wouldn't do to be late to this great new job. "I'm going to go back home. She's shaken up, but aside from that, she's fine."

Kendra leaned down to hug her sister. "I'll be here after work for our lessons. There's no reason to be any more vigilant than you were yesterday. But still reason to be on your guard. You're safe here and safe at work. Don't let him win."

"I'm sorry for dragging you out here when you have to be at work so early."

Kendra laughed at her sister. "You have to be up even earlier than I do. Anyway, that's what family does. I love you. You needed me and I came. End of story."

"I'll walk you out." Galen looked to Jack. "Get her settled,

17

I'll keep the guards. Can't see wasting them since they're here already."

"Great. More guards." Renee frowned.

They couldn't protect her anyway if the attack was a magickal one done over a distance. Still, Kendra knew despite her sister's annoyance, she felt safer in the presence of Galen or Jack and the guards. Kendra didn't blame her either.

"Stop whining. I'll see you later today."

"Love you! Hey, how'd you get here so fast?"

"Max brought me."

Renee looked to her and back to Galen. "Don't forget she rode over with someone. Make sure she's taken care of."

Galen merely stared at Renee for a long moment and she grinned sheepishly. "Right. I'm sure that's already done because I'm married to the most efficient and careful men on the entire planet."

"Precisely." Galen winked and escorted Kendra out to the main room where Max reclined on a chair, very much the king he was in line to be. Relaxed. On the surface. But Kendra had felt his power from the other side of the door in Renee's bedroom. Even then as he sat on the chair, she saw the tension there, the energy bound up in his muscles, waiting to strike if and when it was necessary.

"No one would ever steal a car from him." This made her a bit cranky as her car had been stolen just the week before and found totally trashed some sixty miles west.

Galen looked at her askance for a moment. "Max? Hell no. No one would dare."

She started to laugh, but then the snap of Max's attention landed on her and all she could do was stare at him as he stared at her.

In the background she knew Galen spoke. Max answered. Other big giant males stalked around looking menacing. Funny how Kendra had found herself used to, even comforted by, at times, the new reality of her life in Boston.

Max knew the moment she'd finished, felt the subtle and delicious shift of her magick. He loved that about her. She was rich and spicy with power, a scent so heady it made him drunk whenever he was around her.

The first time he'd laid eyes on Renee's sister he'd been hooked. Hooked on her scent. The sound of her voice. Her prickly demeanor. Oh how he loved that she could be so bitchy. She was a woman who would brook no bullshit, though he had the feeling she hadn't always been so.

As a human, even being a powerful witch wouldn't overcome the prejudice some of his jamboree would feel about her. As such, any woman he'd bring home who wasn't a shifter needed a strong will. When he brought her home the first time, and he would, she'd need to set the tone. He'd talk with Renee about it, knew his parents would be behind the relationship, as would Galen and Gibson. The rest would be hers to win over or scare into leaving her alone.

He had a plan for the future of his jamboree. A plan to leave behind the rules that reinforced the prejudices of the past. Kendra would be integral to that, a partner in the future of his people.

Kendra was it for him. The person he'd been waiting for. His father had always told Max he'd know it when he finally met the right woman. Mainly Max had thought that had been a bunch of woo-woo bullshit. Until Kendra.

He'd been dating someone until right after she'd come to

19

town. It'd taken him a little while to be sure his attraction to Kendra wasn't just about her ass, and God knew it was the finest ass in all creation. Damn he loved each and every mouth-watering curve Kendra Kellogg possessed. Once he'd known it was more than chemicals dancing around between them, he'd broken things off neatly and carefully and given himself some time between the breakup and the asking out. Not that he'd stopped thinking about her, or that he hadn't spent every moment creating a plan of attack. He was, after all, a predator.

Now it was time. He didn't like it that they didn't share enough intimacy to have him come into her apartment and have him stay the night. If she'd been a Were, things would have been different. She'd have either bloodied him for getting too close, or pounced on him if she wanted him. She wasn't a Were though, she was human and his behavior needed to reflect that. He wanted her to be totally safe, totally comfortable, and watching her just then sent his cat pacing with wanting her.

He stood, loving the way she greedily took in how he looked. Sending her a raised brow and a smile, he held a hand out. "Ready?"

Taking his hand, she sent him a look that went straight to his toes. "Thanks. I'm sorry you have to run me home. I'm sure you have to be tired too."

"It's my pleasure to take you home, Kendra. I only need about four hours sleep each night anyway. I'm often up at four so I can work out before I go to the office." He walked her out, sending Galen an annoyed look when he hugged Kendra. Gibson, of course, saw the look and delighted in not only hugging Kendra, but kissing her cheek.

"Come on, let's get you home so you can rest a little before you have to be at work." He shot Gibson a raised brow, promising retribution as they walked past. His brother, nonplussed, rolled his eyes and flipped Max off. *Punk.*

He wanted to drag out his time with her, but saw the fatigue written into her face. "You're not getting enough rest," he said as he stopped at a red light.

"It'll be better in a few weeks, once I get myself situated here better." She blew that little lie with a yawn.

"How's school?"

Kendra had recently started teaching a third/fourth grade combo class at a private magnet school. He knew the school was very prestigious. The judge he was appearing before in just a few hours had two kids who went there.

"I haven't been there long enough to know a whole lot, but from the experiences I've had so far, it's really good. I'm lucky to have the opportunity to work with the rest of the faculty and the students. It's a sister school to the one I taught at back in California, so it gave me a bit of weight in the hiring process. The opening was right exactly what I needed and where I'd fit best." She shrugged. "It was meant to be."

"Yeah. I think so too."

He pulled up in front of her building. It was a decent enough place, had been Jack's before so it would be safe, though probably smelled of wolf. Max managed to hold back a sneer. Not that he didn't like wolves. He just didn't want his woman smelling like one, a male one who'd mated with his brother and sister-in-law.

He could get past that part because he knew for sure she'd be safe there. The place was also close to Renee, which was important to Kendra. Near the T stop she took to the school since her car had been stolen. Well lit, though he'd been looking for those little fuckers who'd stolen her car. He would find them eventually. Gibson was on it. No one stole from their people and got away with it. He hated the very idea of her being without a car, even in a city as mass transit friendly as Boston. And he really hated that she'd been taken advantage of by thugs.

"Is Renee going to be all right?" He sent her that damned raised brow when she moved to grab the door handle and she sighed heavily. "I'll get the door."

"It's really not necessary," she said as he opened it for her.

"Of course it isn't necessary."

"So you're doing it why?"

He laughed, brushing her hair from her face. "Because I want to do it. I like doing it."

"Oh. Why?"

"So full of questions. Because I want to take care of you. It pleases me."

Her frown was more of confusion than anger or fear. She had the sweetest line between her eyes, most likely from her tendency to wear every single emotion on her face. Not that he'd say so. Females tended to get pissed off when you pointed out any wrinkle, even if it was one he wanted to smooth away with his lips.

"It does? Well then. I..."

Fascinating. He'd flustered her.

He didn't resist his desire to slide his thumb over that line between her eyes. She relaxed, slightly leaning into his touch, most likely not even knowing it. "No need to say anything. Right now anyway. Time for rest."

She shook her head with a sigh, apparently letting go of whatever it was she was going to say. "Renee is fine. The wards are holding. She's growing and her control of her power is also growing. I gave the place a look, there's nothing inside that's bad. She's just remembering things. I'm sure Galen told you."

"Some." He frowned, hating that she and Renee had to

shovel the emotional shit their piece-of-crap father had left in his wake.

"The memories she's regaining, well..." Kendra paused, the pain on her face. "I hate to say it, but for a time anyway, it was better she didn't know all this. Probably kept her safe. What could she do as a child with that anyway? But she's not that child anymore and she's fine now. Stronger than most people assume."

He brushed his thumb over the dark smudges under her eyes. What he really wanted to do was to pick her up and take her to his house. Wanted to get her a mug of tea, a hot bath, a massage and lots of sleep. Oh and sex. But mainly the taking-care part because she needed it.

"You're *both* strong. Now, I'm walking you to your door."

"It's really fine. My place is safe."

"I'm sure it is," he murmured as he hustled her up the steps, waiting for her to unlock the outer door.

"You're just going to leave your car?"

"We went over this before."

She snorted. "Some people have all the luck."

He laughed. "We'll get you squared away with this car situation."

"My insurance is getting me a check. No need to square away anything." She unlocked her door and he went in first, taking a deep breath and instantly going hard.

Christ, her scent drove his cat nearly as insane as the man. Not even a hint of wolf. It was all sexy, fertile witch, and it brought a moan he had to tamp down. The cat had more patience because he knew she was his. But the man knew it would take a lot more than being his to lure the sexy Kendra Kellogg into his life and keep her there.

23

"All clear. Just you in here." And now him. He smiled when she couldn't see his face.

"Really? Golly I'm pretty sure I said that already."

God he was messed up. Just the sound of her sarcasm made him have to fist his hands rather than haul her to his body and kiss her until she melted.

"You did. And now I can heartily agree with your assessment. Go to sleep, Kendra. I'll see you later today at Galen's."

He went to the door but paused, changing his course and moving back to her. She looked up at him, her sleepy green eyes wide.

"I forgot something."

"What?"

"This." He leaned down—careful not to touch her or he'd have her clothes off in five seconds—and kissed her.

Just a soft, slow brush of lips against hers. She opened her lips to him, the sweetness of her mouth tempting him to do more.

Instead he made himself stop after one last nip of her bottom lip.

"Sweet dreams, beautiful Kendra."

He left, smiling as he caught sight of her peeking out the window at his car, running, sitting next to the curb.

Inside, she watched him drive away, her lips still tingling from the unexpected and very lovely kiss. She'd wanted more, wanted his hands on her, wanted him to take her to the mattress and be inside her.

Max was the kind of man she'd never imagined would be interested in her. But he was the kind of man she understood without a doubt would know his way around a woman's body.

Despite his broody, bossy ways, she liked him. She just didn't know what to do with him or how to handle him. He wasn't a man to be handled, she understood that, but she also realized he would never stay with a woman who didn't push him back and keep him in line.

That sort of man took work. She wasn't opposed to hard work, she just didn't know if she had it in her to give it to him.

Chapter Two

Kendra watched her sister as magick flowed through her and into the room. Renee's magick was vibrant and green, it soothed and caressed. There was so much within her sister, so much untapped power. She would be as powerful a witch as their mother had been. They'd both been gifted through that line.

Watching, Kendra remained quiet and centered; the hum of her own magick, fiery and bold, a constant as she remained in balance.

She'd never imagined how lovely it would be to be able to teach her sister how to use her gifts, how to be the one who unlocked these miraculous doors for Renee. So much love and trust there between them had helped Kendra immensely. Her magick came to her easier, smoother and with more focus since she'd moved to Boston.

"Try to control the ball on the far table."

Renee breathed in deep and breathed out, a tendril of her magickal energy sinuously moving to the small globe on the dining room table.

The ball rose as a grin of delight broke over Renee's features, Kendra's surely matched.

"Excellent. Now back down."

Renee did so, carefully placing the globe on the table and spooled her energy, taking it into herself once more, and letting it dissipate.

She turned to Kendra. "I totally did it!"

She hugged Renee. "You did. You're doing a great job, I'm proud of you."

"You are?" Renee's smile widened and Kendra wanted to smack their father for the number he'd done on Renee and her self-esteem.

"Of course I am. You're a natural." Kendra shrugged, they both were. Born to wield magick. "You're doing fabulously. You won't need me in a few months."

Renee shook her head. "Now that I have you here, I can't imagine life without you. I know you gave up a lot to come here, more than I can possibly ask you to." Renee tried to look nonchalant, but they were connected, and finding each other again had reinforced that connection. She felt Renee's worry that Kendra would leave.

Kendra took her sister's hands. "As it happens I like it here. I'm afraid you're stuck with me. I can't imagine my life without you either."

She liked the opportunity for a new start as she thought briefly about the protection order she needed to get now that she'd settled in Boston. The fact that Ronnie was all the way across the country was soothing to her.

Renee's surprised look twisted in Kendra's heart. So surprised when people expressed their love for her. Startled to think people loved her. Kendra sighed inwardly, angry at the way Renee had been raised, hurt that it had been without support or love, with hatred and derision aimed at her powers when they should have been groomed and celebrated.

She knew what it felt like to be loathed for her gifts, but in

27

Kendra's case it had been a few years, for Renee it had been daily during all her formative years.

"Thank you." Renee smiled. "What's the news with Max?"

She blushed. "Nothing to report. He's all pushy, lays a kiss on me and then nothing for three days. I'm not being fair." She snorted. "He did call me, just to check in, when he couldn't make the game a few nights back. And then he texted me to say he'd be on some case and couldn't break away, but he would soon."

"He's ridiculously hot."

"He's overwhelming sometimes. I don't quite know how to deal with him."

Renee laughed. "Yeah well, it doesn't really get easier. Shifter males are all overwhelming, pushy, hot to have sex all the time, control freaks who also bring you tea when you're sick and even buy tampons when they're out and about and you need them. It's going to be impossible to resist Max."

"Not that you're biased or anything. He's like the president of your fan club." Kendra sent her sister a raised brow.

"He's certainly a favorite of mine. Those de La Vega men are yummy. Only one is an idiot."

The two of them started laughing and couldn't stop until tears ran down their faces. Kendra cherished this connection more than she could ever express.

Her sister was a good woman, smart, loving, compassionate and as talented as Kendra. They just seemed to click together. The intimacy they'd found, the depth of friendship and sisterhood had startled both women. Sometimes Kendra's affection seemed to overwhelm her sister, but once she acclimated, she took it into herself, feeling bold enough to love in return.

On the other hand, Renee had so much love around her right then it made Kendra a little jealous. Sometimes it was lonely, her new life in Boston. But that kiss three nights before had blown her socks off. The beginnings of something with the very handsome Max de La Vega were taking hold and she liked it. A lot.

"Idiots or not, they're easy on the eyes. If we could only duct tape Carlos's and Beth's mouths closed, it would be perfect. However, none of that matters because neither frick nor frack will be here and visiting your house is like a hot-guy buffet."

Renee grinned, looking a lot like their mother. "I know! Now that they all hang out over here so often, I really love getting home from work."

"And now you're a magickal superstar who can use her power like a rock star."

"I'm working on it. This calls for a prize, a treat, a celebration. Let's go get chili dogs."

"You *must* feel like celebrating." Her sister was a fairly health-conscious woman, Kendra rarely saw her eat what could be termed junk food. "I knew you and I were related."

Renee laughed as they stood and headed out into the living room area of Renee's home. Both women stopped and just took in the sight in front of them as males of all shapes and sizes, though all equally gorgeous, lounged and watched a game on the big screen. Including Max.

"Wow." Kendra blinked at the absurdity of it. At how much testosterone and alpha maleness had gathered all in one place. Max was at home there, in the group, and yet apart as well.

They grinned at each other as the lazy gazes caught the newcomers to the room. Nice thing was that even with a giant screen full of football, they turned to take the women in. A girl could make her way through a pretty crappy day with that memory.

Max sent her a look that tightened her nipples. A look filled with sensual promise. She couldn't remember the last time a man looked at her that way. And damn it felt good.

It was then she felt it, the darkness hurtling toward them. Without thinking, she threw a shield up, stepping in front of Renee. Her lips moved as she began to weave the spell, hoping the protection warding on the outside would stop whatever it was.

"Stop!" She raised her hands as she walked from the main room out onto the landing. Her regular vision had clouded as she used her othersight to keep track of the spell. The interior of the house choked with magick. Magick from the wards, from the spells she and her aunt had put in place, from Renee and Kendra, and all those shifters had their unique sort of magick as well. She couldn't get enough of a read with all that interference, though she was able to use it to strengthen her power, using some of the things Mary had taught her before she'd gone away.

"What can I do?" Renee put her arm around Kendra's waist. The soothing energy filled her as they linked.

Cat and wolf joined them, enraged males in full protection mode prowling around, their growls bringing the hair on the back of Kendra's neck up.

"It can't get past the wards." She relaxed slightly, but never let her attention waver from the threat outside. The fullness of all that magickal energy washed over her, adding to the strength of the walls to keep the darker magics out.

"Is it the same as before?" Jack, Renee's other husband asked—a reference to a series of magical attacks on Renee just a few weeks before.

She listened to it, thought over it before looking to her sister. "What do you see, Ren?"

Renee licked her lips. "It seems...not exactly the same, but similar."

"I agree." She turned back to Jack. "I need to go outside. Keep her in here."

"Oh, no fucking way." A male just slightly smaller than a mountain stepped in her path.

Being kept somewhere by force was a real hot button. Max or not, no one kept her where she didn't want to be. Not anymore.

She stepped back, trying to remain rational. "I have to go out there to get a better read. All these shifters in here have their own sort of magick and I can't see through it to get an accurate estimate of what's going on."

His eyes weren't brown, they were deep black, like obsidian, and they gave him an air of absolute authority and no small amount of menace. He was fiercely beautiful and standing so close to him sent all sorts of signals rushing through her system. She swallowed and blinked a few times.

He noted her deliberate distance and didn't move to close it, but she could see in his body language that he wanted to. Part of her responded, liking it. But not all.

He clenched his jaw and she watched, fascinated until he finally spoke. "Just because Renee was the target before doesn't mean *you* won't be now. You could be in as much danger as she is. Now that it's known you're her sister, how can you be sure you won't be attacked like she was?"

She frowned. "Because what she is, is altogether unique due to the nature of her bond with Jack and Galen. I'm just a run-of-the-mill witch. Powerful, yes, but not that unique. In any case, it needs to be done, Max. With the dream Renee had just a few nights ago, we have way more questions than answers."

She moved to walk around him and noticed the other shifters standing nearby were all watching Max, as if he was the boss of her!

Galen put a staying hand on her forearm. "Maybe you should stay inside."

It was the wrong time for it, it wasn't his intention and she knew it, but she recoiled anyway, hating that weakness in herself and her inability to get past it.

"I need to go," she muttered and tried to get down the stairs.

"Wait! Kendra, are you all right?" Galen followed her and Max moved past them both to block the door.

"I need to go outside." She grabbed the door handle but as Max leaned there, the door wouldn't budge. "It's gone! Let me out." She flicked her gaze up into Max's face and watched his temerity fade into something else. Not so much pity, but he definitely saw into her more than she wanted him to.

"Let me go," she growled at him. He smiled slowly, chasing part of her fear with tingles of pleasure. She had no idea what to make of him. At all.

"Galen, why don't you take everyone back inside and call Rosemary?" Max's voice was a sexy rumble, though he kept his body against the door. His attention shifted back to her. "You and I need to talk."

"I don't think so, buster. Our aunt isn't in town right now and I'm as good as she is at this point anyway. *I'm telling you it's gone.* All this was for nothing because you're blocking my way. I don't like being held someplace without my permission." And she didn't like how her voice broke.

"Max, move out of her way." Renee pushed her way through

the throng of men on the stairs and down into the entry. "Can't you see you're scaring her?" she said far more quietly.

Kendra took a deep breath and rubbed her fingers across her eyes.

"Stop talking about me like I'm five. I need to go and you're going to let me, Max de La Vega, or I will *make* you." She stared him in the face and held her ground even though she knew the headache she'd get in a few minutes would make her sorry.

"Doesn't look so scared to me. Your sister is made of pretty stern stuff." He broke his gaze with her to look to Renee. "Sweetheart, why don't you go back upstairs with Galen and Jack? I'll make sure Kendra is safe." Max's look at her sister was fond, it was clear he liked Renee and Kendra liked that. However, he was still a giant, *hot* lunkhead.

"Kendra, are you all right?" Renee asked, undaunted by all that testosterone.

Not right now. She just couldn't. "I...we can talk about it another time. I'm okay now. I just have to go."

"Max, back off!" Her pint-sized sister pushed at Max, who looked over her head to Galen, who shook his own.

"Kendra, did I hurt you?" Galen asked, concern clear in his features.

"No, no you didn't." She wanted to reassure Galen, but the whole situation was beginning to be embarrassing and she wanted to escape. "Really, I don't want to talk about this anymore. Ren, you and I will get that celebratory chili dog tomorrow, okay? After school is out, I'll meet you at the smoothie bar and we'll go."

"You can stay over tonight if you want. Have pizza with us." Renee took Kendra's hands.

She kissed Renee's cheek. "Thanks. I appreciate it, but I

think you understand about being alone sometimes."

Renee nodded. "Why don't I drive you home?"

"I've got it, Renee." Max stepped away from the door, moving everyone back a step.

Kendra used that moment to grab her coat and head out onto the porch. "Stay inside, Ren. You call me if it comes back. Trust the wards and yourself."

She waved and jogged down the steps, taking a deep breath of the nearly freezing air into her lungs.

At the gate, Max caught up with her. "Where do you think you're going?"

"I'm checking the warding, Dad. That okay with you?"

"As a matter of fact, no. You're making yourself a target right now. What if this thing is still out there waiting?"

"Of course we're being watched! I'm not even a freaking next in line to the throne of a jaguar jamboree and I know that. But we're being watched one way or another anyway. Why not know who it is? Why not work to gain as much information as we can? With all we suspect right now, I can't believe you'd expect me to just pretend and hope it all goes away."

"You know, you're a school teacher."

She blinked up at him. He was so random. "And?"

He growled and paced. "You're supposed to be quiet and gentle and sweet."

She began to wonder if he'd knocked his head on something. "Oh is that how I'm supposed to be? I wasn't aware. You're the one who's totally random. I thought lawyers were supposed to be logical and liked gathering information before making judgments. Did you huff Lysol or something? What's wrong with you?"

He stopped and stared before a laugh erupted from him. A

deep, smooth, smoky laugh that sent her agitation fleeing.

"What? Now you're laughing at me? Haha! *I'm a super sexy jaguar, fear me!*" she mimicked.

One of his eyebrows rose and again with the tingles. The man was a menace. "Do you think the laugh was to make you *afraid*? Why do I get the feeling that when it counts, you push past the fear and do what needs to be done?"

Not like anyone else was going to do it for her. "Max, don't try to analyze me, I'm not that interesting."

He stepped close, not scaring her at all, just sort of stealing her breath with his nearness. "Sexy huh?" Leaning down, he nuzzled at her neck, and she had to trap the groan she wanted to give him for it.

"I'm trying to work here." She hated that her voice had turned breathy like a cartoon-character vixen.

"So am I. You've been here long enough to get to know us, see how we are. It's in my DNA to protect."

"Is it in your DNA to sniff me?"

He did it again and this time she couldn't stop the soft sigh of pleasure from sneaking through her lips.

"It's because you smell so good. Your magick, the way your skin smells right here below your ear, drives me crazy. Three days since the last time I could touch you, taste you." He licked her neck and she nearly came.

Her heart thundered in her chest as she stepped back. "Shut the fuck up while I do this. You're messing with my concentration." She stomped off, annoyance warring with warmth and undeniable sexual chemistry.

She was right, there was no threat outside. Still, Max shadowed her as she moved, giving her the space to work, but keeping close enough to protect her if it was necessary. He didn't hide his smile. He messed with *her* concentration? Every breath Kendra Kellogg took messed with *his* concentration. Even now as she did her magick mojo thing, moving around the yard efficiently, spilling that vibrant red-golden, warm magick in her wake, she took up every bit of his imagination and attention.

She was spirited, a huge turn-on for him. He loved women with an attitude, smart, strong women who didn't take any shit. He liked her sense of humor and the way she stood up to him.

His cat loved her strength. She was fierce, the kind of woman a man could trust.

It probably wouldn't have been as bad if he hadn't scented her. Twice. That was more intimate than the brief kiss of a few nights ago. Now her scent lived in him. God in heaven she smelled like sex. Like sex and comfort; like strong, sexy witch, and his cat practically kneaded his insides to get to her.

No one had affected him the way she did and he didn't quite know what to do with it. What he did know was the idea of her being in danger had set his cat so close to the surface he paced, on guard, just to keep his human skin. He supposed it was simply another piece of proof that she was indeed meant to be his.

"What do you sense?" he asked when she got near enough to hear.

"Nothing. Not even a smear of the dark energy. Maybe I was wrong." She frowned, shivering. He stepped closer, giving her some of his body heat, satisfied when she stopped shivering.

He doubted very much that she'd been wrong about the attack, though. He'd watched her from day one. She seemed to have a good grasp of her abilities. "Do you really think so?"

She thought for long moments before shaking her head no.

"I don't think I was wrong at all."

"Me either. I think you felt it and I think your father has something to do with it."

Her eyes lost their warmth at the mention of her father, not that Max blamed her. He'd be right in line behind Jack and Galen when they finally got hold of Andrew Parcell, or whatever the fuck the man was really named.

"Now that we know he had some involvement in my mother's death, I have every reason to believe he's connected to these other attacks. I don't like that. At all. I don't know what they have of Renee's. That bitch most likely kept her hair or other physical links. I think I found a way to nullify that. When I find them they're going have to deal with me. I *will* find them. And they'll pay. For what they did to our mother, and for what they did to my sister."

Christ, when she got bloodthirsty it only made him want her more. He cocked his head and spoke before he meant to. "You enchant me."

That startled her. "I do? Is that a good thing?"

He laughed. "Yes. No. Hell I don't know, but I like it. I plan to explore that. With you. Just so you know."

She pursed her lips. "Oh." She licked her lips, as if she tasted the words before saying them. "All right."

He shook his head at her when she grinned his way.

She'd hit him like a bus, knocked into his consciousness when he had least expected it. Kendra Kellogg left him dazed and wanting more. Earlier that afternoon when she'd come out of Renee's office he'd just watched her. Fascinated that she looked like Renee, and yet totally different. Her chic curtain of super straight hair, short enough to leave her neck exposed, those eyes, far more green than brown, thickly lashed and God, the dimples at each corner of that fucking delicious mouth—she was the loveliest thing he'd ever seen.

He'd been deep in a naughty fantasy about a hunt to see if she had any more freckles than the ones he'd seen on her forearms, when her entire demeanor had changed, became serious.

His cat had gone on instant alert, dragging all the cats in the room into hypervigilance with him. Jack had as well, the wolves cued to his moods in much the same way. Max had stood, looking to her. Taking his cues from her.

It had been the way she braced her feet apart and took on an onslaught of dark magics that had really pushed him into acting at long last. The kiss had been impulsive, but now he was decisive. He wanted her and she needed to know it. Her ferocity had pushed every last one of his defenses away.

That and the look of fear and panic when Galen had touched her and he'd blocked the door, the recoil she was able to get control of fairly quickly. Someone had done that to her, hurt her so that despite her strength, her first instinct was to try to make herself smaller and get out of arm's reach. Like prey.

Every male on the landing and in the hallway had felt it, seen it, and went into overdrive, wanting to protect her. Max did what he always did, he acted decisively and in doing so, found himself totally off balance and unsure for the first time since he was a teenage boy.

"Whatever it was or whoever sent it, it's gone." She looked around the yard, pretending he hadn't just told her he'd set his cap for her. "It's fine out here," she said quietly.

"Are they safe?" He jerked a thumb toward the house.

"None of us are safe until this is dealt with. But this house and yard will hold safely. I'll go out to Cambridge tomorrow and talk with Mary."

"Mary?"

"She's a powerful practitioner, a friend of my aunt's. Mary's been away for a month, but left a note that she'd be back this week and told me to stop in." Kendra reached for the gate, and in her full view, slowly but firmly, Max put his hand over hers.

"You look shaken. I'm taking you to dinner."

She opened her mouth, most likely to argue, these sisters were quite alike on that front.

"You can tell me about Mary and your plans. Fill me in on just how safe you are at your apartment too. Gibson will only ask me about it tomorrow anyway."

"You're bossy."

"So everyone tells me. It's my job to be bossy. But you're no doormat, I know it and so do you." He reached out and ran a fingertip over the tips of her hair. "No matter who tries to make you feel otherwise."

"Why do you want to take me to dinner? Really?"

Oh she had *no* idea. He smiled at her, slow and assessing. Her eyes widened and then slid a quarter down, sexy and slumberous and all sorts of buttons and levers got pushed at the sight.

"I want to take care of you. You look pale. Got a heavy scare. And I like you."

"Even if I'm feeling like steak and lobster?" She smirked, teasing. He liked it. Only his family teased him. It was intimate and showed she trusted him.

"Mmm, sounds very good." He held out an arm and she sighed before taking it. "What? You thought I'd be scared off by an expensive dinner? I know just the place and you can have the biggest lobster in the tank if you want."

"And cake?"

"Two slices, if that's what you desire. Though they make a mean crème brûlée you might want to try instead."

"If you're sure you wouldn't you rather be inside watching sports and eating pizza with your friends."

"I'm sure. I can get into a fight over football with Galen any day of the week. My office is only two doors down from his. If I need trash talk, I know where to go for it."

He opened her car door and helped her inside, looking up and down the block before he got in on the driver's side.

Her scent rose between them, warm, sharp and vibrant. He breathed deep before pulling away from the curb. *Yeah, that's the ticket,* he thought. He could easily get used to her there in his car.

"Seems to me you two do more than talk trash. Renee and I tease each other, but I've never broken her nose."

He burst out laughing as he navigated through traffic. "You aren't shifters."

"Is that why your sister Beth has been such a bitch to Renee?"

He sobered with a heavy sigh. "Beth has issues. Not because she's a shifter."

"She's a bitch either way," Kendra murmured and he laughed again.

"She is. But something tells me when you come into the family you won't take any guff from her."

"Come into the family?"

"I don't believe in pretending not to see the inevitable. You and I are inevitable."

She made a snorting sound. "You're pretty sure of yourself."

At a red light he turned to face her. "Comes with the alpha

territory. I'm a confident man and you, gorgeous witch, are an intelligent woman. There's something between us. You and I are going somewhere, and I think it's silly to pretend otherwise."

She bit her lip, consternation on her face. "Light's green."

Max grinned and kept driving.

Chapter Three

The place was small, a neighborhood steakhouse with old-school dark wood paneling and leather chairs. Candles in votives cast spare light into the room, but enough to see where to walk. She didn't need light to smell the heaven wafting from the kitchen anyway.

"Max! It's good to see you." An elderly woman toddled over and Max grinned at her before hugging her and kissing both cheeks.

Rapid-fire conversation in Spanish followed. They talked about her. The woman thought she was pretty, told him it was about time he saw women who had curves, flesh, hips made for babies. Max said he liked that too, grinning as he requested a bottle of the house red and the house special for both of them.

After the brief introduction, they'd settled into a booth she felt swallowed up by.

"I don't drink," she murmured.

He looked at her, surprised. A stab of satisfaction lanced through her. He'd had her so off balance she was glad to turn the tables on him.

"What? You think a white girl like me can't speak Spanish? Or are you offended I don't drink?" she teased.

He laughed. "Kendra, I'm pretty sure a girl like you, white, brown or pink, can do lots of things. You're just that able I suppose. As for you not drinking." He shrugged. "What's it to me? What would you like instead of wine?"

"Coffee would be good and then water. What's the House Special?"

"Steak and lobster. Meat is aged, lobster is the size of a compact car. Stuffed mushrooms and a salad to start. Creamed spinach, a baked potato to go with the entrée and crème brûlée to finish. Or you can have the chocolate decadence cake, if you prefer. It's an excellent meal."

"Yeah if you're four people." She laughed.

"I'll eat your leftovers." He looked up as a server brought the wine and some glasses. "Thank you. Can you bring coffee please? And water."

She liked this man. Liked the straightforward way he dealt with everything. He wore his confidence like a second skin. He radiated everything she'd ever thought was good in a man. Everything she'd not chosen before.

A basket of bread called her name though she knew she'd get filled up, she couldn't resist. "Want a slice? This is so good and warm that I'm feeling generous and I'll even butter it for you."

"Who am I to refuse such an offer? Yes, thank you."

Their fingers brushed as he took the bread from her and heat radiated through her. And then he brought it to his lips and she had to clamp down on her nerves to keep from shivering. Cripes she'd never found herself so ridiculously hot for a man that merely watching him take a bite of bread would make her wet.

The food began to arrive at a leisurely clip and Kendra relaxed as her blood sugar balanced. She'd overdone it and depleted her body as well as her magick. If she hadn't had

Renee and the shifters in that room to tap into, she'd be in bed with a blinding headache. Before Mary had left, she'd given Kendra some exercises, ways of gathering the ambient magickal energy all around to enhance her own power. Without that, dealing with whatever had attempted to attack them earlier would have been far more difficult.

"So, tonight?" Max started as he speared a mushroom and ate it whole.

"What about it?" She busied herself with the food in front of her.

"Why didn't I notice your snarky streak before today, I wonder? I mean, I noticed your bitchy streak. And I mean that as a compliment. But the snarky thing..." he paused as his gaze roamed over her face, lingering on her mouth before he spoke again, "...well that's new."

"I just grow on people that way I suppose. Or maybe you never looked closely enough." Most people didn't. Most people looked at the surface and never went any further.

He leaned toward her, giving her that focus she knew shifters were known for. Renee had told her once that when she first met Galen, when he'd given her his total attention she'd been totally swept off her feet.

"Oh I've looked. Kendra, I've looked and looked and looked some more."

She swallowed hard, her mouth suddenly dry.

"Tonight when Galen touched your arm. You reacted. I scented panic when I blocked the door, but you're not afraid of me. What was it?"

She turned her face away, not comfortable with the topic. "I wanted to follow up and go outside. The fresher the trail of whatever magic is used, the easier it is to identify and possibly trace back. In fact, because they possess artificial energy, magic they've stolen rather than magick they've earned, it's easier to use to track them. I was eager and you all treated me like the stupid, fragile woman who didn't know her ass from a hole in the ground. Of course I reacted."

He sat back as they brought her coffee. She stirred and he watched.

"Did you know that jaguars are keen hunters? We'll just wait and wait until the perfect time to pounce." He poured a glass of wine. "This doesn't bother you?"

"No. It's fine. I don't drink, but I don't care if you do."

"Okay then. So, here's the deal, I'm going to let you go for now. But you need to know that I know your answer is bullshit. My nose doesn't lie and as it happens I'm damned good at reading people."

While she loved and didn't fight her physical attraction to him, he seemed to have this power to look right through her. It left her exposed and uncomfortable.

He leaned back in his seat again. "Tell me about yourself. You pick the topic."

"Why?"

"Why are you so defensive? I like you. I want to know you better. You can't know people unless they tell you things about themselves. Help me here. Unless you don't want to get to know me." She might have felt bad, but the look on his face as he said the last bit was so arrogantly confident she couldn't. She was, despite herself, charmed.

"I'm a teacher. I love junk food with an unholy level of devotion." She paused when a plate was slid in front of her, heaped with a lobster the size of a terrier and a steak so beautiful she nearly wept. "Wow. This is...wow."

The server beamed. "I'll pass that on to the kitchen."

Max nodded his thanks, turning his attention back to Kendra. "Why did you become a teacher?"

She ate a few bites, feeling a lot better when she had. "My aunt is a teacher. I grew up around teachers. It just seemed like it was what I wanted to do and be for as long as I can remember. I like my job a lot. This school I just started with has a curriculum I really believe in. My kids are all smart and reasonably well behaved." She smiled, eating more. "Oh my God, I'm so glad we came here. This is the best restaurant dinner I've had in a very long time. This place is special."

He grinned, obviously pleased. "I'm glad you're enjoying it. The owners are my godparents so I grew up coming to eat here. All our family birthday dinners were here. Still are."

That was nice. And it made him even more attractive.

"Why are you a lawyer?"

"My dad is. My mom was, now she's a judge." He gave a one-shouldered shrug, and she tried not to goggle her eyes when they brought him a second steak. She wanted his metabolism. But no. *Her* ass got fat when she ate too much and *her* car got stolen while he could eat eighty-five pounds of food and be all hot and hard. The man left his car running at the curb for heaven's sake! Hers got stolen in less than two months since she'd moved to town. He was gorgeous, intelligent, well spoken, sexy, arrogant, well educated, powerful, and he had a lot of money. Jeez.

"What on earth are you thinking?" His voice broke into her thoughts.

"Just that I wished I had your metabolism."

"Mmm hmm. Anyway, like you, when I was a kid I knew it was what I wanted to be. In high school I was on the debate team and we had a mock trial. I was hooked on trial work from then on. I love my work. I'm good at it and I get to do it with my family. It's a nice continuity in my life. I like it when things work that way for me."

"Somehow I don't think they'd dare to be otherwise. I'd love to see you in action someday." She picked up her coffee and drank, mentally kicking herself for saying that out loud.

He smiled in that way of his and it made her tingly.

"Any time. You're in the building to see Renee just about every day, you should stop by my office." He leaned in. "Have I ever shared this recurring fantasy I've had about you, me and my desk?"

She nearly choked on her potato as heat flushed through her. She wasn't going to let this slip through her fingers not when she wanted him so much. "You haven't. What's stopping you now?"

The smile turned seductive and then secretive. "You haven't told me about these magick lessons you're getting from Mary."

"Are you a tease, Max de La Vega? Hmm? Get me all worked up only to fall back?" She crossed her legs, squeezing her thighs tight.

He raised his brows for a moment as a smirk played around that mouth of his. Mischief lit his eyes and damn it, she fell a few more feet for the man.

"I like you, Kendra Kellogg. You keep surprising me in all the best ways." He took her hand a moment, kissing her fingertips. "Here's the thing, I want to know you. We'll have sex. Lots and lots of it. I plan on taking my time exploring every lush inch of your body. For now? The lead-up will be foreplay."

"Are you always this pushy?" Reluctantly, she pulled her hand back because, well, how could she get to her lobster without it? And if she wasn't going to get laid, she might as well eat some lobster.

"I am. My mother says if she'd have let me, I'd have run the entire household by the time I was six or so. But she's a bigger alpha than the rest of us so I learned from the best. I'm bossy, but not controlling. Yes?"

She held his gaze for long moments as he saw right to the bone. She wanted to run and hide, but at the same time, just having someone know her felt good.

Taking a deep breath she said, "It's not what you think."

"What is it then?" He took her other, non-lobster-eating hand, concern on his face.

Could she tell him that story here? She didn't think so. "No. Not here. Not right now. I'm sorry, I shouldn't have even said that. You unlock stuff inside me and I find myself blurting things out."

"Why don't you drink?"

Gah! "So what did your mother do when you got all nosy and pushy? You know, to get you to back off and let a girl eat her eight thousand calories in peace?"

He laughed. "You and she like each other. She told me the other day that she thought you'd be perfect for one of us. She thought maybe Gibson. I disagreed quite firmly with that."

She'd met his mother twice now and the woman was scary, but also vibrant and absolutely gorgeous. She had this energy, the sort of personal gravity that pulled people's attention to her.

Most shifters felt different to her than humans. Their energy, that personal electricity that was the spark for her own magick, seemed to be set at a lower frequency. A hum she felt in her belly. But most of them, while extraordinary, were of a normal kind of extraordinary. Which, she knew seemed odd, even to her brain, but it was the only way it made any sense at all.

But some of them, the ones who tended to be more alpha in their group structures, possessed the sort of magick laden with something else, unique and delicious. It made them charismatic, some more polarizing than others. Compelling.

Max was this way. His mother more than his father, though his father had something else, a paternal energy that was strong but nurturing and protective. It was rare for her to feel so comfortable around a man his age. His jamboree respected him and feared him because he was the kind of man who took care of things when they needed doing. No matter how they needed doing.

Kendra had to admit she was wildly curious about shifters, most especially the cats. There had been some literature she'd come across online, but not a lot and some of it was mythology. They'd kept to themselves and attempted to keep details of their lives, vulnerabilities and strengths out of the public eye. Too much attention left them dangerously exposed.

As a result, most of what she knew had come from Renee and what she'd seen herself in the time since she'd come to Boston. They didn't mate the way wolves did. There wasn't a mystical bonding that occurred after sex. Instead, cats had this intensity of connection with their imprinted partners. It looked very much similar to the wolves' bond from the outside. The details of the imprint seemed to hinge a lot on the individual cat and his or her partner, but there was some sort of chemical attraction and scenting along with biting. Not like a vampire or anything. A mark of sorts. Kendra couldn't help the warmth in her belly at the thought of Max biting her like that.

Max waited, she knew, understanding she was running through all sorts of stuff in her head. The smile he wore told her he knew she had sexytime thoughts in there too.

"I can't wait until you know me well enough to share

whatever it is you're thinking right now. When Galen first brought Renee around, I thought she wasn't good enough for him. She was human, and despite where we are now, there's still prejudice. And she was, she is, hard to get to know. So they met and Galen left on a trip with Armando. Armando is the baby of the family, he and Galen are tight. Anyway, Galen starts telling me about this woman he's in love with." He worked his way through the rest of his food and she pushed her still-heaping plate toward him before she exploded. And she had to leave room for cake.

"So he brings her to Sunday dinner at the house. Now, as you know by this point, Sundays with us are way more than just a meal. Any given Sunday there will be thirty people there, kids all over the place, lots of playing and physical stuff. So he brings this woman and she's tiny and sort of scared and I took one look and judged. Which is stupid of course. In the first place, Galen is not an idiot about people the way he is about football. And because after about three hours with her, I knew she was so much more than what she appeared to be."

She frowned because he was sweet and a big part of her, though not the part where her clit resided, hated that he was because she wanted to keep him away and he just kept sliding under her defenses.

"I'm telling you this, because I want you to know me too. Because that's how you build something. Story by story, experience by experience. I ask because, yes, I'm nosy, but mainly because I want to figure you out. I want you to let me in."

She didn't want to talk about other stuff, but she could share her plans and the things she was learning. "Mary is teaching me how to channel other energies. She's been teaching for thirty years. Rosemary and she were friends back in the day. She knew my mother too."

She paused when a platter filled with desserts appeared with a flourish.

"I hate to say this, but I am so full. I don't think there's any way I could eat another bite."

"You can have a bite of mine." Max ordered the crème brûlée. "Just one and then I won't pester you again."

"I suppose I can do that. I wouldn't want to disappoint you or anything." She took a spoonful and moaned at how outrageously delicious it was. "You so weren't kidding."

When she opened her eyes, it was to find him staring at her in that way of his, and it sent a shiver through her.

"I love to watch you eat. You know that? You're a sensual woman, graceful and carnal even. It's"—he took a deep breath—"tantalizing."

She fanned herself with her hand. "You're such a tease."

He tossed money down on the table and stood. "Will you invite me to your apartment? Or come to mine? I want to talk with you more and we should probably be in private when we do."

She nodded, pretty much unable to speak because he looked so good and she wanted him so much.

Chapter Four

On the way out, she'd stopped to talk with Lettie, thanking her for the lovely meal. Max liked that she'd shown respect for a woman who was a great deal like family to him. Kendra had ended up at his side, close enough for him to shelter with his body as he walked her to the car.

She'd simply been where she was meant to be. A silly thing maybe, but it spoke to him and his sense of fate.

"I can buckle my own seat belt thanks," she said dryly, slapping his hands back.

"I know you can." He would take her to his house. Let her scent live and breathe in his space. Show her what he could build for her, make for her, keep her safe and happy in. It would be *more* than a house, it would be a home. For both of them.

"So Mary is your aunt's friend and she's a witch like you?"

"Yes. Sort of. Mary, when she was young and left California, ended up with some not-so-nice people. It's where she learned the darker kinds of power and magic. Then she met Craig, that's her husband. He's not a witch at all. A scholar actually. She was a student in his class, using him to get at his access to the museum's antiquities collection. It was all very cloak and dagger. Instead, she fell in love with him and gave up dark magic. But she understands it, understands how energy works, and unlike a lot of other witches, she's not afraid of other traditions."

She said it while looking out the window. His brain was still crowded with all the details from dinner. From her deliberately sexually provocative behavior. Under the surface, Kendra Kellogg was even more interesting than on the outside. She'd rolled with his demeanor, had batted away his overly pushy behavior, but had opened up as he had. Had let him in a little. On her terms. In short, she was proving to be his match on every level.

How could he resist that?

"And she's teaching you? How to deal with whatever is trying to get to Renee?" He paused. "And you. Damn it." Of course. Of course she was a target too, and of course she hadn't said anything. Though it was so obvious he wanted to kick himself. She wasn't only a target due to her proximity to Renee, they'd want her for her, taking the threat against her to a completely different level.

"What's the harm in being prepared? Even for a highly unlikely situation? Anyway, the kind of practitioners we're dealing with, the ones attacking Renee, aren't super powerful. Most of us aren't. So I figure it's a good thing to know how to deal with them. They use magickal properties and energy differently. Hard to fight it if you don't know how. Some of them don't use magick at all, at least not the kind Renee and I have."

Fascinating. Though he was pissed off at himself for missing the clues, he loved how she thought about things. Strategic. Orderly. A lot like he did.

"How so? I mean, how do they use magic differently?"

"In the most harmless of cases, they learn to manipulate other forms of energy to use them in their own spellcraft to supplement what they've already got. Not all of those things are bad. Tonight, for instance, I was able to grab the magickal energy in the house to supplement my own. Shifters have theirs, Renee lent hers to me, and there's power in the wards too. They just go a step more and use negative, but hugely powerful forms of borrowing or theft. Blood. Pain. Fear. Death. All expel a great deal of energy. What I have is natural. I was born to it, it comes to me when I call. That's magick. What they have, when they steal energy to enhance spells is not the same. They call it magic, without the K. It's harmful to the wielder and it's gained without permission. You can't control that sort of energy, not all the time. It's not natural."

"They kill for power?" His cat didn't like that one bit.

"Yes. Or, they hunt around to find people like Renee, who have unique magickal signatures or properties. She, Galen and Jack have this loop, they didn't set out to create it, it just is. But she has this huge draw, which makes her a target. Not that she knew how to use her magick before she mated with Galen and Jack, but her reserves, her infinite possibility has always been there. I believe this is why Susan kept her around.

"Of course, you add in the way Susan tormented her as a child and you get a pretty heady brew of power to leach off. Negative emotions have power too, power enough to have been attractive for these witches. Mages. Whatever they want to call themselves."

"Essentially, they're thugs. Renee's energy is special so she's like extra HP or whatever."

"HP as in video-game power?"

"Haters to the left, Kendra. I like a little video game action to get rid of a hectic day. Who doesn't?"

"People who have sex instead." She blinked up at him, not even pretending innocence.

"You have a one-track mind." Not that he was complaining

about that. Not at all.

"I never claimed otherwise. I like sex, Max. I'd like to have it with you."

He held back a grin, instead sending her a mock frown. "Stay on topic, you're distracting me."

"That's the point." She paused. "Fine. Yes. The last mage who attacked her tried to drain her. I could touch you right now and take your magick. Probably without you knowing it. Hell, I used some of your energy earlier. It's a physical law, right? Energy doesn't dissipate, it merely becomes something else. So all paranormal beings I've ever come across, witches and shifters, though I hear it's the same with Fae and vampires, have magick. You slough it off." She shivered. "He would have drained her and then done a rite to use her all up. Her connection to Jack and Galen included. I don't know how it would affect them, but I doubt it would be good."

He whipped into his driveway, the garage door sliding up as his guard gave him the all-clear sign from his perch on a nearby rooftop. He'd slid into a higher state of alertness as she spoke, adrenaline driving him on. He had to calm himself down or he'd bring the cats around him into that state of agitation as well.

The situation had been calm for a few months. The mage who'd attacked his sister-in-law had been dealt with and they'd been keeping an eye on some men who'd been connected to the attacker.

But the newly recovered memories Renee had resurrected, implicating her father in her mother's death and the abuse that followed, complicated things. He had no idea how to combat this foe. Until Renee, he might have ignored that such things happened. But she was his, part of his family and his jamboree. And now Kendra, who, his cat reminded him, was also his.

"How do we stop this? And keep you safe?" He hustled her

from the car until she pulled her arm free and took a look at the place.

"I told you, I'm working with Mary on it. Our lessons start again and she's teaching me how to draw better on the energies floating around so that I can bolster my own. If I don't, I get sick, depleted. It leaves me vulnerable. Once Renee gets a better grip on her magick, she'll start with Mary too."

"Vulnerable how?"

"Using magick means I spend it, use my reserves. If I get attacked and I'm depleted, I have less to defend myself."

And that was unimaginable to him. "What can I do?"

She paused and looked up, into his face. "You're doing it. You can't fight this with claw and tooth. Or, you can, but only after the magical stuff has been neutralized. The witches have to do that part. I'm encouraging Mary and some of the others I've met here in Boston to get together to try to form a loose organization. Massachusetts doesn't have the best history with witches. You might imagine it's not as easy as one would assume. Many witches pretend not to be, or pretend to be dabblers. New agers." She shrugged. "Nothing wrong with that of course, but that's not what I am."

"You should come out. Like we did."

He led her into the main part of the house. The heart, as he liked to think of the living area where the kitchen, dining and family rooms all flowed together.

"Yeah, that's what we need. A panicked human population drowning us or firing us from our jobs because they worry we'll harm them with our warts and evil ways."

"Come on now, don't exaggerate. We've had our troubles here and there, but it's not all been bad. It's not the same as it was during the witch trials."

He nearly stepped back at the sight of so much anger on her face. Instantly he hated that he'd pushed whatever that button was in her.

"I'm not talking about the trials. Prejudice dies hard. And slow." Her voice was agitated, strained.

"Don't do that." He turned her, tipped her face to his, her expression awash with pain, anger, hurt. Not knowing how to help her, he kissed her forehead. "Don't close up and go away."

She shook her head once, struggling with whatever it was she needed to say. So complicated, his little witch. "What do you want from me?"

He could have softened it. Could have pulled the punch. But it wouldn't have been right. He needed to lay it all out for her because he had no intention of anything but being with her.

"Everything."

Eyes widened, she took a breath and stepped back. "I just got everything back for myself. I'm not ready to give it to anyone else. I don't know if I ever will, Max."

"Remember the discussion we had earlier? About cats being patient hunters?"

"You don't scare me."

She meant it like a tease, but he took it deadly seriously. "Oh yes I do. Not in the physical sense. We both know you could have blasted my ass away from the door tonight if you were truly scared. But in here." He tapped a fingertip over her heart.

"I'd have had a hell of a headache, if I could have made it to the front walk without passing out. Yeah I could have blasted you." She neatly sidestepped the part about being scared emotionally. Still, she'd told him about the physical toll of using her magick. Just a small bit of herself, another piece of the puzzle she gave him.

"So you get sick or feel weak after you use your magick? Mary's teaching you how to feed more power into yourself then. To meet these mages with as much power as they have?"

"I rarely use my magick. That's the way it's supposed to be. I maintain it and practice. I learn new spellcraft and better control. My reserves are good because of that. But when I use a lot of it at once, it can deplete me physically. Bloody noses, headaches, I need to eat or I feel sick. Sometimes a witch can lose consciousness.

"If I don't know how to pull this other, ambient magickal energy from around me, I would lose a direct confrontation if it came to that. They're playing with a totally different set of rules and I have no plans to play nice when it comes to my life or the lives of the people I care about. Rosemary and I fought him off that first time because we were together. But I don't know if I could have stopped him on my own."

He expelled air, wanting to hit something.

"So what can we do? The cats are behind you, the wolves as well. That's a lot of muscle. Tell me and we'll fix it."

She paused, her expression one of surprise. With a soft look, she reached up to cup his cheek. "You can't. I mean, in a normal situation you could. You're strong and fierce. But this isn't normal. If they try to physically harm me, or her or any other witch, and you were there you could stop it. But this won't play out that way. If we, witches I mean, can't defend ourselves, we're meat. I don't want that. So I'm learning as fast as I can."

His cat was of two minds on this. The man however, was far more concerned about the risk this situation posed her.

"Damn it, Kendra. Essentially you're telling me that you're the one who'll have to fight these mages one on one? You're saying it's down to magick. That tooth and claw can't do anything? Because that means you're defenseless and I have a serious fucking problem with that."

She didn't say anything. What could she say? It wasn't that she liked it either. It would be very nice to have a normal life with no one trying to harm her or those she loved. But that wasn't what she'd been confronted with.

"You have to teach Renee this too, so she can help. You can't do this on your own. Teach me. You said we have our own kind of magickal energy."

"You do. I'm of the opinion that it's to do with your change. The power to achieve a totally different form, to change the mass of something, it's indefinably complicated. But you don't use it like I do. You work your magic with that, with your shift. It's not something you can use in any way than how you already do.

"I'm already teaching Renee. Rosemary as well when she's in town. The exercises I have Renee doing now are the bridge to the sort of skills she'll need to even try a magickal draw without hurting herself or someone else. Today though, she instinctively came to me, offered her magick. I think she'll be able to begin some rudimentary stuff with Mary within the next few weeks if she can continue at this level."

"All this time you've been training her. Not telling her about this other depletion-of-magick thing. But readying her."

He tried to lead her to the couch, but she balked. "Hold your horses. This is some place, Max."

"Don't think you can change the subject." He led her into the main level of the house and she blinked, looking around.

"You live here alone? Tour me."

"I'll tour, you'll talk."

She rolled her eyes. "Giddy up."

"The family room, dining room and kitchen."

She walked around the room, looking out windows, touching the spines of the books on the shelves, peering at the framed pictures that sat on every surface he could fit them on. Scenting his things in a way she couldn't have begun to understand the importance of, but doing it nonetheless.

He watched her but stayed in place, content to drink her in. "Tell me why you didn't let anyone know what you were doing."

She turned to look at him, tucking her hair back behind her left ear. Clearly there was an internal struggle, but at last she sighed. "I didn't tell you because, well, I want Renee to be able to use her gifts with pride. She hasn't had that. It's not right. I wanted these first months to be a time when she could get rid of that shame. Why scare her any more than she is already? My sister deserves a break. Even if all I can give her is a short one."

He closed his eyes briefly. She hadn't known where her sister was just four months before. But in that time she and Renee had grown close, had clicked in the way he did with Gibson and, most of the time, Galen. Kendra Kellogg had moved across the country for her sister. Had undertaken her own training to possibly save her damned life and the life of her sister, and on her own.

Of all the things women had done to gain his attention, the dresses, lingerie, makeup, whatever it had been, this was the most powerfully attractive thing he'd ever witnessed. Family was as important to her as it was to him. These weren't words used to manipulate. No, they were deeds.

He pushed from his seat, never taking his gaze from her, loving the way she didn't flinch at all. She waited, breathing a bit fast, for him to reach her.

Rather than continue the tour, he backed her against the wall and leaned in, meaning only to kiss her briefly. Instead she made a sound threaded with raw desire, with need and, as he drew his teeth over her neck, pleasure.

And then he was lost to her. Lost to the call of her scent, of the feel of her, solid, curvy, warm and pliant.

The need for her built, filling him up so it was all he felt. Her taste was right as it settled into his system. "I should stop," he murmured as he slid his palms down her sides, dropping to cup her ass, hauling her closer.

She rocked against him, arching to touch him more. "Mmm. Go on ahead."

He laughed, licking up her neck, finding her mouth and taking. Taking all she offered, needing all she was. Her tongue slid along his, her fingers tangled in his hair to hold him close.

With an iron will, he broke the kiss. "A tour. You wanted a tour."

"No. I wanted sex. You're being coy for some reason though we both know we're going to end up in bed." She swallowed, hard. She stood there, infuriatingly exposed to him.

Comforted by the way he listened, the way he hadn't argued or tried to take over, but still wanted to. She saw the war of it on his face. He'd given her that space, the respect that she had to do it.

At the same time, oh my God did he have the domination in a hot romantic way down. The way he'd crowded her against the wall hadn't alarmed her at all. She was wet and achy and she wanted more.

In that dark place, deep inside, she wondered just how dominant he truly was. For a year, starting the day she drove away from the house she'd been a virtual prisoner in while married to Martin, she'd shut herself down. It had been the only way she could find the space to get over it, to process and be done with it.

And then it had burst open. Her desire, her sexuality and her need to be touched and loved came back with a sudden, shaking fury and she'd decided then to never turn it off again. Sex made her feel alive. She loved it and there was no way she'd feel shame about it again.

Max was someone she wanted on a whole lot of levels. There was no need to pretend with him. To be anything but who she was. It was comforting and jarring all at once. He challenged her. Seemed to respect her ability and independence, while being bossy and nosy and suddenly just in her business.

She should have felt nervous about it. But she *liked* it. She was way more perverted than she'd thought.

"What on earth is going on in that brain of yours?" he murmured, drawing her into a nearby room, a great-room with high ceilings and a lovely view. He settled on a couch and she allowed him to pull her to him, nestling her against his body.

"I don't know how to say any of this. It all seems nonsensical and farcical and yet, here I am, snuggled up against a man who can transform into a jaguar. You're infuriatingly bossy and totally sexy and it feels like you're stalking me, not in a creepy way, but like, gah! Nevermind. I want to have sex with you. A lot."

He snorted. "Working on that. Don't be so impatient. Do you have somewhere to be? I like to take my time. You're worth the effort and I want to hold you right now. I want you snuggled against me. I've longed for this and I aim to enjoy every minute I can."

Snuggling was a very good description of what it felt like to be with him on the couch. He'd enfolded her in his arms, and she fit against him just right. He was warm, hard where he was supposed to be, all big strong man. He made her feel safe. Safe without being crowded, held without being imprisoned.

"If they could bottle up whatever it is you're doing right now, you'd be the richest man on earth," she said without meaning to.

The sound he made was caught between a growl and a laugh. "Don't panic, but I'm imprinting on you like crazy."

"I don't know if I should panic or not. I don't know what you mean."

"I mean, Kendra Kellogg, that I want you and *that* means I really want you. All of you and from now on. I should warn you I'm not a man who loses very often. I like to get what I want."

He nibbled on her ear and she moaned. "I'd panic, but that feels, oh man.... Let's let this thing play out slowly. You don't need to declare your love for me right now. We've only known each other a few months. But I do want you. And I'm quite amenable to being exclusive, as I'd need to harm anyone who tried to pry me from your arms right about now."

He sucked her earlobe into his mouth, skimming it with his teeth. He'd shifted so one of his hands had snuck beneath the hem of her sweater, sliding slowly up her belly to her left breast.

Which was good, as Max de La Vega didn't share. He hadn't lied, he'd gone from like to attraction. And then attraction to intense attraction to the first connections of an imprint in a short time. But long enough that man and cat knew she was the one. He'd never had any intention of having looking for the right woman become a lifestyle. He'd played and fucked, always knowing when the right woman came along, he'd play and fuck her, cleave himself to her and that would be that.

Lauren Dane

He was not afraid of this at all. He knew what he liked, knew what he wanted and he was old enough that he'd gained plenty of skills to make that happen.

He leaned in and kissed her. At the curve of her jaw, at the hollow beneath her ear. "Good. Let me tell you something, *querida*, you never need to concern yourself with me wanting to be pried away. If anything, you'll have to order me to stop being a perv and trying to have sex with you every moment I'm around you."

"Why don't you then? I'm here, telling you I want you. Take a bite. Here, let me get that started." She reached down and pulled her sweater off, tossing it across the room.

He couldn't have taken his gaze from her if something had been on fire right behind where they sat. She sat before him, exposing all that pale, bare skin and a red, lacy bra holding perky, gorgeous tits.

Gaze locked with his, she reached up and popped the catch between her breasts, freeing them from the bra.

"Holy shit," he breathed out. Bold. Take-charge sexy women. Heaven smile down upon them because he loved them.

She cupped her breasts, all while keeping her eyes on him. "You wanted to talk some more? Because, Max, you've been tossing around all that testosterone for months now and you really shouldn't promise what you don't want to deliver."

His eyelids slid partly closed as desire weighed him down, slowed his movements as he stroked fingertips between her breasts. Her breath caught and he scented the spice of her desire.

"You're going to kill me," he said, holding himself in place. Just barely.

She sat, moving forward to straddle his lap so those naked, perfect B-cups stared him right in the eye.

"Only if you don't have sex with me."

The heat of her pussy sat directly over his cock. His cock so hard and sensitive he nearly came when she ground herself over him.

"How is it," he gave in, pressing his face to the hollow of her throat and breathing her in, "I never saw a siren living inside the soft, sweet, feminine school teacher?"

"Maybe you were too busy looking at my ass."

He laughed, reversing their positions, rolling to get her on her back on his couch as he loomed over her.

"Could be. I love your ass."

"Didn't you have a girlfriend like, two weeks ago?"

"We broke things off nearly *two months* ago. Should I be worried you didn't notice?"

She snorted. "I noticed everything else. Enough that I thought uncharitable things about this woman I've never seen."

Satisfaction warmed his belly that she'd been interested enough to be jealous of a woman who he could barely remember at that point. He touched her lips quickly with a fingertip. "There's no need. I broke it off because I knew I was interested in someone else."

She slid her hands up under his shirt, digging her nails into the muscles of his back. "More interest please."

"You're going to scar my fragile psyche with your pressure to go all the way."

Her face lit with amusement. "You can just put the tip in. If it's too much you can stop. I promise it won't hurt."

Laughter shook his sides as he dipped down to steal a kiss. But she gave it freely, holding him to her body, rubbing against him.

"I'd planned..." he paused to lick over each nipple. Her

65

groan echoed with his, "...to take my time with you. To woo you before we had sex."

She reached down, getting his jeans opened up. "I hate that plan. I think the new plan, unless you truly *don't* want to have sex with me, should be having sex with me. We're adults, I don't think you're going to marry me tomorrow morning because we get down."

He laughed, rolling off and springing to his feet. He *would* marry her in the morning if he knew she wouldn't run away from it. That would wait. For a while. "Christ in heaven you look sexy lying there on my couch, your skin flushed, your nipples hard and dark."

He held a hand out to her, helping her up. "Come on then." He sighed dramatically. "Clearly you're a nympho and need some of my special medicine for it."

"Well it's about time."

Leading her upstairs, he pointed things out on the way. "Guest bedroom there. Home office to the left. Full bath. Powder room downstairs just south of the kitchen."

"All kidding aside, Max, your house is lovely. I like it."

He smiled as he turned, sweeping her off her feet and jogging the rest of the way to his bedroom. "Glad to hear that. I want you here, which is easier when you like it." He tossed her on the bed.

"There's more than one way, you know. You can keep me coming back with lots of great sex."

He laughed, pulling his shirt off one-handed. "Single-minded. It's a good trait."

Chapter Five

Holy wow, was he gorgeous. His upper body was beautiful. Muscled, fit. His skin called out to her fingers, her mouth. She gave in, moving to him, needing to touch.

"I'd say something like, how'd you hide this body under your clothes. But I've been watching you enough to know this body was there. Only now that I see it, it's even better than I'd imagined."

He leaned into her touch, moaned at her caresses. But he froze in place when she rubbed her cheek over his chest.

She leaned away from his body to look up into his face. Suddenly feeling awkward. "What? Did I hurt you?"

"No. Not at all." He kissed her, reassuring her. "You rubbed your scent on me. Marked me. It's..." He hesitated a moment. "It's very intimate." His hands went into her hair, sliding through it until he stopped to gather and tug. "And submissive."

She swallowed, hard, knees nearly buckling at the sensation. "Oh. It just seemed like the thing to do."

He pulled her hair to draw her head back, exposing her neck. She closed her eyes, letting herself float. His mouth cruised, finding a spot he seemed to like a lot, where neck met shoulder. She liked that spot too.

"You taste like everything I love the most. Spicy. Your magick makes my cock hard, Kendra."

He was pushing all her buttons so hard she thought it a good possibility she'd come the second he got anywhere near her clit.

So big and raw there, he stood over her, backing her to his bed. When she'd fallen, body splayed on his mattress, his hands went to the button of her jeans.

As he made quick work of them, she kicked off her shoes, helping him get her jeans peeled off.

The way he paused and then growled brought gooseflesh, but in the best sort of way. "Tattoos and a piercing. Each layer I peel back gives me an even sexier woman. It's intoxicating." He breathed it out as he ran his hands all over her, from ankle to neck. Tugging on her belly button ring, leaning down to lick over the words on her side. Kneading and caressing, leaving her a mass of goo, primed and ready to be ravished.

He moved like the cat he was. She couldn't tear her eyes away from him. From the glory of masculinity at its most perfect. "My God, look at *you*."

His skin was burnished bronze. Stretched over hard, flat muscle that bunched and flowed with supreme grace that didn't blunt the predator inside. His power vibrating from him, humming nice and low in her belly. Everything in her turned to him, paid attention to his presence.

His hair was close cropped, only emphasizing the masculine features of his face. Big, wary eyes. So brown at times they were black. He had this way of looking at her and ripping everything away. He saw right into the parts of herself even she didn't want to examine.

His cheekbones were high, an elegant rise on his otherwise rugged features. His mouth was an epic fucking poem.

Tempting her more than she'd ever been tempted. He kissed her hard, breaking away with a snarled, "The scent of your pussy drives me mad." He fell to his knees, hauling her ass to the edge of the mattress and taking a long lick while she still reeled with his words.

She arched, back bowed as a groan ripped from her lips.

"Your clit is pierced?" He spoke, his lips still against her pussy, the vibration of his voice passing through her, bringing her a tiny bit closer to climax.

"No," she squealed out when he tugged on the ring in her clitoral hood with his teeth. "No, no I didn't mean for you to stop." She grabbed his head, holding him in place. "I meant not my clit. The hood."

"This is the hottest thing I've ever seen," he said before flicking his tongue over it, sending bolts of bright pleasure through her body. "Did it hurt?"

"Yes." She paused, letting herself revel in the way he made her feel. "But sometimes, I like that." It had been the first time she'd said it aloud. It was that edge of pain she found herself responding to when she got ink or a piercing.

He groaned, digging his fingers into the flesh of her ass. His tongue swirled through her pussy, fucking into her body only to move up and tease her clit with featherlight flicks.

Climax built, hotter and hotter, closer and closer to the edge until he sucked her clit and the ring into his mouth with just exactly the right amount of pressure. Her fingers dug into the blankets beneath her body as she rode the pleasure tearing through her.

He turned, nuzzled her thigh, nipping it.

Still intoxicated with the taste of her pussy, Max leapt up onto the mattress, rolling her, enjoying the boneless weight of her body against his. "I want your taste." He licked over the line

Lauren Dane

of her collarbone.

"Mmmmm," she hummed agreeably. "You have pants on." Not so agreeable this time. One of her eyes opened and then she turned to face him.

"Your eyes go all green when you're pleasure drunk. Your scent changes, deepens, your magick warms against me as I touch you. Clings like gossamer."

"Wow, you're so good. You must have totally gotten pussy. Like all the time."

He laughed, unbuttoning his jeans and getting them and his boxers off so he could return to her as naked and as quickly as possible.

"No comment other than to thank you for the compliment and to say it's still my plan. I happen to like yours very much."

She rose up, laying kisses across chest, licking over his nipples. "Speaking of tastes, I like yours."

He watched, as she moved down his chest. He'd known they'd have great sexual chemistry, but this was more than great. What they had was combustible, nuclear, off the charts, flat-out perfection.

Inside her was a warrior woman, fiercely protective of those she considered hers to protect. She would stand at his side in all things, hold him accountable to be the best leader his jamboree could ask for.

And sexually submissive. Given the unnamed trauma of her past, he hadn't been expecting that. Given that trauma though, he'd take it with extra care. Each layer he peeled back he found something else unexpected and beautiful about her. Or just plain hot like the clitoral hood piercing.

All that was lost when she licked from his navel to the head of his cock. The wet heat of her mouth drove him insane.

70

Slowly, she took him deeper and deeper. Her tongue sliding around the head.

"Fuck." He may have growled it, but he couldn't be sure. "That's sooo good. Right there, yes, harder."

She made a sound and the scent of her rose, pushing him closer to the edge. She liked the dirty talk. Good. He did too.

"I'm going to come and while the idea of coming in your mouth isn't one I dislike by any measure, I want to be buried deep in your pussy when I come. Little witch." He hissed as she kissed down the line of his cock, licking over his balls.

Her eyes opened and focused on his as she bent over him, her gorgeous ass swaying as she did.

"I think I told you what I wanted."

She blinked, slowly coming out of her pleasure-infused haze. He would have worried he'd pushed her too far, but she smiled then, straightening.

"That so?"

He took her upper arms, watching as her pupils swelled, swallowing up most of the color in her eyes. "Mmm hmm, that's so. I want to lie back and watch you above me. I know your pussy is nice and slick."

She let out a shaky breath as she moved to straddle him again. Oh yes, this was going to work out so very well.

She grabbed his cock at the root, angling it against her pussy. She hummed low, the sound laced with pleasure and tension. "Condom?" she murmured.

"You and Renee don't, um, compare notes?" Damn it, her breasts were so beautiful. He cupped them, flicking his thumb back and forth over her nipples.

Her dreamy look faded a bit and her lip curled. "If you tell me you've had sex with my sister I'm so out of here."

He laughed. "No. I love Renee, but not like that. I mean, we don't carry STDs and you're not ovulating."

She frowned, though she continued to hover, the head of his cock bathed in the wet heat of her gate. "Sexy. For the record, Renee does not share the details of her birth-control situation with me. Though, you de La Vega boys have quite the reputation."

"You still with me here? We got a go for launch?" Even he heard the strain in his own voice. He wanted inside her so badly his hands may have shaken if he hadn't been rolling and tugging on her nipples.

"Yes," she gasped.

He angled himself and thrust up into her body, the shock of it, of how tight and slick she was nearly sent him over the edge.

She moaned and then, while her gaze was locked on his, began to circle her hips. "Now *that's* sexy."

Not as sexy as what he was looking at. In addition to the spectacular tits, an ass that went on for days and that face of hers, the ink on her sides, curling up and around her stomach, turned him on beyond measure.

The dangling jewel in her navel ring and the one in her pussy drove him nuts. He pinched her clit, gently, tugging on the ring every once in a while, just to watch her face change, to see her nipples darken, her eyes grow glossy.

"You're what's sexy. Gorgeous. Your pussy feels so good I may die from it. But I'll die happy."

"If you die, I can't have sex with you. People tend to look down on that sort of thing."

"Very good point."

She moved over him as he watched her, content to get his

fill of each curve as his gaze roved over her body. She was graceful and strong and he couldn't seem to get enough. Good thing he was a patient man and could happily spend the next decades filling himself of her.

She hadn't been so full, well ever. It was the combination of the girth of his very fine cock and the way he looked at her. Looked at her like there was nothing else in the room worth looking at.

Every part of her he touched was on fire for him. And the way he touched her! It pushed her buttons in a big way. Dominant. Sure. Just an edge of rough, but still clearly play and not meant to harm.

All that muscle, all that coiled power and strength, and he used it to play. To incite and turn her on.

She found herself smiling down at him and those eyes stared back. They were dark, but not a flat darkness. A darkness filled with promise, with endless energy and strength.

His hands on her body stroked, soothed and excited at once.

Needing more, she leaned forward, bracing her hands on his shoulders. The change in angle brought the line of his cock to brush against her clit and the ring, sending shivers of pleasure through her over and over.

"Fuck, fuck, your cunt is squeezing my cock so tight. So good. I'm nearly there and you need to be there with me."

She closed her eyes a moment, getting ready to deny it was possible. And then he reached between them and flicked a finger back and forth over her clit and made her a liar.

She gasped, sucked under by the intensity of climax with him so deep inside. Dimly, she was aware of his snarled chant of her name, his fingers digging into her thigh, the flex of his abdominal muscles as he thrust up into her over and over until

73

he pressed one last time and came.

"Good thing you're strong and stuff, because I wouldn't be able to move on my own steam for another few minutes."

He chuckled, moving her beside him on the mattress, keeping his arms around her.

He traced over the symbols on her skin. "What are these?"

"Protection spells. Runes. Words of power."

"Is this something all witches do? Does it work?"

How could she explain it? How the ink had given her power and control over her situation once she'd walked out on her broken marriage?

"I like to think so. They're frowned on in many circles." She stretched and smirked when she caught him staring at her boobs.

She moved to sit up, but he tightened his arms around her. When she nuzzled into him, tasting the salt at his neck, he actually purred. Like a full-body vibrating purr.

"I like that," she said, her face still buried in his neck. For all his cuddly ways, she'd seen him in full battle mode, knew he was more than a human man. A big cat lived inside him. And yet, he held her gently, *purring*. Lord, he got to her.

Of course he purred! Was she crazy? He'd just had the best sex of his life, with a woman he was totally convinced was the one and she nuzzled his neck. He loved the way she felt, the scent of sex and magic mixing in the room.

She felt right. *They* felt right. It pleased him, even as she stirred everything inside.

"I don't purr for just anyone, you know. Now, you have this way of lobbing a bomb and then skirting away, changing the subject and rubbing on me. This is distracting, to say the least, as your parts were made for rubbing. So, what's frowned on?"

"A lot of witches of Rosemary's generation and older have lived in fear of exposure. Of being misunderstood. I'm sure you understand this."

And he did. So he nodded.

"We learn from each other, from our mothers and fathers, from cousins and friends. We're insular."

That was another thing he understood firsthand. Cats were one of the more insular shifter groups. And it meant great suspicion toward outsiders.

"What I wear on my skin is not solely from my own tradition. There's magic older than what Rosemary and my mother were taught by my great-grandmother. My grandmother has no magickal gifts, though she grew up with magickly gifted people so she nurtured that within my mother and aunt.

"A few years ago, I realized there was more to my gifts and powers than what I'd been taught. After I got divorced I spent a lot of time simply learning about myself, about what I was and who I was. I started reading, seeking, learning from other traditions."

"And some in your community are threatened by that."

"They don't trust it. It can be manipulated, used to harm. But I think they're throwing out something they could actually benefit from. Fear is good to a certain extent, but then it becomes something more, something worse. It paralyzes and makes people paranoid. That's not helpful. People like Mary have a lot to teach."

"Does that translate into them not trusting you?"

She heaved a sigh, wriggling until he let go.

He watched, waiting as she sprang from bed and began to pace. The moonlight through the window played over her skin with silver fingers.

"What have they done for me anyway? My mother had to pretty much abandon me. She was murdered, most likely by our father and Susan, God only knows what she is or who she's working with. Renee was emotionally abused and as we've discovered physically too."

She had to move when she thought. Interesting.

"So what then? Doesn't sound to me like you want to separate yourself entirely or you wouldn't give a crap what they thought. You do."

She rounded on him, eyes narrowed. "Are you playing lawyerball with me?"

He laughed. "I'd never dream of such a thing. Though, if you wanted to play something, you can come by and we'll use my desk to all the best ability we can. My chair would hold our weight easily."

Her annoyed look melted away as she bent to find her clothes.

"Why bother getting dressed? I'll only have to take them off again when we fuck in an hour or so."

"I need to go home."

He wanted her to be here. Wanted this to be their home. Not that he'd share this with her just then. Another shifter would have understood, but he'd need to take things a little slower with her.

"Why is that?" He sat up and moved to her, enfolding her in his arms and holding her close.

"That's what people do," she said, her voice muffled as she made no move to leave his embrace.

"Which people are here with you and me right now?" He began to sway, smiling against her hair as she moved with him.

"You run with some pretty stunning male specimens

should you, you know, want to bring any of them around." Though he couldn't see her face, he knew she smirked.

She broke into full-throated laughter as he swept her up and tossed her on the bed again, scrambling atop her.

"Galen's situation is different. I don't like sharing what's mine. And you and I both know you're mine."

One of her eyebrows rose imperiously and his cat approved. "I know we have great sexual chemistry. I'm willing to concede we're dating even. Yours though? I'm no one's but my own."

"Not to own, little witch. Never that." He kissed her softly. "To cherish and take care of."

"I still need to go home."

"I'll sleep there then." He rolled off and tossed her clothes in her direction. "I'll pack a bag. What are your plans for tomorrow?"

She pulled her panties back on and he sighed. "I do like you naked."

"You're full of it. Cripes." But she smiled as she said it.

"Tenacity is a gift, little witch."

"It's a pain in my ass, that's what it is." She snorted. "Tomorrow I have to work and then I'm going to meet Renee. We're going to B&G Oysters for lobster rolls. It was supposed to be chili dogs, but she texted me earlier to suggest an alternative plan. She tells me I have to try them there and who am I to turn down such an offer?"

"Am I invited? I love lobster rolls."

She rolled her eyes as she struggled into her bra and pulled her sweater back on. "I doubt you've eaten a lobster roll. Ever. Look at you." She waved her hand his way.

"Shifter metabolism, my beautiful witch. As it happens I'm a big fan of lobster rolls, though not to argue with your sister, but I like Neptune Oyster Bar better. Perhaps we'll go there next, you know, just to be sure. Come on. It'll save us the charade that you won't have guards trailing along."

"*Renee* has guards trailing along. I, on the other hand, am free of that." She smirked and he laughed, pulling his jeans on.

"Yes, well. I think you're a woman who prizes honesty so I'm going to tell you right now, you'll have guards too. Gibson has no doubt worked out a plan for when you and Renee are out to keep the number of guards low enough not to attract a lot of attention. But it's going to continue for the foreseeable future."

She spun, narrowing her eyes. "You what? You can't send fucking werewolves and jaguar shifters with weapons to an elementary school. That's ridiculous. *I have a job.* I'm trying to build a life here and I won't do that with henchmen at my side." She sailed from the room and he followed, grabbing his suit bag and the toiletries kit he always kept at the ready.

"I'm not sending werewolves or jaguars to the school with weapons strapped to their bodies like Rambo." He stepped into his shoes. "They'll be discreet. They know how to do their job."

"Why are we talking about this like you have an option?"

He nuzzled her neck, scraping his teeth over her skin, loving how she leaned into his touch. Probably without even knowing she did it.

"We're not because I'm not asking for permission. There are people out there trying to harm you. This is not acceptable to me. I have the ability to protect you, and I will. Period."

She pushed at him, but he stayed long enough to kiss her neck again before stepping back.

"I can protect myself too, you know. Also, newsflash, I'm not one of your cats. You're not the boss of me."

He laughed. "Of course I'm not the boss of you. You don't need me to be your boss. That's not what this is anyway and we both know it. It's happening, I have no plans to make it stop. Now, on to happy things. Will you make me breakfast in the morning before you go to work?"

"You better sleep with one eye open."

"All this sex talk just makes me hotter for you."

Chapter Six

She didn't really know what on earth to do about Max. Other than indulge him, which, she had to admit, was fun and usually a win for her. Over the last two weeks or so, he'd simply become part of her daily life.

He called, texted, stopped by, paid attention. He wanted to know what she thought about things. Wanted to hear her opinions on every subject imaginable. They'd spent more time simply wrapped in each other's arms on his overstuffed couch than in his bed. Though they'd spent a lot of quality time naked as well.

She'd never been so well matched with someone before. In bed, they burned up the sheets. He was inventive, attentive and had a seemingly unending well of energy. Out of bed, they poked at each other, played, teased and discussed.

He'd become essential to her. It had felt as if she'd looked up and found him there. And she liked it.

Oh sure, she'd seen him several times a week before that. He was Renee's brother-in-law after all. But *this* was different. He had a way of taking up space, in her head, in her apartment and in her heart. He took care of her. He touched her in a way that made her ache, filled her up, made her feel beautiful, strong and capable. And yet, he sheltered her when he could, and sometimes even when she told him to back off.

He was infuriatingly pushy. Nosy. Bossy. So intelligent it set her back on her heels at times. Sexy. Nurturing and loving.

It freaked her out, even as she loved it. Even as she wanted to get used to it, wanted to count on it.

And no matter how much she tried to hold him off, he simply flowed in.

"Like the tide."

Renee looked up from where she'd been making Kendra a blueberry smoothie. "Huh?"

"Sorry. Max, he's like the tide. He's coming into my life whether I want him to or not."

Renee laughed, pushing the smoothie her way. "I put extra protein in it. You'll need it." She gave Kendra a look so Kendra gave in and took a drink.

"Thank you. It's actually good."

Renee's smile was mischievous. "I should be offended that you sound surprised every time you come here and drink my smoothies."

Kendra laughed. "I'm sorry. You're right. I'm so proud of you and I say goofy stuff."

Renee's grin softened. "No need to apologize. I know you're proud. Now, back to Max. Here's the thing, you don't want him to *not* rush in like the tide. I've seen you two together. You're connected. Like whoa. And, like Galen, only worse, he's a right pushy bastard."

"Lucky he looks so good. I don't think he'd get away with half of it if he wasn't so handsome," Imogene de La Vega said as she came to stand next to Kendra. "My, don't you look pretty today." She leaned in to kiss Kendra's cheek and then squeezed Renee's hands across the counter.

Imogene, of course, looked flawless in her chic business

suit that probably cost a month's salary. The woman was nearing sixty and she didn't even look thirty-five. Tall, taller than her husband, her thickly braided hair was held back with an equally chic band at the back of her neck.

"I do? Please. Look at you!" Kendra waved at her.

Imogene laughed. "Oh this thing? I just threw it together on my way out this morning." She paused and laughed some more. "I lie. I had a luncheon today with the law students I'm mentoring. This is my successful judge suit. Cesar gives me side eye when I wear it. I swear the man is wearing the same suit we scraped together the money to buy for his first day in court."

"Should I be worried about this gathering of my favorite women?" Max sauntered in, wearing a suit that did far more exciting things to her insides than Imogene's had. He looked smooth, elegant and yet, even with the dapper suit and nice shoes, that edge of danger in him was still obvious. In the eyes, the set of his mouth. Damn it, he was irresistible.

"I was telling your Kendra that you only get away with as much because you're so handsome. Of course, I hope you're giving her more reasons to stay than to go."

He bent to kiss his mother's cheek, rubbing his own along her jawline. Kendra had seen it before, affectionate and also a sign of rank. She liked that Max respected his mother the way he did.

"Kendra doesn't let me get away with much, *Mami*. Why do you think that is?" He grinned as he leaned over the counter to kiss the top of Renee's head.

"Because she's not a pushover. Nor is she wrapped up in all this jamboree ranking business. She's your match. This is a good thing for you and for the jamboree."

Kendra blushed furiously. Dealing with his family always

seemed like, well, like a job. There were so many of them and every one of them came with some sort of list of issues. They were fiercely loving and loyal but the most political group she'd ever dealt with. She wasn't sure she was up to the task, though it did make her happy that everyone else seemed to think she was. "Well, let's not be hasty. We just started dating and everything. But also, he's so pushy that it sometimes happens that I oppose whatever he's trying. He brings it out in me."

Max laughed, taking her cheeks in his hands, tipping her face up and kissing her soundly. "There's hasty and there's fate, little witch. You're my fate." He shrugged, like it was that easy.

"You're going to scare the girl away, Max." Imogene shook her head at Max, though her eyes seemed to be lit with the same mischief his were. She turned her attention back to Kendra. "How about you come to dinner on Sunday? It's time you came around. You may not believe in fate, though I bet you do, but you know this thing between you and Max is serious. You may as well come to dinner and meet everyone. I know they want to meet you."

She didn't give Kendra any time to say no. She just dropped a kiss on her cheek again and squeezed her hands.

Imogene winked at Renee, who laughed and blushed. "You too. You know how much I love to look at Jack. He's so pretty."

"Wouldn't miss a Sunday. And you'll spoil Jack more than he already is with all this attention."

"Max will give you all the details. I'll see you soon." Imogene sailed out, holding the coffee Renee had made her.

Kendra turned her attention back to Max, whose smug smile made his lips look even more delicious. "Your mother is scary."

Max looked down at her, stepping close so he ate up all her personal space. And she didn't make a single move to stop that from happening. Having him that close made her dizzy in a most delicious fashion.

"She likes you. She knows you're going to change things, shake them up. Aside from her first impression of Renee, which she admitted herself was wrong, my mother has a very good gut sense about people."

"Nothing like having unrealistic expectations of the new kid," she mumbled and he bent, kissing her quickly.

"You're special. She sees it. I missed you today. I got yelled at by the judge for my client's stupidity. I didn't have time for my afternoon snack and all I could think about was you."

She frowned momentarily, worrying that he wasn't getting enough calories. And then realized he was trying to change the subject. "You're trying to distract me."

"No, I'm trying to entice you. Then I can say, *Kendra, please come to my house for dinner tonight. Stay over. I love it when my sheets smell of us.*"

A shiver ran through her and Renee busily wiped the counter down just to their left, totally eavesdropping.

He grinned, knowing he was embarrassing her, and she gave in and smiled at him. "I'm worried that if I keep giving in, I'm only making you more spoiled."

He pretended to be crestfallen, the rogue. "You know I'm your servant in all things."

Renee made a gagging noise. "You're worse than Galen and I thought that was impossible. Anyway, she can't have dinner at your house, she's having it at mine. Galen was supposed to tell you earlier today." She narrowed her eyes at him, looking him over. "I don't see any blood, but with you two, who knows? Did you two punch each other at lunch or something?"

He winked. "Not today. But tomorrow is another day." He

laughed. "I've been in court since nine and I just finished about fifteen minutes ago. I'm sure there's a message on my voice mail. I walked into the building when I scented my lovely Kendra. I needed to make my way here to rub myself all over her."

Kendra looked back at Renee, who rolled her eyes at her sister.

"Galen is a good cook. I'll bring wine for us." Max tipped Kendra's cheek, kissing her again quickly. "For you? Rosewater lemonade. I made a little trip down to my favorite Middle Eastern grocery and found the rosewater."

He was impossibly good at this. Rosewater lemonade was one of her most favorite things in the world.

She tiptoed up to whisper in his ear. "You're very good to me. I notice these things, and appreciate them. Even if I don't let you make all the decisions. You're so getting lucky later. Just so you know." She went back to her heels, but he banded an arm around her waist to hold her.

His eyes lit with something only for her. A smile touched his lips. "Already *am* lucky. I like making you happy. Come up with me so I can get my things and I'll give you a ride home?"

"Thanks. But, I need to go by Mary's for an hour or so before dinner. I'd planned to leave from there. I'll meet you at Renee's. I'll bring a bag," she added, to soothe and to affirm. Funny how they both seemed to need that. She hadn't told him the insurance money came for her car and it sucked. Not nearly enough to replace her old car with something as nice. She had the money but she didn't want to dip into her savings right then. She'd moved cross country, and until she built it back up, she wanted to leave the money in there alone in case of an emergency. She'd keep on taking the T and save up for the car she really wanted. But he was a man who simply wanted to

85

make things happen for his people. If she didn't keep him reined in, he'd buy her some giant luxury armored car or something.

She hadn't told Renee either. Not so much because she worried Renee would tattle, but she might mention it in front of Jack or Galen who, also being control-freak males, would want to step in and handle it as well. Which would have meant some mess of three alpha men all trying to manage her.

"Come up and I'll go with you to Mary's and then drive you to Renee's." He brushed his thumb over the curve of her cheek and all her promises to herself to hold him off dissolved like smoke. Sneaky, sneaky man. "It'll save gas. And you won't have to take the T all the way out there. You know, defenseless and alone on a train when fucked-up crazy people want to hurt you?"

She snuck a quick look at Renee, who nodded at her.

"All right. Don't think that saving-gas comment was even a factor. You can't interfere with anything I do there. Got me? It's important."

"Do I look like the kind of guy who would interfere with your lessons?"

She and Renee both snorted a laugh. "Yes. Yes, you do." She turned to her sister. "I'll see you later. Can I bring anything but the cake I made?"

"Nope. Just you two. We'll take the wine though, Max. You have good taste in wine and in women." Renee looked back to Kendra. "Tell Mary I'm excited to be starting lessons with her."

"I will. See you in a bit." She walked around to the end of the counter and hugged her sister. "Love you."

"Love you too."

Max watched her, his lovely witch, as she interacted with her sister. Their magick swirled around them. He and Jack had likened it to pixie dust, but Galen called it catnip. Galen was probably closer on most days. Heaven knew he loved to simply roll around with her, her skin under his hands, against his lips, her scent wrapped around him.

The shifters who guarded Kendra and Renee both loved to hang about and chat with them. Max understood it, he liked to do that too. Beautiful women who gave off magick like perfume in their wake. Of course his men wanted more of it. Luckily for those men who were entrusted with the care and safety of these two women, they also knew and respected the connection between man and animal, witch and woman.

"You're beautiful today," he murmured as they got on the elevator. "I love you in that color blue."

She looked him up and down. "I'm certainly glad to wear casual clothes instead of suits and all. But you look like you stepped out of a magazine ad."

It wasn't as if others hadn't complimented him on his looks or his clothing. It had happened before she came into his life. But when she said it, when she noticed him and said so, it meant more. He wanted to preen around for her, silly as that sounded in his head, he still wanted to do it.

The elevator doors opened and oh, his lucky day, Beth stood in reception talking with their father. He tried not to bristle. Despite her flaws, he loved his sister and wished she'd let go of her past and embrace the women Max loved so much.

Their father who turned, saw Kendra and...*beamed*? Indeed he did. Smiling like a fool, Cesar de La Vega made his way to them, his arms open.

"Kendra! It's lovely to see you." He wasn't as big and braw as his sons, but he was a presence so large he could steal the air from a room, command a jamboree without question or hesitation. But that wasn't who his father was right then.

That man, that cat softened and drew Kendra into a hug, the sort he only used with family. The importance of the gesture squeezed around Max's heart, warmed him.

"Cesar, how are you?" Kendra, smiling, took his father's hands in her own after the hug broke.

"Better now that I have yet another beautiful woman brightening my view." He turned to Beth, whose sour expression made it clear what she thought of Kendra. "Doesn't Max's lady bring something special to a room every time she enters it?"

"Now you're just poking at her, Cesar," Kendra teased.

"I don't need your help," Beth nearly snarled, bringing Max's protective instincts to the fore.

"I'm sure you don't." Kendra looked Beth over. "Pregnancy suits you." She turned back to Cesar. "It was lovely to see you. I need to run now, but I'll see you Sunday at dinner."

Cesar continued to smile. "Oh good! Imogene said she was going to ask you today, so I'm glad she found you already."

Beth, robbed of her moment to be a bitch, sniffed haughtily and stomped off.

Kendra heroically held her bland facial expression and the next-in-line part of Max loved it. Loved that she would run the jamboree at his side and he'd know she could do it.

"I'm going to pop my head in and see if Galen is around." She hugged Cesar again and to Max's surprise and total pleasure, she rubbed her cheek along his father's. With that, she waved over her shoulder to Max and disappeared down the hall.

His father raised his brows and nodded approvingly. "She's a hardass. You wouldn't know it to look at her, but she's tough.

I like that." He paused a moment. "Sunday will be important. Does she know how much?"

"She understands a lot more about us, about our culture, than I thought she did at first. She asks questions, observes. I imagine she'll know, yes."

"You have to let her do it on her own." His father's eyes darkened. "It won't mean anything if she doesn't do it herself."

"She has magick, *Papi*. Unlike Renee and some of the other humans others have brought around, she *will* defend herself. And she can. I've seen her do it. She can handle herself and once she does, they'll back off."

His father tsked. "Some won't ever accept her and you're the one who needs to be ready for that. It was hard on Galen. Still is. He loves Renee and can't understand why everyone can't see in her what he does."

Max growled low and his father growled right back. "Don't you growl at me, boy. Don't you forget who runs this ship."

"This isn't about that and you know it. I'm going to be sure she knows she should feel free to knock anyone who fucks with her on their asses. I haven't discussed the issue of taking on a cat, haven't asked if she'd be willing to change. But she can handle herself either way. However, if a single claw is unsheathed in her presence I will do my job. She is mine, *Papi*. Mine to protect and I will. These cats are mine as well. Yes, yes I know you're in charge. But I will be some day and I will not tolerate any threats against my woman."

"You've begun imprinting."

Max laughed, but it was rueful. "From the first moment I laid eyes on her. In the midst of Renee being harmed and threatened, chaos all around and she stalked in and helped. Even got bitchy with me and Galen at times. She made Renee better, stronger, accepted her sister in a way that told me she was special and strong. I haven't marked her. The past, her past, stands between us. She's human, they like a slow courtship."

It was Cesar's turn to laugh. "Boy, if you can't see the love written all over her each time she looks at you, you're a fool." He headed to the elevators. "I'll see you Sunday."

He could see it. It was the reason he was content to give her space to figure it out herself. Smiling, he lifted his face and found the trail of her essence. Her scent, the magick she shedded as she moved.

And followed.

Beth thought she could out-bitch Kendra? Pfft. Kendra's former in-laws had been the most vicious people she'd ever met, and they did it while smiling tightly and holding their religion in front of their behavior like it excused them rather than condemned. She'd lived around those people for three years and she was still standing.

No one would ever take her humanity from her again, least of all some spoiled, snotty jaguar shifter who thought the world revolved around her. Worse, the woman had messed with her sister and that could not be tolerated.

Her annoyance melted when she caught sight of Galen standing in his doorway speaking to his assistant. When he noticed her there, he smiled and headed toward her. "To what do I owe this visit?" He hugged her.

"I'm here with Max. He's still talking with your father so I thought I'd cruise past your office to say hello."

"Renee told me she's starting with Mary this weekend. I wanted to tell you thank you for all you've done. She's so much more confident now when she uses her gifts. She's finally believing she's worthy of using her magick, that she can and do it right."

"You don't have to thank me. She's my sister and more than that, she's a witch. None of us should be ashamed of what we are and what we can do. Our mother can't teach her, she barely taught me. But I can help and that's the way it's supposed to work. Mary will be good for her."

"And do you? Believe you're worthy?" he asked softly.

"Most of the time." She shrugged. "We're damaged, all of us human beings. But it's about getting past that and being better than the people who try to harm us. Being better than they expect. That's revenge."

Galen looked at her for a long time without speaking. "I'm glad you're here, Kendra. I'm glad to be your family."

Max loped down the hall toward them, her attention snagged on how he moved. She'd been in denial really, or on a deliberate *I'm not going to think about that* kick when it came to him.

It wouldn't help her. She was already in so deep with him that there was no turning back.

"Got my stuff. Ready to head out?" He slid an arm around her shoulders when he reached her, kissing the top of her head.

"Yep. I was just saying hello to my brother-in-law." She looked back to Galen. "I'll see you in a few hours for dinner."

Galen snapped his fingers. "Crap. I forgot. I'm supposed to invite you both to dinner tonight. I left a message with your assistant." Galen smirked at his brother and she snorted at how they were together. It was cute. Though she'd learned from Renee the two brothers would sometimes end up in physical dust-ups, she had no doubt there was deep respect and love between them. And they were predator animals under the skin after all, even if they were dumb dudes for punching instead of negotiating.

"Yeah, yeah. I got it. Renee invited me too just a few minutes ago downstairs."

"Catch your ugly mug later then." Galen turned back to Kendra. "Nice to see you. And thank you again."

"So," Max began as he pulled out of the parking garage and headed across the river to Mary's place, "I think you should let me replace your car. It'll make me feel better to know you have it. I worry about you."

Christ, already? How had he learned? "How the hell did you know?"

He paused a moment and she realized she'd jumped to conclusions. He'd probably only thought she hadn't gotten the money yet. Damnation.

"Know what?" The ease in his voice was such a ruse. She knew he was on the scent and wouldn't let go until she told him everything.

"Nothing. Nothing." No one ever said she was smart all the time.

He continued to drive with that ease of his, even though Boston was the craziest city she'd ever driven in.

"You know I'm not going to let it go. So tell me. Though, well interrogating you could be quite entertaining. I could lick you and lick you until you begged me to let you come."

Even annoyed, she couldn't stop the shiver that worked through her at that visual. "Fine. Fine. I'm just taking my time to find the car I want. The insurance company's check arrived already."

"So why wait? I can take you to a great lot one of our cats runs out in Brockton. He'll be fair."

Gah. This was totally her own fault. "I want to save up a bit more to get exactly what I want. When I get to that point, I'll be happy to use your friend though. Thank you."

He growled, the sound thick with annoyance. "They didn't give you enough money to replace the car with one you want."

"It happens." She shrugged. "I'm fine with waiting so I can afford what I really want."

"This is stupid, Kendra. I have the money, why not let me help?"

"I've already said no thank you. And really, Max, how many people ride mass transit every day? It's safe and easy to use. Totally convenient from my place to the school."

That damned smile of his took his lips, curving them upward in a most alluring way. "What if you get stranded?"

"I can take a cab. Or, if all else fails, call my boyfriend to come get me. But where do I go that late anyway? I'm not twenty-two hanging out at after-hours bars. I'm tucked up in bed by ten. Or if you're with me, midnight or so." Max loved to spend hours on sex, and who was she to complain about that?

"What if you borrowed my car? You know, just until you get rest of the money saved? Or, you could take a loan from me for the rest if you won't let me pay for it."

"Max, it's very sweet that you're concerned about me and all. But I'm fine. It shouldn't take me very long, another two months or so. Jack hadn't let go of his lease for the space at his apartment so I even have a place to park." She'd moved into Jack's old apartment. Had tried to resist, there was no way she could really afford it if he'd charged her market rate. But of course, like everyone else in her new family, including Renee, they'd appealed to safety and space. And relative closeness to Renee's house.

"Concerned is a very soft word for how much it freaks me out that these fucking witches are out there looking to hurt you, to rob you of your power and your life."

"If they come for me, they'll come for me in my car or on the T, or in my house or when I'm getting groceries. Whatever. It's not a lack of a car that exposes me. I'm learning how to defend myself."

"And then what?"

She turned to him. "And then I plan to teach those skills to every witch I know and who is interested, because we shouldn't let fear of other kinds of magick cripple our ability to protect ourselves."

"Which will piss off some of your people, right?"

"Yes. I imagine when it comes down to it, I'll face a lot of criticism. But at least they'll all be talking, even if it's only to criticize me. We are not safe the way we are now. It's far easier now to track us, what with computers and readily available digitized information."

He muttered in Spanish and then caught her looking and cursed, in English.

She laughed. "You keep forgetting I speak Spanish, don't you?"

"So you're taking on a revolution. You know that, right? You're taking on a huge fight."

"Yes. I know staying silent and protecting only myself and my sister is a cowardly, selfish thing. There are too many others who don't know enough and will be at risk. What would you have me do? Keep quiet? Is that what you'd do?"

"I hate it when you do that."

He pulled around behind Mary's small house as she directed him to.

"Do what?"

"I hate it when you're doing the right thing and I have to

admit that even when I know it's dangerous and I could lose you."

She sighed inwardly. No matter how she tried to hold him out, he simply found a way in, leaving her defenseless against him.

"I'm not going anywhere but inside to learn some stuff. I asked Mary if it was all right to bring you, by the way, so she knows you're here."

Max wanted to meet this woman anyway, being welcome was a good thing.

He wasn't expecting what greeted them at the door though. Why he'd imagined this Mary as a tiny, bent, shriveled woman, he didn't know.

A tall, elegant, dark-haired woman with pale green eyes that didn't miss a trick opened the door, smiling when her gaze locked with Kendra's. "You're here and positively glowing." She looked around Kendra to Max, giving him a slow perusal. "You're Max de La Vega, and I imagine, the reason for the glow. I'm Mary Pierce, please be welcome and come inside."

Another surprise greeted him as he followed Kendra into the small house. He'd expected clutter. Books and crystals and stuff. Instead, it was spare, clean lines, white furniture, dark woods.

"I think it would be good for you to watch Kendra work. You have a lot of power, a lot of magick in you. It's tuned to hers as hers is to yours. This feedback loop has helped her, though I don't imagine she's told you. It means she has to articulate how much she cares for you."

He smiled, more at the sigh of affectionate annoyance Kendra had made than anything else. He knew she cared for him, it was obvious in everything she did, in the way she let him take over at times, the way she made room for his need to protect and love her.

"I'm glad to hear it. Glad to hear I'm helping, because I have to tell you this whole business makes me very nervous. I'm not a man prone to sitting and letting things happen. She's being threatened, my sister-in-law is being threatened. These are my people, I need to know they're going to be protected."

"I'm giving her the tools to protect herself," Mary countered, still wearing that smile of hers. His cat liked this woman very much. She was strong and utterly capable. This meant she had the ability to protect Kendra in her own way. Mary was part of Kendra putting down roots in Boston and the man approved mightily.

Kendra, obviously annoyed, huffed the smallest of snorts. Knowing she respected Mary, Max understood what an act of willpower it was that she hadn't snapped a comment or two at them. Max held his grin back.

Kendra stepped neatly between Mary and Max, taking control again. "I appreciate you seeing me in the evening, Mary. We need to be somewhere later, so if you two are done discussing me?"

Mary just patted her hand. "Go on through. I put a chair in the corner for Max. I'll be right in."

"Through here." Kendra led him down some steps and out into a garden room of sorts. Lots of natural light from the large windows.

He took her hand, pulling her back to him. She allowed it, looking up into his face. "Thank you for letting me in. I know it's hard for you and I know there's a good reason for it."

"Like the tide," she said softly. "You sweep in and I tell myself to tread water. To go to higher ground and I just...don't. I like it, apparently."

She pushed him gently back before he could say anything.

But he didn't need to. She'd said it for him. "Now, go sit over there. This will be a short lesson tonight."

He obeyed, but he smirked for good measure.

Again, things he hadn't expected. Mary's magick was not like the lessons he'd observed between Kendra and Renee at all.

Mary bent and placed her palms against the floor. It was as if she was...not there. Her eyes were open, but saw a far-off place.

"Use your link with Max, draw on his energy."

"No."

Max sat, waiting to see where that went.

"I haven't asked and it's not an emergency. I won't do that. I don't even know if it will harm his ability to change. I won't endanger him like that. Especially when I haven't even asked."

So fierce, his little witch. He kept quiet, letting her handle it. Of course he'd let her draw energy from him. She'd done it before, though, as she pointed out, it had been an emergency.

Mary shrugged and looked to Max. "So ask him."

"I didn't bring him for this. I'll take the energy he's giving off, but none still within."

The two women's gazes clashed as will met will. Mary nodded once. "I don't think I asked to negotiate this."

Kendra stood tall, back straight. "I'm not asking your permission. You are my teacher and I respect that. However, how I use my magick is my business, and it comes with ethics and rules. I will not wild all over the population to steal their essence for my amusement. That's not who or how I want to be."

The tension stretched taut until at last Mary smiled. "I'm glad to hear it." Mary nodded once and Max realized Kendra had passed some sort of ethical pop quiz. "Now that I know you'll be ethical even when you have access to a well of deep magick, let's talk about how to collect ambient life energy from your surroundings without taking it directly from any living being while they're using it."

Max hid a smile, though only barely. He spent the next hour watching Kendra draw things like sunlight dappled off water into herself. She looked tired by the end and he reminded himself to ask her later what sort of toll it took.

Mary put her forehead to Kendra's as they finished up. "Be sure to eat some protein. It'll help with the headaches. I'll see you tomorrow with Renee." She looked to Max. "It was lovely to meet you. Can you please excuse us for a moment?"

He waited for Kendra to give him the signal, and at her nod, he moved to wait for her in the hall just outside the room. Of course, he could hear the conversation anyway.

"What's wrong?" Kendra asked.

"Not wrong really. It's...Kendra, your connection to Max has opened up the taps of your magick in a wholly new way. What we did tonight was something that would have taken at least a month to pick up. You did it the first time you tried. He makes you stronger."

"I can't harm him. I won't do any magick when he's nearby."

Max leashed his frustrated growl, but only just. If he made her stronger that was a *good* thing.

"That's the thing. I monitored you both while you worked. The way between you is wide open. You draw on it, but when you expend it, it returned to him. You two are like one being in several ways. The tenor of your magick is different. Not weaker at all. I think...I don't want to say what I think until I do some research. We can talk about it next lesson. Rosemary will be staying with me when she's here in Boston. I'll put her to work on it too."

"If it has something to do with him being a shifter, it's integral no one gets wind of it. We'd be putting him and other shifters in danger if it got out. They'd start hunting shifters to leash to mages." Max heard the fear in her voice. "I can't have that. This is my family and I won't do anything to hurt them." There she was, the fear had melted into anger.

"Of course. But you know the others are going to resist even more if it gets out. They're fearful enough of outsiders as it is. If they learn about some sort of connection between shifters and witches, many of them will see it as a threat."

"They're already afraid of what they are; it won't surprise me if they're afraid of what others are. We both know it's going to be an issue no matter what we do. I have to go, but thank you for your help."

They began to walk toward where he waited, so he pretended to look out the window at the tiny but plant-filled backyard.

"Ready?" He held a hand out, his love for her filling him up, overflowing.

She took it and their connection seemed to click into place on a level she hadn't experienced before. Their eyes met, hers wide and surprised. He smiled and stole a kiss as he escorted her to the car.

"Wait." She paused, looking at his car and cocking her head.

"Problem?" He scanned the immediate area, not seeing anything out of the ordinary, not even sensing it.

She turned back to him. "Do you have a knife?"

"Why?"

"Because."

"I'm sure I'm going to regret this." He pulled a Swiss army knife from his case and handed it to her. And she proved him right when she sliced her upper arm open, near one of the tattooed marks he liked most. The spice of her blood filled his senses, rich, ripe with magick, thick and velvety. A lesser cat would have had a harder time with the lure of it. As it was, he had to fight the urge to scent her more deeply.

"Don't crowd me," she said prissily as she dipped her finger in the welling blood and traced symbols on his tires.

He wanted to grab her, shove her in the car and take off. Instead, he had to satisfy himself with a growl as he moved closer. "Take some of my fucking energy, will you? What the hell are you doing? You're going to be sick when you finish."

"God, you're an old woman," she muttered, surprising him but amusing him anyway.

He followed her, keeping watch over the area. His cat paced, agitated, concerned for his female.

After a few minutes she stood, paler, but otherwise all right as far as he could see. Certainly all right enough for him to allow some of his temper free. "Damn it, Kendra." He pushed her into the car and rustled around through the first aid kit in his trunk. "Hold still and let me get it wrapped."

She held her arm out, not moving as he cleaned and then bound the wound.

Kendra realized she wasn't even that tired. Usually after her lessons, all she wanted to do was go home and nap for a bit. But just then, tucked into the soft-as-a-whisper leather seats of Max's car, she was content, and while not in any shape to run a marathon, she was without a headache and feeling well.

He tended to her cut, gentle as he touched. But she felt his temper coming off him in waves. "You want to tell me what the fuck that was all about? Do you think I want you spilling blood for me? I want you at one hundred percent! I want you healthy and always able to defend yourself. I know it weakens you to use your magick. How much?"

She found her water bottle and he made that cute little growl as she drained it in seconds. It was dreadful of her to be so entertained by his temper, but it was cute and she was utterly defenseless against it.

He slammed the trunk lid down and got into the car, belting in and staying silent for long minutes.

"Should we stop and get you something? Are you all right? I heard Mary tell you to be sure to be hydrated and to eat protein. Should I stop and get us dinner right now?"

"Do you have any question you'd prefer to have answered first?" She knew she was poking at him, but it amused her and he always looked dangerously hot when he was agitated with her.

"Kendra." One dark eyebrow winged up and she knew it was time to give him a break.

"I'm fine. When we get to Renee's I'll get some juice and grab some cheese and crackers to fill me up until dinner is ready."

"That's question one."

She'd driven with him enough to know she shouldn't watch the road, cars, pedestrians and whatever else he careened around. Instead she turned, resting her head against the seat while watching him. Much better than the road any day.

"I put protective sigils on your car. My blood will carry the magick better. I gave it freely. It didn't harm me. Blood is a carrier agent. It can be used negatively, but not all of it is bad. It just hit me that you're out and about and our relationship is pretty public knowledge. I want you to be safe."

He frowned, but not for long. "You're going to take years off my life, you know that?"

"Pfft."

"Pfft? Don't blow me off. This is important!"

"Hey, buster, fuck you. I'll do what I want when it comes to protecting the people I care about. And you can't stop me so get that right out of your head. Don't tell me what's important. Like I don't know myself? Like I'm too stupid to figure it out?"

"When have I ever said you were stupid? Never. Because I don't think so and I wouldn't say that."

"I'm not some weak child playing with spells because she watched *Charmed* or whatever."

"Hey, that's not my doorbell, Kendra. That's not even my neighborhood."

"Yes, but it's mine." Oh God, she was going to cry. She dug her nails into her palm, feeling the blood seep into the bandage as she flexed, opening the wound again. Shit.

"If you told me what it was, I could avoid it in the future. I'm not going to judge you, you know." He paused, nostrils flaring. "You're bleeding."

"I hate that," she muttered.

"Too fucking bad. You wrote on my car with your blood and you did it at harm to yourself. I don't like that."

"And I don't care."

"Why do you have to be so stubborn?"

"We're here. We'll talk later."

"We'll talk now." He turned toward her, pushing her sleeve up and re-dressing the slice she'd made. His hands gentled and he looked to her and she saw it. Stark fear. For a man like him, it had to be a pretty unusual emotion.

Max was a fixer and she wasn't a problem easily solved.

She took a deep breath. "You once asked me why I didn't drink. I drank too much at one time and I made mistakes. Big ones. I don't blame the alcohol, but it doesn't make me a good person."

"This is about your ex?"

"I *really* can't do this right now. I have to go in there and there'll be at least five other people, and if I'm all emotional, Renee will notice and feel bad and want to fix me. And I'll be pissy because I've had enough of people trying to fix me."

"Don't you understand? I love you. I want to know you. I want to understand you. This is part of what it means to truly be with someone. To be my family and let me be yours. Family shares stuff. You're part of that for me."

She closed her eyes. She should tell him he couldn't love her, but it would have been disrespectful. And a lie. And she knew he did. Knew he was sure of how he felt about her. She couldn't say with a straight face that she didn't want or need his love. It was a lie. She *did* want it. She did need it. No matter how impractical, or silly. She'd wanted it for as long as she could remember, and *that* was the crux of her fear.

The stuff about what happened with her ex, that was part of it, but a blip really. She was over it, past it for the most part. But there was this place inside her, the insecurity at times was powerful.

Deep within there was the girl whose mother had left her. The girl whose sister got to have that mother every day. And then she was gone, and Kendra couldn't get past feeling alone, even surrounded by people. Even having a grandmother and an uncle, being raised by Rosemary, who loved her without question hadn't quite quenched that unspoken question. Was she a burden? A problem to be solved? Or was she a gift?

103

It was stupid. She got that. Her family, her mother's family, loved her. She saw that love in Renee's eyes, felt it in everything her sister did for her. But what you knew and what lurked inside were sometimes very different.

How could she explain to him what it was like for her to see him with his family? When Renee had had a horrible childhood and Kendra at least was raised by her aunt who loved her? Kendra felt selfish and guilty for even thinking it. He'd never not known what it meant to wonder where he fit, if he was loved. He was next-in-line, the golden boy who achieved, the male who fixed things. She was entirely sure he'd been that way the moment Imogene gave birth to him.

None of those things were subjects she wanted to delve into. Especially then and there.

He cursed. "Shit. Renee sees us. She's waving from the porch." Thank the heavens for her sweet, nosy sister.

She grabbed her bag and he growled when she put her hand on the door. "Oh for God's sake, Max. I can open my own door."

"Why do you have to try to push me away when you know you like it? You like it when I take care of you and I like doing it. Sit there or I'll tell her about the cut and she'll make you drink some nasty-smelling tea."

"You're diabolical."

He snorted and got out. She waited.

Chapter Seven

He hovered, making sure she kept drinking and staying hydrated. Happily, she seemed to accept his need to do it. She did eat the cheese and crackers, and he brought over some fruit too. Renee noticed, her eyes narrowing as she took in the scene. He wasn't kidding, he would sic Renee on Kendra if his little witch even thought about not taking care of herself.

Jack came in with Akio and a wolf Max had never met before, though he scented alpha right away.

"Renee, I brought a guest. Hope that's all right."

Renee turned, tipping her face up to receive a kiss. "Of course. We've got plenty. Galen's in charge, you know he always makes enough for five or six extra people."

Jack sent an affectionate look to Galen before turning back to Renee. "Gorgeous, this is Gabe Murphy. He's one of the Alphas of Pacific Pack. Before that he was the National Mediator and we worked together. In fact, the place Grace and Cade live is where he lived for years. He's in town for a few days, and as Grace wouldn't stop singing your praises, I figured I'd better bring him by so he could see my beautiful mates."

"He hasn't shut up about you and Galen since I arrived so I figured I should come over and see you two in person." Gabe bowed slightly. "It's my pleasure to meet Jack's mates. I'm in a triad as well so it's always nice to see another working relationship like mine."

Renee blushed. "You're mates with Grace's sister-in-law Tracy, right? She was telling me about your little girls. Do you have pictures?"

Gabe's face lit at the mention and Max's estimation of him rose.

"That's us." He pulled his phone out. "Always happy to show pictures."

Kendra joined them, looking over Gabe's shoulder. Max knew wolves mated for life, had heard this one was mated not just to one wolf, but two, and he had no romantic designs on Kendra at all. And yet, her proximity to another male stirred his agitation, even as logic told him it was silly to feel that way.

"This is Rose." Gabe smiled down at the picture on his phone of a little girl with mischief in her smile, what you could see of it around all the chocolate. "She just turned two. She looks so much like Nick, he's her other daddy, it's not funny. This is Lianne, she's going to be five soon and ready for kindergarten. The older two in this one are Chris and Haley, Nick's niece and nephew. They're ours too. We're very fortunate to have such a beautiful family."

"I was raised by my aunt. She's more of a mother than the one I was born to could have been." Kendra's smile at Gabe was filled with emotion and Renee hugged her. Max moved to her, Renee stepping aside so he could touch Kendra.

Gabe looked up, met Max's gaze and nodded, getting it. "We're happy to have you with us tonight, Gabe. Please make yourself at home. You have a lovely family, just as Grace said. Would you like a glass of wine? Juice? Soda?"

Jack indicated a chair at the large table. "Have a seat Gabe. I'll get you some juice. Renee squeezed it this morning."

Galen stepped forward as Max let go of Kendra, who

relaxed against him one last second.

"I'm Galen. Nice to meet you. This is Renee's sister Kendra and my brother Max."

"Two witches. Interesting. One of the humans who just mated with one of my wolves is a witch. He hasn't taken the change. Are you going to?" he asked Kendra after taking her hand in his.

"Max and I haven't really had that conversation. I...I hadn't considered it. I'm not opposed to the idea. How did it work out for him, do you know? I mean when he bonded with a wolf. Did his magick grow or feel any different?"

Max smiled briefly, Galen caught him and his smile echoed his brother's. Kendra hadn't argued being his. Ha.

"I can give you his contact information, if you like. He's open enough, I'm sure he'd talk to you about it."

Kendra smiled. "Thank you. I'd like that."

Gabe turned to Max and nodded. "You're alpha."

Max nodded. "Next-in-line."

"Kendra, can you help me with something?" Renee called out.

Max put a hand on Kendra's shoulder, a gentle caress and she leaned into it for a moment. He asked Renee, "What do you need, babe? I'll do it."

Renee rolled her eyes at him, she knew his game. "Girl stuff. I believe tampons may be discussed."

Kendra snorted a laugh and the two of them disappeared off into the bedroom.

"I have no idea why you thought you could hide Kendra's pallor or the fact that she's been bleeding from Renee. She doesn't need our sense of smell for that. Or that you could sway her from getting an answer." Jack plopped down at the table.

107

"She all right?"

"Magick lesson." He wasn't going to go into detail with Murphy there. He trusted Jack like the family he was. But he didn't know Gabe Murphy from Adam, and there was no way he'd take a chance and expose Kendra to any danger if he could help it.

"Magick makes her bleed?" Akio spoke then. Max liked the wolf who served as Jack's right hand in Boston. He'd taken up a lot of the slack, doing much of the travel across the country as a representative of the National Pack since Jack had mated with Renee and wanted to stick close.

"No. She cut herself after the lesson. I field dressed it. Tried to get her to go to the doctor but she refused. It's a shallow cut."

"You're so gone for her I should laugh. But I remember the early days when I first brought Renee around and you were the first to stand behind us. I'll tease you, but not enough to make you cry like a pussy." Galen snickered.

"Shut the fuck up, pretty boy." Max shook his head and tried not to laugh. "I am gone. Like beyond gone. She lets me be. It works out."

Galen and Jack burst out laughing. "Those two may not have grown up together, but damn, they're so much alike it's not funny."

"You wanna tell me why you're so pale?" Renee demanded once they'd gone into the bedroom and closed the door.

"You know they all have super hearing, right?"

Renee waved a hand. "Yes, worse than a bunch of old ladies with the eavesdropping. But since Max obviously knows what's up, you can tell me. Also, Galen has good manners most of the time. They'll listen in, but feel bad about it."

"I'm fine. I just had a particularly draining lesson. I cut myself." She motioned to her arm. "Needed to ward Max's car. He took care of it there, so stop glowering at me. I had to do it the strongest way I knew how. I'm worried for everyone." And she was. It hit her as she'd walked out of Mary's, hit her that while she and Renee had some means to ward off an attack, the others relied on tooth and claw, but the assholes out to steal magick didn't care about that. They cared about power. Kendra didn't want them to figure out how much energy shifters possessed.

She patted her sister's arm. "Get your frowny face off. You'll get forehead wrinkles. Anyway, the cheese and crackers really did help. Hey, and dinner is almost done so I'll pig out and get to blame it all on magick depletion. Bonus. I'm going to bed early tonight and I promise to get lots of rest. To be totally honest with you, everything is...I don't know, different. My ability to spool up energy is better, smoother. It feels different, but I can't describe it just yet."

"Interesting. What does Mary have to say? Did you talk to her about it? Or to Rosemary?"

"Mary said she felt something was different too. She's going to look into it and talk to me after."

"I don't like that you're doing all this alone." Renee's chin jutted out. "It's not fair for you to take all this weight on for the rest of us. Look at you. You're pale and bleeding!"

"I told you, I'm already feeling better. And eventually, you can handle more as you learn. I need to rest more, I know I do. I don't have to be up early tomorrow and Max will make me breakfast in bed because I'm that lucky in life. Don't worry. By the way, Mary wanted me to tell you how excited she was about you starting with her tomorrow."

"Well for heaven's sake, let's get you some more food.

Galen's out there looking all delicious as he cooks enough for three dozen people, he'd look even hotter getting you a snack with some protein." Her sister looked her over again, catching Kendra as she tried to keep her composure intact. "There's more to this story than you're telling me." Renee crossed her arms over her chest and glared.

"Today has been...a lot. Just a lot and I'm asking you to back off enough for me to process it all. Please. I'll talk to you more when I figure it out myself. I need the time to get it straight in my head."

The anger was gone then, replaced by worry. Her sister simply enfolded her into a hug and the first sob broke. "Let it go. You're here with me. Safe. Surrounded by people who love you."

"I'm going to be swollen and red." But the tears didn't stop.

Renee sighed, hugging Kendra, smoothing a hand up and down her back. "How long has it been since you've allowed yourself to cry?"

"Long enough I remember how awful I feel while doing it, which is enough to keep me from letting myself cry usually." She gulped in air, and something in her chest loosened as the tears fell.

Max simply waltzed in with a brisk knock. She smelled him, that rich, dark scent laced with sex, desire, strength and masculinity.

He stopped just an inch or two away from her, close enough that she felt his heat. He caressed her shoulder and spoke so very gently she was able to rein in the tears even as the tenderness in the way he treated her broke through her.

"Ah, *carino,* why don't I take you home? We'll get you tucked up in bed. I'll feed you and you can go to sleep. Let me take care of you."

"He totally does that all the time," she mumbled into Renee's sweater.

"He called you sweetheart to soften you up." Kendra knew Renee smiled as she said it. "Galen and Jack do it too. The barging-in thing. Welcome to being in love with an alpha male, huh? They mean well. But sometimes you need to smack them in the nose to get them to back off."

Kendra wanted to die from embarrassment. The place was full of people, most of them with super hearing so they knew she was crying.

"Can you please leave us alone for a few minutes?" she asked Renee who simply kissed her forehead and left the room.

Max hugged her. "Baby, I hate to see you sad. Let me help you. Tell me what to do and I'll do it."

"Unless I tell you to wait outside while I talk to my sister."

He snorted a laugh. "Busted. I'd say I can't help it, but I just don't want to." He swayed from side to side, holding her as she melted against him. The simple act of touch sent comfort and warmth through her system. "You hurt and my heart breaks. I want you to be happy all the time. I want you to smile and know you're loved."

Oh he undid her.

"I can't leave. Renee invited me and I want to be here for her."

"Let's get you a cool cloth for your eyes then." He led her into the adjoining bathroom and she sat on the side of the tub while he got her a washcloth.

"Thank you." She took the cloth, pressing it to her eyes. He hadn't tried to sway her to leave, instead he'd accepted that she wanted to stay for her sister. It wasn't the big house and the luxury car, it was his heart that attracted everything inside her.

"I love you. I want to take care of you."

He did. She knew that and despite the craziness of the situation, it was good.

After what had turned out to be an enjoyable dinner, Max took her back to his place with every intention of cosseting her and making her rest. Once he got her inside his house he breathed easier. Felt safer with her there at his side, in the space he knew without a doubt he could defend. His cat eased back a bit.

She even allowed him to carry her up to his bedroom, burrowing her face into his neck as he moved.

When he put her down on his bed, she fit, like she was meant to be there. And she was.

She yawned and allowed him to take her sweater and bra off. He quickly put one of his shirts on her because the sight of her skin drove him wild.

"What do you look like as a cat?" she asked, half-naked, her hair tousled, his shirt inching up her creamy pale thigh.

"You haven't seen me that way?" It hadn't occurred to him, but he supposed she hadn't. She shook her head. "Do you want to?"

Her eyes lit and he felt it to his toes. "Now? Oh yes! I mean, if it's not too tiring or what have you. I understand it takes a toll on the shifter when they change forms."

"Lower-ranked shifters, yes. If I had to shift say ten or twelve times in a few hours, I'd be very tired and it would be difficult unless my father or another alpha forced the change. But like you with your magick, I don't use it all the time. It's fine." And he wanted her to see his other self. His cat liked that very much.

She sat on his bed and he tucked the blankets he'd added for her—his body temperature ran very warm so he hadn't much use for blankets until his little witch found her way into his bed—around her legs. "I'll change and we'll have hot tea when I change back. And then we talk."

She frowned with a sigh, but nodded anyway.

After he'd stripped off and he'd preened for her, he crouched and let his cat come. Next time he opened his eyes, the world was different, sights and scents were a symphony. Hers brought a rumble of pleasure from his belly.

She watched him, a smile on her face. He moved, slowly, butting her hand with his head and purring when she stroked him.

She spoke and the cat realized hers were words of wonder and awe. She spoke of his beauty and strength as she touched his shoulders where his muscles bunched. Her hands on his fur, stroking over his body pleased him.

She was small, soft and fragile. The cat wanted her safe and the man agreed. She smelled like his. He licked up her hand, over the delicate nip at her wrist, the magick she wore delighted him.

The beast, the cat knew from her touch, knew its heart's mate and all was well.

When the man came forward again, he found himself in her arms.

"Well hello."

She kissed him. "Thank you for that. Your cat is amazing. Beautiful, strong, powerful. Also, wow, you're like, huge." After a snicker she composed herself again. "Well yes, that way, but you know what I mean."

"Tell me. Tell me what broke from you today in sobs so sad they nearly shattered my heart to know they lived inside you." He settled in bed beside her and she found his side again.

"I'd just had a day with a crap-ton of stuff going on. I realized a lot of stuff and it stirred up things I like to think I've dealt with. I don't like not being in control of myself."

He kissed the knuckles of the hand he held. "You can let yourself be flawed. Just for a few minutes. Tell me."

She cleared her throat. "I know you think I was physically abused. What I was, was controlled and emotionally beaten down so that I ceased trusting myself, ceased understanding myself. So I drank. A lot. Enough to ignore the way my father-in-law would bump into me, or slam a door and sometimes I'd be near enough to get hit.

"I took it to my husband but he reassured me it wasn't on purpose. That his parents were very religious and didn't know how to handle my being a witch. So could I, you know, dial it down a little?"

He tried to maintain even breathing, even though rage began to build within.

"I don't want to tell you all the gory details. It's over now and I'm done with it, with who I was then. But..." She paused, licking her lips, her bottom lip trembled. "I didn't know up from down at the end."

"You don't have to say any more. I don't want to upset you any further."

She shook her head. "He kept me locked up. He said it was to cleanse me. He joined with them and their crazy movement. You know them, the same people who want to be allowed to kill all shifters."

He did know them. The angry humans who protested outside hospitals that treated shifters, outside churches where they worshipped or schools where they were educated. The same group of people who used to spend their weekends outside funerals of young men and women who'd died of HIV, holding up signs about how they were hated by their creator.

"At first I allowed it. It was easier to do than fight. And then I began to realize what a weak, unworthy person I was being by allowing it to happen. The last thing I wanted was for them to be right about me. So I began to plan to get free."

Pride, the feeling was pride, and she couldn't have known how much he felt for her at that moment. "And you did."

"I hurt them. I hadn't used my magick for some time and that day I used a lot. It was unwieldy, but still mine. I took it, I realize now, I took it from everything around me because my reserves had been so low. I was a mess. Angry. Afraid. I lashed out at my father-in-law, who blocked my path, and my husband who stood on the lawn screaming that he'd kill me if I tried to leave. A neighbor saw it and called the cops. When I drove away with my aunt that day, I vowed I'd never, ever allow anyone to make me ashamed of my gifts or to take my humanity."

He understood. He'd accepted before, knew she had buttons, but now he got hers on a totally different level. What's more, he realized the way she allowed him to take over and protect had been an immense gift of her trust.

"You're so beautiful, Kendra. Powerful. A witch, a woman who deserves nothing but love and kindness. I want to give that to you."

She turned into his body, hugging him tight. "You *do*."

He wanted to mark her. Wanted to sink his teeth into her skin the way Galen did with Renee. Wanted her to accept all of him, including the imprint.

"What is it?" she asked, her lips against his skin.

"You know me like no one else does. It should be scary. It's

115

not. I'm imprinted, you know that, right? Know what imprinting is to us?"

"Sort of. From what Renee has said about Galen, it's the way the cat within the human identifies with another person as theirs. As their husband or wife. Like a mate I guess. You don't do it like the wolves though, right?"

He kissed her, tasting the salt of her grief, the spice of her happiness, the musk of her desire. Every part of her excited the man and the cat.

"That's the gist of it, yes. We don't have that instant bond like the wolves do when they have unprotected sex. Ours is slower to build in many ways, though no less deep and certainly no less permanent. You're not scared?" He wanted to laugh, he'd been so worried about it and she seemed to be taking it just fine.

She took his face between her hands. "You told me a few weeks ago that you were imprinting on me, it's not like I didn't know. As for fear? I'm scared all the time. But not *of* you. I worry I'll fuck things up. I worry I'm not worthy of you. My God, Max, you're going to run the jamboree, and I know enough of the politics there to understand my being human will be a detriment to you. I don't want to make things harder for you."

Without missing a beat, he slid her panties off and she laughed. The laughter faded as he rolled over, her thighs automatically opening to him, long, lithe legs wrapping around his body.

Satisfaction slammed into him. "Wet already."

"Always. Any time I even think about you."

When he began to inch his way into her pussy, her eyes darkened, lips parted, gaze only for him.

"You don't get it do you? I don't care what Beth thinks, or Carlos or the other small group who have issues with humans.
116

You're mine. That's what counts. My cat is set to run the jamboree and my cat wants you as much as the man does. If they can't trust my judgment on something as important as my wife, I hardly think tossing you aside for a shifter would make a difference for the better. It would weaken me as a person and as a leader. I would die for any of my cats, but I won't give up my heart. You're my heart. And you're eminently worthy of running the jamboree at my side."

He didn't miss the way her eyes glimmered with emotion and unspent tears. Her smile was for him alone. "I never imagined loving like this. It's improbable. And ridiculous." She laughed. "You know what I mean so get that look off your face. I mean I've known you for five months now, we've only been dating a very short while."

He frowned, annoyed to be going over the same ground. "I know what I feel." And right now, he had to fuck her or he'd lose his mind. He pulled out and pressed back in, loving the way her breath stuttered and she caught her bottom lip between her teeth.

"Oh, that's very nice. One of your finest qualities."

He laughed, gathering her wrists in his hand, stretching her arms above her head and holding her in place. Her back arched, thrusting her breasts up. But it was that delicious little gasp she gave him that made him weak-kneed.

"Mmm. Yes, that's the way. I may just have to hold you like this for a few hours, torturing you with climax after climax until I'm sated of you." Given how his every waking thought was of her, he wasn't sure that was possible. Not that he'd turn down the chance to make her come for hours.

"You look far more handsome this way than frowning." Her voice was breathless as a pretty flush built on her neck. Taunting him to sink his teeth into her flesh. "As far as you knowing how you feel, of course you do. I mean, look, you turn furry and run around in the wilderness. I can bend energy and use it in all sorts of ways. It's not like I don't already live an improbable and ridiculous life. Why not this too?"

"Why not indeed?" Joy filled him in a way he'd never experienced before at her acceptance of the situation. "On to fucking. Then we can talk more."

"Bossy."

"As Renee would say, duh."

After a quick nip of that fleshy bottom lip of hers, he got back to work. Deep inside, her body was hot, wet, ready for him. He kissed and licked over her neck, across the blade of her collarbone, into the hollow of her throat. She writhed against him, pulling against his hold on her wrists, but only in a playful way. If she wanted to be free, she'd say so, he knew that much.

"More. God, please, deeper. I like it harder."

He obliged, thrusting harder and deeper, always remembering the relative difference in their strength. If he ever hurt her, he'd hate himself.

A sound broke from her lips, desperate, needy, so laced with sexuality it sent a shiver through him.

Kendra was sexually bold in a way he'd never expected just from a glance. She knew what she liked and wasn't afraid to ask for it. Ask? Demand. It meant more to him than he could express that she trusted him with herself, with her body and her heart.

She moved her head, exposing the long, pale line of her throat and the place his mouth watered to mark.

He licked it instead and felt the ripple of her inner muscles all around him.

What had she done to deserve such a man?

Kendra shivered as she pulled against the hand restraining her wrists. Her entire body hummed as he thrust into her pussy and dragged out slowly. His weight on her was just right, enough to cage her, hold her in place, but not too much that he harmed her.

He was so ridiculously sexy when he got all controlling in bed. More so because she knew he held back to keep from hurting her. That edge of control, the vibration from him, the way his muscles flexed and played as he fucked, nothing in her life had ever been like this.

Little bone-deep orgasms skittered through her, keeping her on edge for a big one. And all she could do was hang on, knowing he'd take care of her, knowing her pleasure was on his mind.

Knowing he found pleasure in how she responded to him.

"I love how you look at me," she managed to say, needing him to understand he meant something to her in ways she couldn't always articulate.

"You're the most fucking beautiful thing I've ever witnessed."

She groaned and then he pulled out.

That got her attention, dragging her back up from that pleasure-seeped place he always took her to. "Hey!"

He chuckled as he kissed his way down her body and she wasn't complaining at all when he pushed her thighs wide and dove in, licking her pussy, teasing, flicking and generally devastating her with his mouth.

Orgasm hit, far harder and much quicker than she'd thought. Flooded her until she had to close her eyes and let it take over.

Her muscles still jumped as he pushed his way back inside,

setting off more waves of pleasure.

"I needed your taste in my mouth, on my lips and tongue," he growled in her ear, holding her hands above her head again.

She was past words so she managed a "mmmm" and left it at that. He said the best stuff. From wicked dirty/bad/wrong to sweet and romantic. Man oh man, he must have a swath of women in his wake a mile wide.

"And you're all mine," she mumbled.

"Don't know what brought that on, but yes, *querida*, I am." He hissed. "You're so slick and hot, I can't hold off. I need to come inside you."

"Yes."

Chapter Eight

Rosemary met Kendra and Renee at Mary's door the following day. Their aunt smiled widely when she saw them, pulling them into a hug. "You're here! Oh good. We have some positive news. I think we found it." She opened the door wider, ushering them all inside.

Max, Galen and Jack stood just behind them, having insisted on accompanying Renee and Kendra. Rather than waste time arguing over the inevitable, the women had simply thrown their hands up and allowed it.

"They wouldn't let us come alone," Renee explained. Kendra knew her sister was really nervous and excited about the lessons. She was proud of how far Renee had come in such a short time.

"Of course. They want to protect you. Come in. Mary is in the kitchen getting some tea." Rosemary tipped her face up and the men dropped kisses on her cheek as they walked in.

Kendra had wanted to speak with her aunt about Max, but she hadn't been able to other than to say she'd been seeing him. Either Rosemary had been too busy to sit down and listen to the story when she'd called, or Kendra had been too busy or never alone long enough to tell it. Clearly though, her aunt saw the way he watched her, saw the connection between them without too much effort.

"You and I need to have some dinner this evening." Rosemary sent Kendra a raised brow, and Kendra laughed, linking an arm through her aunt's.

"I know. We have a lot to catch up on. Now what do you think you found?"

They walked deeper into the house and Mary came out with a tea tray. "Hello everyone." The bracelets on her wrists jingled together as she turned to smile at Galen, Jack and Max. "My goodness you three are fine examples of masculinity! I figured you'd be here today. My husband is just down that hall, first door on the left. I believe there's some sort of sporting event on the television. And beer served with junk food of every type."

Max looked to Kendra, concern in his eyes.

Mary must have noted it. "Nothing can get in here. You have my word."

But he waited for Kendra to speak. She hid her smile, but moved to him, needing that contact as his hands went to her shoulders, caressing down her arms and clasping her hands.

"I'm fine. You're very close by and it is safe here. And, let's be honest, there are four pretty powerful witches here, I think we could manage to hold them off, at least until you all arrived."

His lips quivered as he held back an amused smile, and her mouth watered to taste them. "I can feel you, partially, through the bond we're growing," he said quietly. "We'll talk more about that later." He winked at her, knowing he'd lobbed a bomb her way, inclined his head, Jack and Galen following suit, and disappeared toward games, beer and chips.

"My. The two of you certainly have your hands full in the man department." Rosemary smiled, putting an arm around each of her nieces. "Max isn't like him." Her aunt never said Kendra's ex-husband's name, believing it gave him more power and recognition than he deserved.

"I know."

They followed Mary down the hall as she led them toward her practice space. "I have a friend. She's hard to locate unless she wants to be located. She's an encyclopedia of sorts. She brought me a location spell." Spells of this sort were hoarded, traded, searched for and honed over time. Sharing a spell was an intimate thing. "We don't think Renee can do it. At least not alone. It's going to take a level of focus and skill that she's not quite at yet." Rosemary looked at Renee. "Sorry, sweetie, but you're going to be a help here. And eventually, you'll have the chops to do this sort of ritual work."

Renee shrugged. "Not insulted at all. I'm just excited to learn."

Kendra removed her shoes and socks, preferring the closest contact to the earth she could get when she worked her magick. "Why can't you do it?" She paused and realized the answer. "You need the biological link. That's it, isn't it?"

Mary nodded. "Yes. Smart cookie, you are. Your mother was like that. Intuitive."

Yes, well, their mother was dead so how much good did it do her?

"All right. So let's make a circle. You and Renee in the innermost circle. Rosemary and I will be just outside that one in another circle. You need to keep your focus at all times. This is old magick, Kendra. Blood magick. Family magick. The ties that connect you will bring us answers. But projecting the ties leaves you open to danger. Which is why we're doing it here and also in two circles."

"Are you all right with this?" Kendra asked Renee, whose eyes had gone wide.

"Heck yeah. I mean, it's spooky and all, but I trust you. And you trust them. So it's all good. Just tell me what to do and

123

I'll do it."

Kendra would work the ritual so she drew the circles. Calling them to her, invoking protection and clarity of thought and purpose. Mary gave her the instructions and she barely felt the slice, into the same place she'd used to ward Max's car. Her blood, mixed with Renee's, would carry the spell, create the connection to find their father.

She threw open her othersight, the day-to-day world falling away, replaced by the wisps of color people carried around, their energy, their emotions, their personal brand of magick.

There were darker things just beyond, darker things looking for her. She knew it without a doubt. Knew they looked for Renee and would harm her if they could. Still, she kept her focus as she spoke the words, moving her feet the way the woman had said to. The dance was old, the steps not choreographed until they were being performed. They came to her, one after the next.

Exhaustion seeped into her bones. She drew, carefully, of the air around her, of the plants, the garden just beyond the windows, and found Max, a bright shimmering energy there just for her. His scent surrounded her, filled her as she steadied and continued to move her way through the spell.

It caught her up in its own rhythm and sway, like a song she heard in her head. She let it in, spun it back out. This was what it felt to be one with the energy, it felt right as it consumed her, used her to make her intentions reality.

Until the last words were whispered, the last steps taken and she let go, falling to her knees.

Max barreled into the room, barely leashing his fury as he saw her, pale and sweating, on her knees. The scent of her magick painted the air, heady, sticky-sweet. His cat relaxed a tiny bit, but the man felt the bite of the claws reminding him to stay vigilant. The cat didn't give a fuck about anyone but her.

"You mind telling me what the hell just happened?"

Rosemary looked him over quickly. "Your agitation won't help right now. She's been working a spell. It took a lot out of her. But she drew on you. Took that spell farther than I could have and I've got thirty years on her. She's changing, growing in ways I hadn't imagined. I'm so proud of you, Kendra." Rosemary pushed the hair from Kendra's face, and man and cat had had enough.

"All this time? One spell?" Christ, they'd been there two and a half hours.

Renee nodded. "She was amazing," she said to Galen as he edged into the room, Jack on his heels. "I just was the backup. She did this thing, this sort of dance, and she spoke in a beautiful language."

"You were a lot more than backup, Renee. You and she worked together totally seamlessly. She needed you and you helped so much." Rosemary smiled up at Renee.

Max scented her blood, his cat snarled inside, urging him to action. "She's bleeding." He stood at the edge of the circle, knowing enough not to break it. "Can I touch her?"

Mary stood, brushing her hand over the edges of the two circles. "Broken." She looked to Max. "Touch her."

He did more than that. He picked her up, cradled her against his body, tamping down his desire to run out of there with her. She turned into him, snuggled against his chest and he gave her touch. Gave her affection and strength. And she received.

"Here, let me get at her cut." Renee knelt, Jack touching her shoulder, Galen watching over the room, his thigh against Jack.

Kendra took a deep breath and sighed, some of her bonelessness gone.

Renee looked up at Max from where she cleaned the slice *he'd* cleaned only the day before. "Touch. It helps her too. Don't need to be a shifter to let yourself be comforted by the ones you love."

"Take her home. I tucked some tea that should help into her bag. Make sure she rests until tomorrow." Kendra's aunt touched his arm before she squeezed Kendra's hand again. "I know you don't know me very well. But I love these girls like they were my own. This won't cause her any lasting damage, Max. I wouldn't do that to her. It's part and parcel of using great reserves of energy. She'll be more efficient at it over time."

He wasn't sure he could take this sort of thing on a regular basis. But she was worth the effort and he knew he had no right to ask her to stop. Even if he'd felt like he was having a stroke when he came into that room and saw her just moments before.

Rosemary smiled up at him. "I'll see you both tomorrow at your parents' house. Your mother called to invite me. I'm very much looking forward to it. Tell Kendra I'll be checking in on her later."

"She'll be at my house. Renee, babe, can you get your aunt that number?"

Renee nodded, leaning forward to kiss her sister's forehead. "She did great, Max. Totally kicked ass. She'll be fine. I promise."

He said his quick goodbyes and took her away from there, loading her into his car and taking her home. His home and he wanted it to be hers. Somehow the sight of her there, so fragile and wan, without her shoes, huddled in a coat tore him to pieces, even though he knew she'd recover.

"I'm all right," she managed to say as he pulled into his driveway. "Just need a nap."

"You'll be getting one." He didn't bother asking to help her from the car and she didn't bother arguing. A fact that alarmed him.

He picked her up again, heading upstairs, straight to his bed. She didn't complain when he quickly undressed her and slid her under the blankets. "I'll be right back. I'm going to make you some of that tea. You'll drink it and then you'll sleep."

She nodded, her eyes drooping as she rested against the pillow, the spill of her hair against the pale green of the pillowcase appealed to him, even though he knew how wrung out she was.

A task. That's what he needed to keep his mind off the bad outcomes he couldn't seem to stop envisioning.

He brought the tea and made her drink it all even though she flipped him off twice and gagged a bit at the end. "Nice to see your attitude is back. It's how I know you're going to be okay." He kissed the top of her head and tucked her in. "Now you go to sleep. I'll be within earshot and check in. Just say my name, baby, and I'll be right here."

Her smile lightened his heart.

When he got back downstairs, he made himself a cup of tea, Earl Grey, not that crap she had to drink. And then he allowed it to come. The fear of losing her made him shake.

That's when Gibson came in.

"Galen called. She okay?" All lanky six plus feet of his tattooed and dreadlocked brother fell into the chair across from his.

He didn't want to do this. But Gibson, unlike Galen, was blunt and pushy. He knew Max better than pretty much anyone and there was no way he could hide his anxiety.

"She's sleeping. I made her choke down some tea that smelled like the bottom of a birdcage. Her color is already beginning to improve as well."

"So why are your hands shaking?"

"I had no idea that it would be like this. I figured she'd do her witchy thing here and there. Like she does with Renee. Moving shit with their magick. Not fucking passing out and bleeding. Not thugs hunting her down so they can kill her and steal her magick."

"So you're going to break up with her then? Move on to a nice shifter female who, by the way, turns furry and has sharp claws and teeth? I can see how the worry might distract you from work and running the jamboree after *Papi* steps aside."

Max sniffed and growled. "Yeah, yeah, aren't you all emo and shit to use reverse psychology on me. You know I love her. You know I've imprinted on her and you know I have no plans to break up with her."

"Yeah. I know it. And I know your hands are shaking just thinking about what could have happened. But—and I hate to get all *emotional and shit*, so if you bring this up I'll deny it—it's supposed to feel that way. You're supposed to feel as if you'd die if she did. Why on earth would you want to be with someone who didn't feel like they were an integral part of you? What's the fuckin' point of love, Max, if you don't feel it in all its glorious intensity, both the good and the bad?"

"It sucks when you make sense."

Gibson laughed, but kept it quiet so as not to disturb Kendra.

"I like her. She's got a warrior's soul. She's good for you. A woman you can count on. And let's be honest, this just makes her even stronger to be at your side. She is totally worthy of

128

running the jamboree with you. She can protect herself and those cats. My cat is comforted by this. You have to understand the rest of us will feel similarly.

"You and Galen both lucked out. Too bad they don't have any cousins or anything. I put some extra people on her. On the school and her apartment. Since her place was Jack's before, it's very secure, though she'd be better off here. I expect you'll propose that one to her soon enough. Can I do anything else?"

"Yes. I want you to look into her ex-husband and his family. I want to know where they are and what they're up to. Full search. I'll handle helping her transfer the protection order locally so don't worry about that part."

Gibson's demeanor changed, hardened. "Oh so it's that way? Yeah, I'm on it. If we need to make our point in person, I'm good for that too."

"We may have to. But let's just be sure they're far the fuck away from here first. Then we can go from there."

Gibson stood. "Unless you're up for a beer and some television, I'm going to get started on that work for you. We have some of it from when she came to town originally so it shouldn't be too hard."

He stood, clasping his brother's forearm, sliding his cheek along Gibson's. "Thank you. For everything. I appreciate it."

His brother nodded once. "I'm family. Comes with the subscription package." He walked to the door before turning back. "I got your back."

For a long beat after Gibson had left, Max stood in his entryway. Listening, letting himself center and focus. He would know if someone came in, would feel if a threat breached the outside security.

Satisfied that it was safe, he moved to where she was, needing to see her, taking the stairs quickly until he came to stand in the doorway to his bedroom, looking at her in his bed, watching the rise and fall of her chest, feeling it echo within his own. She'd become more than a woman he was in love with. She'd become necessary to him, integral.

He'd have to find a way to get through the fear and support her. She had a gift, even if it put her in danger. And she'd experienced others trying to take it from her, trying to shove it away and make her into someone and something she wasn't. He would never do that to her.

He'd need to figure out how to do that and still protect her.

Chapter Nine

When she opened her eyes, he was there. She knew he'd been there watching over her the whole time she'd been out. It was one of the reasons she found herself able to let go and totally fall under, letting her body recharge. He was there to protect and defend, and while it might not be politic to admit it out loud, she found it a very fine quality. Loved how he took care of her. Loved that he gave her the space to be who she was, but made room for himself in her life as well. Took up a lot of space, more each day. And she loved that part too.

He wasn't sleeping anymore. She knew he was awake, though his eyes were closed. She touched him anyway, loving the hardness of his muscles against her hands. When his lids lifted, his eyes locked on hers, and she didn't fight the rush of pleasure at the recognition there.

"How are you feeling?" His voice vibrated through her. She stretched, luxuriating in the pleasure of it.

"Pretty good actually. I was drained, but now I'm not. And I opened my eyes to behold a tall, sexy man in bed with me all naked and everything. Handy."

He'd been on his back and turned to face her. She moved to him without a thought, seeking his heat and his touch.

"Well then I'm feeling even better." He held her to him, the thud of his heart beat where her head lay on his chest reassuring.

"You're so warm. I may never want to get out of this bed."
She wriggled, smiling at the hardening cock at her belly. "Seems
like you're good with that plan."

He growled, his cute and not-very-scary gruff growl. "You're
going to rest. Then I will make you dinner. Then you will go
back to sleep."

"Grr. Arrgh. Grrr. I'm the big tough alpha cat, grrr. I won't
have sex with you!" She said it while laughing and he joined her
after a groan.

"Smart ass. Talk to me, Kendra. Tell me. Share what scares
you, what makes you happy. What brings the shadows in your
eyes sometimes."

She tipped her head back enough to see him better. It was
go time. She could open up to him, accept this wonderful thing
between them, *all* of it, or she could back off and make him wait
and hurt him for no real reason. She had been a coward before
and it wasn't her. It didn't fit right. And he deserved all of her.

"You don't just love me, you possess me. No, that's not the
right word either. Or maybe it is. Gah! I'm messing this up."
She tried to wriggle free but he tightened his arms.

"If you really want to get up, I'll let go. But if you're just
embarrassed, it's only me. I like you here with me, against me."

She couldn't help but smile at him. How could anyone
resist this man?

"I've never been with anyone, not ever, who made me feel so
wanted. You look at me and there's no room for anyone else.
You touch me in a way I know you never have with anyone
before. It's so very big and bold and all encompassing." She
paused, forcing herself not to hide her face. "I like it. I'm scared
of how much I like it. I'm scared I'll get used to it and then I
won't have it. I can get over a lot. I've gotten over a lot. But I

don't know if I could get over you."

"You undo me. So strong. Bold. Gibson came by earlier and he said you're a warrior. He's right. You are. But beneath that, there's softness, vulnerability, compassion. This is it for me. Do you know what it's like, how hard it is for me not to mark you when I'm buried, balls deep in your pussy? When everything I am is wrapped around you, bound to you?"

She thought of Renee and the mark she had on her neck. She shivered and had to close her eyes a moment. "Like what my sister has?"

He bent and nuzzled her neck. "For a shifter, it's more than a love bite. A mark like that is a ritual. It ties us together with our partners. It's also a public declaration, like a wedding ring or what have you. I want to mark you. I want you to be mine all the way. I'm afraid of freaking you out. It's not the same as with wolves, no, we don't mate that way. But with us, imprinting is similar, marking you would seal that for me, in the eyes of my family and other shifters. I'm not going anywhere. Even if you're uncomfortable with me marking you, I'm still here. I will always be here."

"Can I tell you something I've never said out loud before?"

He shifted so that he could take her hands. "You can say anything to me."

"What scares me is not ever feeling like I belong to someone. Like I'll die without experiencing that connection. I know people are married and have kids and love their partners. But I want more than that. I want to be indelible to someone."

Her voice was so small it cut him up inside. He got it then, understood her. The woman was a warrior, but inside her lived a girl whose mother had left, whose father never cared to see if she was alive. A girl who was raised with love, but clearly with a feeling of loss that never got filled.

"I know, right? I'm such a cliché. The girl with the dead mother. I'm textbook. And look at Renee, she's done so much for herself and she didn't have half of what I did. I had Rosemary, I had my grandmother and my uncle. I grew up with cousins. I was raised to love my gifts. I had everything and it's not enough. I'm selfish. I'm not fixed. It's...something I struggle with sometimes. You don't need that."

He wanted to laugh, but he sure as hell didn't want her to think he agreed with the stuff she just said.

"You belong to me. You're indelible to me. Written into my heart, my flesh." He said it quietly, but with conviction. "From the first moment I saw you, in the midst of all the chaos, the worry over Renee, you were there and no one else existed. I stalked you like prey." He snorted. "That sounds creepy and I suppose it could be in another context, but I knew I wanted you so I listened to myself and watched you. When I was sure, I freed myself from all relationships and set out to woo you. I want every bit of you. I'm a greedy bastard and I don't share. You're not broken, Kendra, and frankly the last word I'd associate with you is selfish. The things you've experienced have shaped you. That's how everyone is."

The glimmer of a smile on her lips buoyed his confidence, made him believe they were moving in the right direction.

"Let me be your family. Let me possess you, but let you be free to be who you are. I respect that you have a job to do, even if it does scare the crap out of me. I will be at your side when you find and confront your father. Let me love you. Be mine. Will you? And I'll be yours. This can be our house. Our bed. The seeds of our family right here. I won't pressure you anymore about it, but I want you to know it's what I'd like to have with you. What I want to build for the future."

The ache she felt wasn't from sadness, not anymore, it was

the good sort of ache. This was it, the right choice, the right man. The right everything, and who was she to turn her back on perfect? "Where did you come from, Max? How can you be so perfect and wonderful?"

He did laugh then, kissing her forehead. "I'm not. Weren't you telling me how bossy and pushy I am just this morning? But I'm perfect for *you*, and that's what matters."

She licked her lips. "So, um, this biting thing, does it hurt?"

He hardened from head to toe. "I've never been bitten. Not sexually. My parents nipped us when we got out of line, when we were in our other forms that is. Are you afraid of pain?"

He heard her swallow, saw her pupils grow larger as she shook her head. "I like it. Sometimes. Not real pain, I don't want to be slapped in the face or hit or anything. But sometimes when I'm getting inked, it sends me to another level of consciousness. I like to ride that edge where it hurts just enough to feel good. I think...I think I'd like that. For you to mark me."

He let out a breath, long and slow, hoping to steady himself but it didn't really work.

"It can wait until you're better. And you need to know this connection we have between us, the way I felt that spike and then sudden bottoming out of your energy today? Well that's the bond and it'll deepen, strengthen after I mark you. My cat will be married to you. In the eyes of my culture, my people, we'll be married."

She sprang up, pushing him onto his back and scrambled atop him. "Well, wow. All right. Go big or go home, Max de La Vega. I'm just fine. I told you. I needed the rest and now I'm ready to go."

He'd planned to at least symbolically urge her to wait, but

instead she reached down, spread herself open, stroked her middle finger over her clit and that barbell she wore, making a soft moan that set him on fire.

"You're a menace," he growled as she reached back with her free hand and angled his cock perfectly. He lost his mind when she slid down on him.

"So you've said. Shall I stop?"

He growled, rolling her over so that he was on top and in control of the depth and ferocity of his thrusts. "That's better."

"Whatever you say." Her lips quivered as she struggled not to smile. He bent and nipped her bottom lip, bringing a ragged moan from her and his own in response.

"I say get your hand back down and make yourself come."

She moved quickly as he held himself away from her to give her the room. Her inner walls tightened, the muscles fluttering as she began to play with her clit.

"I love it that you know what you want and that you take it." He said it before he licked over the spot he'd been toying with marking and she writhed, arching into him. Of course that movement around his cock and the slide of her nipples against his chest only brought him closer to blowing.

"If I don't know what makes me hot, how can I be sure to get it from anyone else?"

"Beauty, you undo me."

"I'm not sure anything can undo you. Mmmm, that's so nice. You feel so good inside me. You're always in control. I can count on you. I like that."

She added a circle of her hips when he pushed all the way back into her pussy, ripping the last of his control to shreds. But it wasn't until she gasped, sucking in air with a ragged cry, her pussy tightening around him as she came, that he let himself lean down to her neck.

He breathed her in as she came, breathed in her magick, her scent, the scent of her arousal, the basic clean, spice of her skin, the scent his body made against hers. He scored the edge of his teeth down the tendon at the side of her neck and she whimpered.

Not a bad whimper at all, but the sort of whimper a woman made when she wanted a man to go on about his business, a needy whimper.

He answered that need with one of his own, a need so large it filled him from head to toe. And bit. Bit where her neck met her shoulder.

Her back arched as she cried out, a shout of delight, edged with a bit of pain, but not alarm. His cat shifted inside, reveling in her taste, in the way she submitted to him, the way her fingers dug into the muscles of his shoulders, urging him on, urging him closer, all while he continued to fuck into her body, so hot and slick.

Their connection, the beginnings of the bond created through his imprinting and now the physical mark he gave her, blew open. He knew she felt it too as she froze a moment and made a soft sound, a sigh of satiation.

That's when he came, buried in her physically, swimming through their emotional bond and knowing what he had was monumental. Knowing he'd keep it, cherish it and protect it for all the days of his life at her side.

Kendra lay, limp, sweaty and totally satisfied. Her muscles still twitched from the climax and now, each time he licked over the mark he'd given her, he sent a cascade of sensation running through her system.

He lived inside her, which was odd given how alone she'd felt for most of her life. Not in an intrusive sense, but he was there nonetheless. "I can feel you in me. Not physically, though that's always a treat with you. Your emotions, your general level of satisfaction. It's sort of there in the background."

"Over time, it'll strengthen. The longer we're connected, the more we know each other and love each other. My parents have been together, imprinted, for forty-five years. They have the kind of bond I'd only dreamed of having. And now I think we've got it, the seeds for that sort of forever."

She smiled at how sappily romantic he could be at times. Didn't say a whole lot in public, not unless it needed saying. But when it was just family, just her, he opened up and showed her his creamy center.

Touching the mark sent sparks of pleasure through her. Interesting.

"Do I get to bite you?"

"If you want to." He pulled her close.

"I may just."

That's when everything went sideways as she gasped, back bowing, eyes closing. Fur and fang, the scent of warm bark, trees in the afternoon sun. Golden energy rushed through her, filling the reserves of her magick she'd depleted. And more.

Sensation of a wholly different sort rushed through her. So much feeling it arched her back, filled her and filled her until she could no longer breathe without drawing in more.

Magick. So much fucking magick, more than she'd ever felt in her entire life and it lived inside, sparking, brushing against her heart and lungs, stretching her to the point of pain.

It scared her for a moment and she resisted, trying to read it before she let it in any further. But it kept coming, more and more until she drowned in it. And yet there was no end to it.

The roar of it filled her ears, greater and greater, it took over, smoothing things out in its wake. She let it go, let it settle in. Once she stopped resisting, the sharp slice against her ribs eased.

"Kendra!" Max held her upper arms, his face close to hers. "Come back to me right now."

When she opened her eyes, he jerked back, a growl on his lips.

And she answered with a growl of her own. Where had that come from? Panic threatened, but somehow being with Max calmed it, kept it at bay. Something loomed, big, lifechanging. Inside her belly there was a rumble, an expansion that felt as if her entire being was stretched until she couldn't stand it. Thankfully, at last, it settled.

Max sat up, eyes wide, watching. "Kendra? What is it?"

The rushing in her ears muffled the sound, muffled what he said though his lips moved and she noted the concern on his face. He reached for the phone and she shook her head.

She didn't know what the fuck was going on, but it wouldn't be helped by a phone call. Deep within there was a sort of knowing, but she couldn't connect with it.

She was not one anymore. But two. Which wasn't accurate either. Time stretched as she floated, disconnected and yet not.

And then it exploded. The world lived in color and sensation on a wholly new level. She could smell everything. *Everything.* For long moments she simply breathed. In/out. So much sensory input she had to let it wash over her before it drove her insane. Instinct was there and she grabbed it, let it take over and once she did, the waves diminished and she went with it, rather than let it threaten to drown her.

She turned her head, opening her eyes, and caught Max looking utterly stupefied, standing next to the bed where she...crouched. Gingerly, she moved, realizing how different it

139

was to move with four legs instead of two. With the mass that had to be triple what she normally had.

Her cat was in charge, reminding the human to back off and let her be in charge. Because she was curious, fascinated and stunned, the human part of herself stepped aside and let the cat lead. The cat was satisfied by this.

She was still Kendra and yet not. More than what she'd been. But the cat was not interested in any distinctions as she sprang from the bed and headed toward her man, toward the man within which her cat lived.

He touched the cat, fingers digging into spots her cat liked very much, butting against his thigh for more.

The man knelt, rubbing his jaw along hers and satisfaction rumbled deep, vibrating outward. This was hers.

"Come back, Kendra," he whispered in her ear and suddenly she was there, back in her human skin, his arms around her.

"Holy shit." Her entire body trembled, muscles spasming, the burn of a great deal of hard physical activity pulsed through her muscles. He picked her up like she was light and settled with her in the bed again. "Wh-what happened just now? I was a cat! A-a jaguar. Like you." She reeled with it, with the wonder and excitement of what had happened, the utter miracle of it. Oddly, there was no fear, just a sense of rightness, of being what she was supposed to be. And so she went with that.

He held her tighter a moment, breathing her in, in a way she understood on a totally different level now. "I have no idea. What just happened shouldn't have happened." He rubbed against her, that low purr vibrating through her body. "My cat likes it."

"I've taken the change. I don't know how, but hello, big giant furry cat just a few moments ago." She wasn't upset as she told him this. Confused, caught off guard as she hadn't really thought about the change at all and now it was there.

"That can't be. I can't transfer this to you with a marking bite. It didn't break the skin. I wouldn't do that to you. Not without your permission." He licked over the bite he'd made, sending pleasant tingles straight to her clit.

She laughed, hugging him. "I'm not mad. Just, well sort of surprised I suppose. I know you didn't do this on purpose and while I tend to scoff at the idea of fate, it's certainly a recurring theme with us, isn't it?"

He kissed her neck and her cat telegraphed images to her, satisfied, pleased images. "She likes you. My cat."

He exhaled. "My cat likes you too, and certainly likes that you've got a mate for him as well." He laughed, but it was careful and she hurt for him.

Turning to face him fully, she took his face in her hands. "I hadn't planned on this. But I hadn't planned on you either. Plans aren't life. Life just happens sometimes and this is where we are. I'm on board, do you understand? This doesn't hurt us, it strengthens us. I know this down to my toes." And she did. She also knew her magick had changed, deepened and strengthened. She was a wholly new kind of witch. "Something else. My magick has changed. I'm filled with a totally different sort of energy now."

Max's emotions were all over the place. Good ones definitely, but they were a tumult in his belly. Relief mainly ruled then as she assured him she was all right, even pleased with this shift in their relationship. Christ, what a beautiful cat she was, tawny gold with black rosettes, big green eyes. His cat, and the man, approved of this.

"For better? Or worse?" Had he made her less safe? His phone rang. His father's ring and one he couldn't ignore. "I have to take it."

She nodded. "Yes you do."

He scrubbed hands, hands that smelled like her, over his face before he answered. His father, in full alpha mode, bellowed into the receiver. "You did not have permission to change anyone, Max. Why is there suddenly another cat in my jamboree?"

"*Papi*," he started out, not knowing much himself. So he just told his father what happened.

His father paused, Max knew weighing all the options, certainly not missing what a huge coup this would be to the jamboree's power that Max could bring the cat into another person without even breaking the skin. His mother would see that right away, she was savvier in some ways than her mate. Max had learned from the best, growing up with them as an example. Without hesitation, he would use this to keep the others in the jamboree back and respectful of his woman and of his position. His cat knew politics just as well as the man did.

"Interesting. I'll get Gibson on it, to get some answers. Truthfully, I've never heard of something like this. *Mami* either. There are elders, we'll speak with them too. I feel her, my new cat. I suppose tomorrow we'll be celebrating more than you and my new daughter marrying, eh? Be here early. We have to talk. Bring Kendra." He hung up without another word and Max tossed the phone into a drawer.

Max turned back to her, his lovely woman. Magick flitted around her as always, like dust motes in a shaft of sunlight. But now, now his own energy connected, reached out and caressed.

He found his voice enough to speak to her. "I don't know what to say."

Her face fell and he realized she'd been nervous about his

reaction.

He quickly moved back to her side, touching her, stroking over those long, pale limbs, so strong and feminine. "No. This is amazing and wonderful and more than I'd hoped for. Don't think I'm not thrilled. Both to be joined with you and to have you a cat too."

She nodded, rubbing herself against him, taking his comfort. His cat eased back, though the man felt the slap for being careless of his partner.

"I just don't know how it happened or what it means. I worry about you."

"I have the number for the witch who mated with the wolf in Gabe's pack. I should call and see what the results of their bonding were. Gabe said he didn't take a wolf, but maybe later? I don't know, but he might have information we could use."

"You're awfully matter-of-fact," he said, following her as she headed for his bathroom.

"What else can I do?"

He leaned against the doorjamb as she moved, pulling out towels, knowing where he kept everything. That pleased him a great deal.

"I could be upset, which is silly because, well, because I'm not. Maybe it's because I'm already different, already not quite human. Maybe it's because my cat trusts yours and that's keeping me mellow. I don't know. What I do know is that freaking out never solved a damned thing. Obviously I have questions. I wonder how my magick will work, clearly it's different now. I wonder what it'll mean to Renee, who made the choice not to change. I worry about your family and I don't want to mess with your status."

"Fuck that. Listen, if you want me to be brutally honest? It strengthens me. You're not only a witch, which brings me

143

status, you've taken on a cat. And she came to you in her own, totally improbable way. My cats will see this as a sign that fate meant you to be at my side. They will see you as my destiny and as the destiny of the jamboree."

She turned to him, a smile on her face. "I prefer brutal honesty any day. I'm not fragile, Max. I need to know the details. I can't help you if I don't know the details."

Of course he forgot what he was going to say next as she bent to turn the water on in his shower and the curve of her pussy caught his attention.

"I haven't had you from behind yet," he murmured.

She looked back over her shoulder at him, mischief on her mouth. Bracing her feet apart, she then leaned forward and gripped the side of the tub. "What's stopping you now?"

He should have resisted.

But when he sank back into her heat, he couldn't feel guilty. Especially when she arched, pushing back to meet his thrust.

His cat wanted to roar with satisfaction at the primal act of possession. At the way she reacted to his touch. He wasn't ready for her cat though, at the ferocity of her response to his. He needed the support of the wall, held on as everything she was filled him, settled in and took over.

He might have marked her with his teeth, with his seed and his intent, but she marked him just the same.

And when he came, he fell into her totally. She owned him in a way he doubted he'd ever be able to articulate fully.

Gentle hands soaped her up as she leaned back against him. She didn't bother opening her eyes, instead, she experimented with her newly enhanced senses.

"This is amazing. Part of the magick I work is called

othersight. Anyone could see it if they could toss aside the barriers we erect from birth to close out all the external stimulus. Anyway, it's a lot like this. Do you see like this all the time?"

She paused as he soaped her pussy, detouring to play against the barbell. "Answer this first," he murmured. "What made you pierce yourself this way?"

"I came out of a shitty marriage with a lot of frustrated sexuality. I repressed it for years, but it's not natural to do that. We're all sexual beings. So I sort of threw myself into a sexual reawakening. I got the navel piercing first, before I'd married. And I remembered liking the edge of pain. I saw a clitoral hood piercing in a movie, yes a porn movie." She laughed. "And I liked how it looked. The place that did my tattoos also had a piercing station. I gave it a try."

"Mm. Well, my cat's not so thrilled with some strange man with his head between your thighs playing with your clit. But I do like the results."

"It was a woman."

"Even better. The other humans I know who've taken the change, and there aren't many, we like to keep to ourselves, say it's like all your senses are at twelve. As for what I see like, I've never seen any other way so I don't know how to explain it. I see the inner light in people. I can sense a lie. I know when you're turned on because your body heats up and your pussy gets sticky for me."

He said the hottest stuff.

"What will happen tomorrow? Are you in trouble with your father?"

"No. We have to get permission to change a human. I didn't get that. But he can feel the birth of a new cat into his jamboree. He knew you'd transformed because it was another being he was connected to and responsible for. My mother felt it as well. But I didn't lie, they know I have no reason to lie. So I'm not in trouble at all. They're going to want to speak with us tomorrow before the dinner so we have to arrive early."

"Great." She hoped things wouldn't get worse because of this.

"The dinner will be far more than a normal dinner now. You have to understand that. I've marked you, which means we're married as I explained. This will be a huge celebration because you're my wife, and I'm next-in-line. On top of that, you've taken on a cat and at the end of the evening, you'll transform."

"Nothing like a first meeting with your family turning into a wedding party and a meet-the-new-cat party. No pressure or anything."

He kissed her. "You'll be just fine. You were born to be right here, right now. Trust that and trust me. We'll have to work on you making the choice to transform rather than have it take over when you aren't ready. You'll need to change with the other cats in the jamboree present. It's part of your ceremonial and physical entry into the jamboree as a member. I'll be with you, as will my father. He's your alpha and he'll guide your cat forward. It's hard the first few times for the newly changed."

"It sucks that I've got to deal with these messed-up witches. I'd love to spend all my time experimenting with these changes."

She turned in his arms, kissing his chest.

"We've got time. You'll have more physical strength now. My cat is comforted in part by that. We'll deal with the witches and then get on with our lives." He helped her out, handing her a big towel to wrap up in.

"You seem disappointed that I'm not upset," she teased.

He paused, taking her arm and turning it. "*Querida,* look."

She glanced down and saw the slice in her arm was gone. "Cool."

His look of surprise melted away into a smile. "It is, actually."

Chapter Ten

Max checked in every few minutes. Just seeing how she was feeling. Which amused her. He seemed befuddled and sweetly happy that she'd accepted him and this change. She'd meant it when she'd told him earlier that she never found much point in railing against the random chaos that fate often threw in your path.

In truth, she felt...satisfied. Safe. Comfortable in her own skin. Part of it, she imagined, was from him. Max was the kind of person who just went through his life totally sure of himself and his place. This was endearing, even when he was a pushy butthead.

She'd been loved over her life. Rosemary loved her, definitely. Renee did. Her family did. But that part of her that had felt unmoored wasn't unsettled anymore. Because she did belong in a way she simply didn't question.

That stability of thought enabled her to look honestly at her life and know for certain she'd always belonged to someone. Still was a daughter, a sister, a granddaughter and now, unexpectedly enough, a wife.

She began to laugh and he looked up from his computer where he'd been working for part of the morning. "Should I be worried?"

"I was just anticipating the look on Beth's face. Makes me

want to rub my hands together with glee."

"You're now a higher rank than she is. That ought to make you giggle some more. Sadistic woman."

"She hurt my sister. I don't like that."

He looked up from the screen again. "I don't either. This isn't going to be totally easy, you know that, right? Galen will be behind you, as will Renee. Gibson. Armando."

"Pretty much everyone but Carlos and Beth." She waved a hand as she stood. "Pffft. Don't care. I have things to do. I need to work on some lesson plans. How about I meet you at your parents' at two?"

"How about no. I thought you were going to move in here?"

"I am. I just figured it would take some time to get that all organized. In the meantime I still have a job and stuff. I have to water my plants and do laundry. I'm also totally in need of some maintenance. I'm sure you'd love me with hairy legs. After all, you're all furry sometimes. But I need some girl time."

"Gibson told me to inform you he'll get you all boxed up and moved in one day. You're safer here, so he has an ulterior motive."

"Listen here, bossy, I need to be, you know, consulted on this stuff. Yes, yes, I agreed to move in here. And why not? Hot cock on tap whenever I want it."

He laughed.

"It's a big-assed house. There are like super bodyguards all over the place. You have a great view, and when I get my car, I can park it in a garage. So all in all, I support that. But don't think that just because I'm furry now and your mate or wife or whatever you want to call it, that you can push me around."

"I'd never dream of it." He continued typing, and she knew he would shine her on to do exactly what he wanted because he was that way. Luckily, she was that way too and would push him right back. It made for pretty hot sex and she knew it was all well meaning. If she had a man who let her push him around, it would be boring. Max was her equal, that was exciting.

"I'll speak with Gibson today. I'm sure he'll be at dinner."

"Speaking of that, my mother called when you were in the shower. She made me promise to tell you tonight will be a full jamboree gathering."

"What? I haven't even told Renee yet!" She headed to the front door but of course he got there first.

"Where are you going?"

"Okay, here's another thing we can't be doing. I need to be able to come and go without a list of permissions. I have a thing about that. You know why. Also, back off. I can't tell my sister about all this on the phone. Duh. I need to see her face to face. If she hears from other people, it'll hurt her feelings."

"Call her first. My father and mother know. Gibson knows. It'll trickle down. Then we can go over there."

She closed her eyes, seeking patience. "Max, I don't need you to go with me everywhere."

He stepped closer, nuzzling her, licking over the bite mark she'd left exposed. "I know. But I like to look at you. I like to watch you move and know I've touched every part of your body. I like you and my cat isn't quite ready to not be with you a lot."

"Oh your *cat*. Poor cat, gets the blame for all your bossy ways." She smiled, knowing he couldn't see her face, but would feel it anyway. "Get your keys and let's roll. I'm going over to Renee's now whether you are or not. Your cat will have to deal."

"Sorry to get you guys up so early," Kendra said to Jack, who looked adorably rumpled. "I need to talk to Renee."

"You're welcome here anytime, sweetness." He kissed the top of her head and paused a moment. "I think I see why you're here."

"Yeah. Don't let her talk to anyone on the phone until I tell her myself. Apparently the cats are a gossipy bunch and there's a hootenanny tonight to celebrate."

Max snorted. "There should be. Hey, Jack, got any coffee?"

"Just made a pot. Go on through. Galen should be back shortly, he went for a run. Renee is in the shower."

"Ren?" she called out as she entered the bedroom.

"Kendra?" Renee came out of the bathroom on a puff of steam. "Is everything all right?"

"Yes. More than all right. I wanted to tell you myself." But Renee saw the mark and grinned widely.

"Get out! Yay, I'm so pleased for you both." She hugged Kendra tight. "This is so awesome. How awesome is it that you found your Mister Right and he also happens to be my Mister Right's brother?"

"There's more."

Renee grinned. "There's *always* more with the de La Vega men."

"It looks like I took a cat. I don't know how. We were, well you know. He bit me and it was, wow, awesome and all, and then it just happened. I mean, one moment I'm in his bed all sex-exhausted, and the next I'm a freaking jaguar. I felt their magick, the energy of all the cats in their jamboree. My magick is...changed. Max says he's never heard of anything like this. Ditto with Cesar and Imogene, but Gibson's on the case so I'm sure we'll have answers soon. He's one of the most accomplished and together people I've ever met. Anyway, I need to talk to that witch who mated with one of Gabe's wolves. Maybe he can tell me something, give me some insight. Rosemary and Mary might be able to help too."

Renee simply stared at her.

"God. Do you hate me for not telling you right away? Are you mad that I took on a cat?"

Renee burst out laughing. "No! I'm trying not to be petty and not doing a very good job of it."

"Beth?"

Both women laughed for some time about that.

"She's going to flip her lid. If she wasn't pregnant, I could be happier and maybe even taunt her. But now, she's bearing the next generation of jaguar or some stupid shit like that, and I have to pretend she's worthy of something nicer than a kick to the face."

Kendra grinned at her sister. "She's snotty. But there has to be a reason why. I mean, all the siblings except for her, even Carlos, find a way of at least being civil. Anyway, she sucks on lemons and we don't care. Plus Max says I rank higher than she does. I love that. I may have to mention how I had no idea of that when she can hear it."

"You're such a bitch. It's why I love you so much." Renee kissed her forehead. "Max is out there? I bet his cat is doing the pee-pee dance to come in here to check on you."

The laughter started anew.

"He can hear everything anyway. The nifty thing is, so can I."

"Yes, I can. And I'll have you know my cat does not do any such pee-pee dance, thank you very much, Renee," Max called out from the other room.

"Come on. Let's go out there. I need coffee. Then I need to go back to my place and work a bit. Or my old place. Whatever."

They walked out and both of them paused at the sight of Galen, mopping his bare upper body off with his shirt, as he stood laughing and talking with Jack and Max.

"Hot damn. I think I just had some really dirty thoughts about your husbands."

Renee nodded. "Go on ahead, I have 'em all the time."

"Well, you're not involved, though Max is. I promise there's no brother touching in this particular filthy fantasy. Not between them anyway."

They looked up, three sets of wary, sexy, alpha male eyes locked on the two women. Kendra waved. "Don't mind us. We're just objectifying you."

Max rolled his eyes but Galen walked toward her. "Christ. Max was right." He took her hands. "Welcome to our family, Kendra. Max needed someone like you. No, that's not right. He needed *you*. And this cat of yours, ahhh, there she is."

Kendra felt it then, the distinct brush against her insides, that otherness coiled within. "Wow," she breathed out. "I felt her. My cat."

Max was there at her side suddenly, pressing against her. "Mmmm." He nuzzled again, that spot he'd marked and it drove her crazy. "I can scent her now. Stronger than before. It's more than a ghost."

"Stop that," she murmured. "You're stirring me up and this isn't the place."

He laughed, his lips near her ear. "I'd apologize but it'd be a lie."

"Gah, you're incorrigible." She stepped away from him. Galen, smiling, handed her a mug of coffee.

"And you, stop looking so good. Put a shirt on." Renee pointed toward their bedroom.

"No need to cover up on my part." Kendra winked at him and Max swatted her ass.

The taste of her laughter was still on her lips when everything fell away and a new kind of sight jerked her into another level of consciousness. Numbers, numbers, numbers, they fell from her lips as she scrambled for the table. "Pen. Paper. Now."

No one questioned her. The items she needed appeared and she began to write.

"Call Rosemary," Renee murmured as she read over Kendra's shoulder. Max hoped his brother or Jack planned to do that because he wasn't moving from Kendra's side. Her magick had taken over in a way he'd not seen thus far, and he needed to stick there to be sure she would recover without a problem.

When she'd gone into this odd state, his bond with her had changed. He knew she was all right, but the way between them had been flooded with her energy and it changed his perception. Fascinating, even as he worried, he was certain she was fine.

"What is it?" Jack asked as Galen picked the phone up and began to dial.

"It's...looks like streets and maybe a town? Numbers."

Jack examined the paper. "Looks like coordinates. Latitude and longitude."

"The spell," Kendra said on a gulp of breath as if she'd surfaced from being underwater. "This is where he is."

Rosemary and Mary glanced at the paper and agreed.

"This worked very fast. It usually takes at least several

days." Mary spoke as she studied Kendra intently. "And you have a carrier in there. A beast. You took on a cat?"

Rosemary looked up from the map Akio had brought over. "You've had all sorts of adventures we haven't talked about."

Kendra's face fell a bit and Max glowered at her aunt. "I'm sorry. It's not that I've done it on purpose. It's all happened so fast and you weren't here and I wanted to talk to you, but you have your own life to live right now. For the first time in forever you have your own life and you're not responsible for me. I just wanted you to have that."

"Let's go for a walk, shall we?" Rosemary held her hand out and Max, though he wanted Kendra to confide in her aunt—it was clear they both needed it—he also didn't want her out there without protection.

"Why don't I accompany you both?" Akio bowed deeply. "I'll refrain from eavesdropping." He made an X over his heart and Kendra's smile brightened the room.

Jack's gaze moved to Max, checking in with him about that. Max nodded once. "We'll need to put together a plan and a team to go out to these coordinates to investigate anyway. You have the time."

"Good idea. Why don't all us witchy types go to breakfast and fill each other in? Akio can sit with us because, well, come on, look at him." Renee put her arm through his.

"I can make breakfast here," Galen muttered.

"Not the same. They need this time," Max said quietly.

When they'd all left, Max called Gibson, who quickly put another two guards on the restaurant and said he'd be right over to discuss the situation regarding Renee and Kendra's father.

When they had ordered, Rosemary turned to Kendra. "Before we talk about this extraordinary man you've fallen for, I want to talk to you about something you said back at the house. You're part of my life and you always will be. I don't want you to ever feel like I don't want to be involved in your life. You're only my niece in name, in reality you're my daughter and so is Renee. I cherish that. Being part of it is not an imposition, it's my pleasure."

"How do you always know what I need to hear?" Kendra asked her aunt.

"I've told you this from the start, silly woman. But now you can hear it and for that I'm grateful. I can tell what you need to hear because I know you." Rosemary looked to Renee. "I'm only just getting used to having you around again, and it's wonderful to grow together and build a family with me in it. I love you both and I always have."

After some hugs and the arrival of the food, Kendra told Renee, Mary and Rosemary the whole story of how she'd come to have a cat living inside her. Aside from the fucking parts that is, she wasn't going to share that with her aunt and Akio, for goodness sake.

"I didn't plan it at all. It just happened. He didn't do the change on purpose. In fact, he didn't even break the skin when he bit me." She pulled her shirt away a little bit more to show the mark.

Akio's mouth turned up into a smile. "Always looks so beautiful," he said before going back to his giant plate of eggs, bacon, sausage, pancakes, breakfast potatoes and two bagels.

Mary jotted down notes as they spoke. "I'll see what I can find about this sort of transference. It can't be too common because we'd have heard of it. But it's not entirely out of the realm of possibility. Perhaps it's because the mix of magicks between different types of others is loaded with possibility. It could be that Kendra had been opening herself to him, to his energy and also other energies and essences as she trained with me. That could have made such a transfer of magicks far more powerful than it would be otherwise. It seemed to me that she'd changed when she was at my house on Friday, even. The way she worked her magick had changed."

"Interesting. I'll speak with Imogene this evening to see if their history has any such stories." Rosemary stirred her coffee.

"If I may interrupt for a moment," Akio said. "The oldest Warden female is somewhat of an elder among her people. She may be a good resource as well."

"Oh great idea. Yes, I'd love an introduction." Rosemary looked back and forth between Renee and Kendra. "I'm sure she'd be a lovely help and perhaps in the future we can work together." Again, her aunt paused. "I've been thinking about moving here permanently." Rosemary sipped her coffee.

Kendra's heart lifted. "Really? That would be wonderful. But what about your job? Your house? Uncle Roger?"

"I miss you, sweetie." She smiled at Kendra and then to Renee. "And I want to know you more. I can't do that if I'm on another coast. Your uncle has his own life, his own kids and family, grandchildren now. He's happy in San Jose so I don't see any reason to disrupt that. But there are airplanes and he likes the east coast so he'll visit. You two are my children, and one day, you'll give me grandchildren. My job is a job, I can get another job here. In fact, Mary and I are thinking of expanding her shop and we wanted to talk to you two about how you'd feel about it. We'd need your help."

Kendra smiled. "How we'd feel about having you here with us? Duh. We'd love it. I miss you. I do want you to have a life, but I can't deny that I've missed you." And she had, so much.

The talk she'd had with Max had really cleared things up in her head.

Rosemary looked back and forth between Renee and Kendra. "We'd like you to help us work with others like us. To train them in other forms of magick, defensive magick."

Kendra laughed. "Yeah, I want in on that. I was telling Max about this too. I think it's criminal not to admit we need the help and we're not prepared for what's coming. He's worried, it's what male shifters do. But he respects my space, respects what I believe in. He'll be behind me on this, though we may have to endure extra guards."

"I'll do whatever I can too," Renee added.

"Part of it will be for you to learn and then teach others. That's a manageable task. We don't have the resources to undertake something huge. So we teach and those we've taught will teach."

The excitement of what her aunt and Mary were speaking of began to build. "This could be a way to unite and work with other groups who'll be possible targets as well. Why shouldn't witches learn the magicks of other paths when it comes to healing and defense? We've erected so many walls and right now, that's part of why we're such big targets. There are more of us than them and yet, because we don't interact, the balance shifts away from our favor."

"I'd love that!" Renee leaned in closer. "I would love to learn healing magicks from other traditions. There's so much out there, wow, this could be massive."

Kendra realized this could be a great way for Renee to continue to gain confidence with her own magick. She'd be an excellent teacher and leader. "You'd rock that job, Renee. You have so much you've learned on your own. You created your own form of intuitive healing magick."

"That's right! I hope those boys of yours are prepared to share you in your spare time." Mary grinned. "The shop has plenty of room for you two to participate in all this."

"Of course, that makes you not only a visible target, but an extremely attractive, visible target." Akio leaned back in the booth. "You would be like a buffet to those out to find you and take your energies."

"Maybe so. But we can't all hide. It's not protecting anyone. They're finding us anyway. And we're weak in our ignorance. They don't hesitate to learn and use whatever energies they can against us. It's insane not to at least work with others who share our goals and philosophies to protect ourselves. I'm not advocating that we go out and use magicks that are derived from pain or despair. But we damned well better figure out how to pull ambient energies from the space around us so that we can do it when they make a move against one of us. If not, we're just being victims. I'm not a victim."

The corner of his mouth twitched up. "Indeed. But I am not your mate." He looked to Renee. "Your mate, an alpha werewolf and your other mate, an alpha cat. Oh and yours, Kendra, the next-in-line alpha. What you propose to do will put you in more danger, especially in the beginning. It would be wise to remember that when you speak of this to your men."

Rosemary nodded. "Their safety is paramount to me as well. I'm moving here to be part of keeping them safe. And many others like them."

Mary spoke then. "The shop and the house are warded. Both are totally safe. And Kendra is right. Our own silly prejudices have kept us ignorant. We have to do something or we'll be in far more danger next year and the year after that. Our children will be in danger. Shifters too. Any of us who are imbued with magickal energies."

"Let me talk to Max about it before anything else gets planned. He'll feel like I'm going around him and I'd feel the same in his place. He'll resist. Big time. But in the end, he'll respect me and support my choice."

Renee agreed. "Me too. Galen and Jack have been on high alert with all this stuff for months so I need to approach the subject with caution. They're smart men, they'll hear me out, but I have to do it my way."

"Good idea. So, is tonight like a wedding ceremony?" Rosemary asked.

"I have no idea. Max just told me it's some all jamboree meeting thingy. I'm sort of reeling. Not that I doubt any of my choices. I don't. But it was totally unexpected. I can't quite believe it, but I'm glad for it."

Chapter Eleven

"No." Max stalked into her apartment where she'd only moments before tucked her finished work into her case.

She knew he'd be this way, so she just looked up at him. "You know, I said we could *discuss* it more fully when I finished my work."

She'd laid out the plans they'd all made over breakfast as he'd driven her to her apartment. She'd only gotten him to agree to table the discussion for the time being so he could think over everything she'd told him. Oh and that she'd move in with him. Worked out pretty nicely, she'd thought. He got what he wanted—her aunt could take over Jack's place when Kendra moved in with Max. And she could finish up her prep work for the coming week.

"Discussion does not equal you storming in here saying no. You're supposed to have mellowed after you thought over things for a few hours."

He looked at her, blinking his eyes and probably wondering why she hadn't simply done exactly what he said. It was almost cute the way he just assumed everyone would do his bidding without question.

"No. Kendra this is fucking insane and you can't possibly think I'd support it."

"Pfft. Of course I think that. And you will. You know it.

Right now you're all, grrr, she's unsafe, let me wrap her in cotton and hide her in my sock drawer. It's who you are. But you're *also* the guy who is a keen lawyer, an intelligent, accomplished man who understands what it means to lead. I have to lead here, Max."

She felt him through their link, his agitation, annoyance, his fear for her. But also his pride in her.

"Damn it." He took her hands, drew her close. "Don't do this. I can't get behind any plan that puts a big, neon target around you. Complete with a map."

She fought for patience. "We all have paths to walk. My mom's path was short. And tragic. But it led me here. *To you*, Max. To what we have. I'm not stupid. I'm not going to be careless. We both know Gibson put more guards at the school anyway. And I'll be living with you, in our house. At the side of a seven-hundred-pound jaguar encased in a man the size of a redwood tree. I'm safe with you. I'm safe at school and I'm safe at Mary and my aunt's shop. I need to do this. This is my path. I get that you're worried. I understand it's dangerous. But we both know I can't *not* do this."

This is what pussy got you. Max knew trouble would come from this little slip of brunette heaven at his side.

Let me do this, Max. I need to do this, Max. Damn it all to hell. Yes, he knew, he'd known from the moment she began to talk about the danger witches faced without understanding their full potential. She'd have to do something about it. It was her way. He admired it even. But how could he sit by and watch her put herself in danger this way?

And then of course, when he'd been about to resist, she'd brought up all that stuff about honor and leadership.

He was pissed off that he could do nothing but go along

with this stupid plan. Because she was right and he hated that too. Fuck the rest of the world, she was his and she would be in danger even more after this. Perhaps from her own people.

So there he stood on his parents' doorstep, utterly beguiled by a woman who was totally insane. Worse, he admired her strength, her fire and independence. She wasn't going to just turn tail and run, she wanted to fight.

She noted his annoyance. Most likely feeling it via the link and gave him the side eye. Stupidly, his cock thought she was even sexier when she was annoyed right back.

"Stop it. Your parents are going to see how pissy you're being. Geez, we had sex twenty minutes ago, you promised it would cheer you up. Now I'm going to figure out it was just a diversionary tactic and a way to have sex all rolled into one. You're destroying my fantasies about you."

He would not let her make him smile, damn it. "Don't think you can get out of this by referencing the sex, which you clearly remember exactly how much I enjoyed."

She turned, her body brushing against his, those big, green eyes wide and sexy. "Do you think I'd do that, Max? A man like you could *never* be distracted by sex." Of course she used her sexy voice and rocked her hips forward, grinding herself against his cock.

"Witch. Be careful what you go stirring up there." He tried to sound gruff, but she knew as well as he did that she got to him.

"Or what?"

"Oh for God's sake. When will one of you start thinking with the right head?"

"Hi, Beth. Lovely to see you. I only have one, so I'll volunteer." Kendra poked her head around Max's body so he turned to keep himself between them. "Thanks so much for coming tonight to celebrate me and Max. I feel very welcomed to the family. But you're early. Is that to celebrate me even more?"

Max wanted to smile, but he didn't. Beth's sneer was a mar on her otherwise lovely face. Her issues with humans had simply become part of her, like a sickness. They'd all tried over the years to help her, and by that point, Max was done. He'd let Kendra deal with most of it, but if Beth got out of line, *he'd* handle it. He and Galen were united on that point now that the full extent of what she'd done to Renee had come to light.

"We'll see you inside." Kendra waved before turning back into his arm so they could go inside. Immediately the sound of family surrounded him, righted his sense of being off balance after his disagreement with Kendra. Helped him find his center and there she was, had been all along.

"You're the center of everything for me." He kissed her temple.

She smiled, bright and full of pleased surprise. "What a lovely thing to hear. Thank you, Max. I love you."

She tiptoed up, her hand on his chest, her lips brushing against the side of his neck as she pressed herself to him, hugging him tight.

She hadn't come out and said it yet. But it sounded natural from her lips and he knew it lived there, even before she'd said it. Still, he needed it.

"I love you too."

"Let's do this." She winked.

"Kendra!" Cesar de La Vega came into the living room from the kitchen, clapping his hands before holding them open.

Kendra hugged his father. "You look very snazzy tonight."

"Thank you, baby. Imogene loves me in the navy pinstripe and who am I to refuse her when she looks so pretty?" Cesar waved to Max's mother, who appeared to be refastening a barrette for one of Max's numerous nieces. She smiled at the sight of them and indicated they come over to her with an imperious tip of her head.

Cesar nodded at Max, a father to his son saying you did well for yourself.

"We'll grab your mother and head into the office for a few minutes before the rest arrive." Cesar took Kendra's arm, winking at Max. "I'm stealing your woman. I promise to give her back. Later." His father drew Kendra away, her hand tucked in the crook of his arm.

"He wants to say no. He can't." Cesar laughed at that. Kendra had to grin at how well father knew son.

"I'm sure he trusts your ability to protect me if it came to that."

Still, Max trailed along, right on Kendra's other side.

"Smart girl." Cesar patted her hand as they reached Imogene, who strolled along with Max, right behind them.

"I see your father has fallen for your wife." Imogene cocked her head as she looked up at Max. "Whole lot of stuff for you in just a few months, eh?"

"True, *Mami*. All that came before was training for now."

They entered his parents' massive home office, closing the door behind them. Here, in the heart of this house was the jamboree's power center. Gibson had a full office on the grounds as well, right next to Max's. His father rarely invited his children into the office, instead doling out occasional meetings there as incentive for good behavior. Old school and very clever.

The office of the jamboree, the job leading it was bred into him, heart and soul, blood and bone. He'd been raised to honor it, to understand it for the gift and responsibility it was. Both to him and to the cats he'd lead someday.

Kendra would have no way of knowing this and yet, she gave the space respect the moment they entered.

"First we wanted to say welcome to our family. As Max's parents. Our son is a good man, a strong cat, and he'll lead this jamboree into the future. That's a tough job, one that will oftentimes put him in conflict with his own and with humans. We trust you to have his back, to lead with him and hold this jamboree close. We couldn't ask for more in anyone our children brought into our family." Imogene leaned down and Kendra, eyes downcast, rubbed her cheek along his mother's jawline.

"See there? Already she's a queen." Cesar took Kendra's hands. "Now, as your alphas, we wish to welcome you to our family. To our jamboree as not only our daughter, but as the next alpha here. We have every confidence in your values, your judgment and your abilities. There will be trouble. I'm sorry to say it, but I believe it. Kendra, you're going to have to underline the point yourself. This is how our culture works. They'll respect you if you can handle yourself."

"Max told me what to expect." She held her back straighter. "As did my sister. What happened to her is inexcusable. She didn't know she had her magick to protect her. I do. And I will. No matter who it is. I will not be threatened."

Imogene looked to Max, her smile was sly.

"Of course, I'll do my level best to win them over with my sparkling wit."

Cesar laughed, kissing her cheek. "Of course you will." His father looked to Max. "Now that you're married, the jamboree will look to you more and more for leadership. You've done a fine job so far, but at this point you'll need to be my proxy at the intra-jamboree nation. You'll fill the seat in Imogene's place. Kendra, once you've got a better grasp of our national and international political situation, you will need to accompany Max to these meetings. You will need to choose your own committee assignments. Imogene will begin to instruct you on all this."

Kendra nodded. "I'm eager to learn."

His parents then cracked open some champagne and explained how the evening would progress.

"He's protective, but you're higher ranked than he is, he knows you're capable of protecting me. Still, he'll find a way to stalk us, just in case."

Cesar laughed again, a buoyant, booming sound that drew the eye of many in the room as they sailed through. The house had filled up considerably more in the time they'd been in the jamboree office.

As they'd all exited, he'd told Max he was stealing her again and would see him later. Max hadn't liked it, Kendra knew he wanted to check in with her to see what she'd felt about what had gone on. But Cesar was the alpha and he had a plan.

"You know my boy pretty well. The last time you were here, there had been trouble. You didn't get the tour. Do you trust me, *niña?*"

She was one of his cats, she realized. Max hadn't said it that way, but that's what it was. And she realized, she did trust him, understood at even the deepest part of her, Cesar de La Vega would put his cats before himself, always. She was still shaken, excited, touched, by the meeting they'd just had. True to his word, he was opening his family to her, readying her to lead.

The responsibility was frightening, but at the same time, she was honored that they felt she was worthy of that sort of trust and responsibility.

"Yes."

He squeezed her hand, clearly pleased with her answer. "Ahhh, Mando! Come and meet Kendra, Max's wife."

The famous baby de La Vega, Armando was an artist who traveled all over the world. She knew he and Galen were very close. Renee adored him and had nothing but positives to say about him.

"Talked to Max on the phone three weeks ago and he raved about you the whole time."

"Raved? Max?"

"Well, raved for Max. So more words than his usual one and two syllable grunts." Armando took her hands and rubbed his face along hers. Pausing.

"Double congratulations are in order, I see. I didn't know you'd taken the change. Welcome to the jamboree."

"It just sort of happened. We weren't expecting it."

Armando's brows rose. "Really? Darling what have you and my brother been doing that the change was a surprise?"

She laughed, blushing from the tips of her toes upward. "No. God. I didn't mean it that way. I just meant he didn't do it the regular way. His bite didn't even break the skin."

"Really now? Wow, I want to hear more of this story. But as I can see everyone getting impatient that they haven't been formally introduced, I'll let you fill in the rest later."

"How did you know? That I'd taken on a cat?"

Cesar interrupted then. "They'll be able to scent your cat. Lean in to Mando's neck. Take a deep breath."

Kendra did so and realized he smelled like Max. Not exactly

168

the same, but elements, the warmth of bark, the scent of leaves, fur.

"Eh?"

"I see. He smells sort of like Max. May I?" She indicated Cesar's neck. He tipped his head a bit and all speaking around where they stood stopped immediately. If she asked him what was happening, it would make her look weak. She knew that. He'd given her his neck, a huge honor.

She breathed in and realized there were elements of his scent that also mirrored Max, but some were sharper, stronger.

"Do you scent the difference?" he asked when she stood back.

"I do. Thank you for that."

"It's my job to teach the newly changed. My job to help you understand us. Your sister opened doors for you, you know that. You and she are so good for my boys. Immi and I know you will lead at Max's side with strength and courage."

He said it loud enough that all those straining to hear got an earful. His enthusiastic approval of her as a match for Max, and as an alpha to succeed him and his wife when the time came.

Max came down the steps into the backyard and after embracing Armando, he turned to his father. "*Gracias, Papi.*" Max hugged his father and then put an arm around Kendra. "We need to make the rounds. Introduce you to everyone." He was happy, she felt it humming between them, the heat of it, the warmth of belonging.

His father waved a hand at him. "That's what I was doing, boy. It's not the first time I've done this."

Max dipped his head, but kept his arm around Kendra. The two of them, on the outside, seemed very different. Scratch the

169

surface and they were the same man, just in different packages.

The more she got to know Max's family, the more she liked them. Well—she gave Beth the side eye—most of them anyway.

"Of course. Thank you."

Imogene came out, making sure everyone saw her head straight to Kendra to embrace her. Max had coached her for part of the afternoon, so she knew to rub her cheek along her mother-in-law's as a sign of obedience and respect.

So much was going on and she had to bite her tongue. She wanted to whisper stuff to Max, but since they all had great hearing, she couldn't risk telling him she thought things were going pretty good.

Across the back deck, she caught sight of Renee, Galen and Jack arriving. Renee had a big bouquet of flowers. Touched, Kendra blew her sister a kiss and mouthed a thank-you. It strengthened her, knowing her sister had arrived and had her back. Safe and way less alone.

One by one she met all seven of Max's siblings. According to the ritual Max had described, his parents would introduce her formally to the family and any other elders or cats of very high rank, and then they'd introduce her to the jamboree at large.

How much she was accepted and her relative place in a jamboree would be determined by how Cesar and Imogene handled the introductions. The more effusive they were, the better it would be for Kendra. So far they'd both held her hand and had taken her arm or caressed her shoulder.

Renee hadn't gotten this much support when she'd come around with Galen. For a long time Imogene hadn't liked Renee, but a few years back, the two women had a showdown, and Imogene had announced she'd been wrong about Renee and was fully supportive of her place with Galen.

170

Kendra was really glad she didn't have to endure that sort of cold shoulder. It was just another example of how amazing her sister was, how strong. She'd won over nearly everyone through years of relentless politics and wary extensions of trust and affection.

When they got around to Galen, Kendra gave a big hug to Renee, who beamed at her sister proudly as she stood at Galen's side. Galen gave Max his throat before they embraced.

As they turned to head toward Carlos, Kendra paused, cocking her head and listening.

"There's something wrong." Max spoke before Kendra had figured it out.

Gibson streaked past on full alert. He hadn't changed forms yet and still brought the hair on the back of her neck to standing.

Rosemary, who'd been in the crowd, rushed forward, but guards blocked her out. Kendra turned. "Let her in."

"No one gets near the alpha couple or the next-in-line."

"I'm the next-in-line too and she's my aunt. Let her through or let me to her."

Max was at her back. "We need to get you out of here," he said into her ear.

"No." Anxiety crept into her belly and she realized it was her cat. Her cat wanted to seek shelter and watch. But she knew one of the thieves was nearby. The magic in the air was amateurish, nothing natural lived in it at all. It was as if its user had bought it in a box like macaroni and cheese.

She moved toward her aunt. "What's going on?"

"Let her through. They're trying to help," Max called out and the wall of guards let her pass, Renee on her heels.

"This guy is a joke." Rosemary looked around, shaking her

171

head. "That's some D-List magic. Nothing of him at all in it. Even if he could lure any of us out, he's too weak to do anything with us."

Gibson shielded Max, who moved him over to shield Kendra. She rolled her eyes at them both.

"What if he's pretending to be an amateur? To lure you out and then he's all BAM super witch or something?" Galen looked from Renee to Rosemary.

"That was my question too. Though of course I couldn't lend it the poetry you do." Gibson bowed his head to his brother and Galen scratched his nose with his middle finger, flipping his brother off on the sly.

Rosemary thought it over for a moment. "No. Not unless he was uproariously good. And if he was, he'd be in here. Any witch with that kind of power doesn't need to bother with luring. He'd come in and take."

"Let's go grab him." Kendra turned to Gibson. "Come with me, or send another guard. I only need to be there because he might try something on you. I can stop him easily. Then you can grab him and bring him here."

"And we can take him to the dungeon and beat the truth out of him." Gibson said it with a straight face, but Kendra heard the joking tones. "Kendra, in another situation I might agree with you. But what if some of these more skilled witches are using him as bait to get you out there and then they'll strike? I'm not even saying this because you're next-in-line. You're a courageous cat, beautiful, but there are people in the world who will sink to any level to win. Create any level of pain and destruction to get what they want. If we're going to face that kind of being, we need to be prepared."

"It is my suggestion that we simply continue with this party," Cesar said. "Your Aunt Rosemary has warded the house quite well so they can't get in. Why let them harass you? Why let them win on such a lovely evening, eh?" He held his arm out. "Gibson is right. We don't know enough to move just yet."

Rosemary nodded and Max heaved an audible sigh of relief when she took his father's arm.

"Let us continue! We have a new member of the jamboree to introduce." Imogene stood, the fading light against her skin. She held a hand out and Kendra stepped forward to take it. "This is Kendra. Kendra is the other half of Max's heart. I have seen this face"—she cradled Kendra's cheeks—"in his eyes. She wears his mark and has accepted the space at his side."

The gazes in the room sought Kendra. Some were friendly, some were hostile, all were curious.

"She has taken on our Max, and a cat."

The voices in the room rose. "He had no right without permission!" Beth stood forward, anger slanting wrinkles of fury into her face. "He did not seek the council to request bringing another cat over."

Imogene blithely ignored her daughter to continue speaking. "He had no need. Her cat has come to her in an altogether unexpected way. He has marked her."

Imogene looked to Kendra, indicating she show the bite and she did.

"But the skin has not been broken. Look at her. She was with people until late afternoon yesterday. Others saw her before seven this morning. Even if Max had broken the rules and put her through the change, there is simply no way she would be in any shape to stand, much less be up and ready for breakfast in a restaurant full of people less than sixteen hours after that happened. Even the strongest among us in our history have not had that sort of recovery time."

"Then how do we know she's even got a cat?"

173

It hadn't been Beth that time, but Carlos. He shoved people aside, heading toward her. Part of her knew he'd never be allowed to touch her. Max wouldn't allow it. But she didn't need him. In fact, it was necessary she do a lot of this on her own or none of them would see her as an equal.

"Don't touch me. This will be your only warning." Her cat rose, even as Max made to shove his brother, Kendra dropped away and her cat growled while the magick filled her.

Her voice hadn't been her own. The knowledge of that should have scared her. Yet she found herself fascinated instead.

Carlos's eyes widened and he dropped his head.

Imogene growled at her son before speaking to the crowd again. "One of these days, a child of mine is going to bring home a spouse and we will not have all this drama. Carlos, you're being rude and now you have been warned. Beth, sweetheart, the baby. Take a deep breath and try not to be so angry. I worry about you."

And just like that, everyone went about their business, talking, eating, drinking, as if this sort of thing happened all the time.

Renee sidled up to her. "Yes, it does happen all the time."

She must have looked surprised because Renee laughed. "I could see the question written all over your face. Well done, by the way. That growl thing was awesome."

"I don't even think I could do it again if I tried."

Max hugged her from behind. "You could. Your cat will protect you and yours. You let her do that. You'll find you get along better if you listen to each other."

"All this is going to take a lot of getting used to. Also, I hate standing here eating meatballs when our target is right out there and we're not going to get him."

Max squeezed harder. "No. Gibson is right. It's too dangerous. Be smart about this."

She sighed. "All right. All right. I deserve some of that cake tempting me from the buffet table, you know, for showing all that restraint."

Max stayed glued to her side every moment he could. He was fully agitated with the situation and wanted to take her home. To their home where she'd be surrounded by four walls and much less a target than she was out in the open in a crowd.

His mother kept sweeping Kendra off to meet this or that person, usually with Renee on her other arm. The two sisters filled the room with their own kind of light and energy. He and Galen sort of orbited around their women as the evening went on.

Right then, though, he saw something he needed to attend to.

"Carlos, a word if you please." He'd worded it like a request, but no one made the mistake of believing it was optional.

"I know what you're going—"

"No." Max cut him off. "You don't. Which is why I'm next-in-line and you're not. Don't speak. You're not here to speak. You're here to listen. Kendra is my wife. She shares my position and rank, and she is welcome in our world. Whether you like her or not is utterly inconsequential to me. You have a right to like whoever you please. You don't have a right to invade Kendra's space without repercussions. And by that I mean from her. She's not only carrying a cat, she's a powerful witch in her own right. I've seen her use it, and you would be wise to keep your mouth shut and leave her alone if you don't like her."

His brother began to speak but Max held a hand up. "I said, no. You have been warned, by Kendra herself and now by me. Do not do this. If you push her to react you will shame yourself and the family."

"She'll shame herself if she can't handle a challenge. I know the rules, Max. Do you?"

He let his cat show in his eyes, let him glint in the lengthening incisors. "I'm warning you. After she's done with you, I'll be right there. Do not attempt to harm what is mine or I will defend it. There can be no mending that rift. I will no longer have you as a brother if you do this."

"And if I shame her, she's not fit to lead. She's not one of us. She's not human. She's not even fully a witch because she's taken a cat. What does that make her and why do you not see it as a threat?" Carlos stormed off and Max rubbed his hands over his face.

"It had to be said." Galen stood next to Max, his arms crossed over his chest as he watched Carlos leave the deck.

"He won't listen."

"Then she'll make him. You know she can." Galen paused. "Over time, I've come to believe this behavior in the jamboree is beyond destructive. You can't have this sort of attitude toward the spouses our cats bring into the jamboree. Renee handled it and she's proud. But she shouldn't have had to. Now that I know the extent of what she endured, I have to say, Max, if Carlos calls out a member of this jamboree's ruling line, he needs to be triumphant or weeded out. Not a single member of this jamboree should ever doubt that another member has his or her back. This is bigotry backed by bullying. You're the next generation. The change is starting, don't allow us to backslide."

Max realized Galen was right. Gibson had said something similar only a few days before. But he didn't want Kendra to

Beth materialized at her side and Kendra did her best to ignore her. Of course Beth wasn't satisfied with that. "You might want to have some vegetables. Max has never gone out with a fat woman before."

"You're like herpes, you keep coming back. Beth, please don't take this the wrong way, but you're a bitch. Excuse me while I take my fat ass to grab another chicken skewer. I'll think of you while I'm eating it. Also, Max isn't *dating* me, I'm your new sister. Please try to contain your excitement."

Beth grabbed her arm, digging her fingers into the skin. The crowd who'd been talking and laughing grew silent.

"I'd knock you back into the fence if you weren't pregnant. Do you care nothing for the child you're carrying? What kind of crazy, vicious creature are you?" Kendra pried Beth's fingers back, harder than she had to, but breaking a finger wouldn't hurt the baby, just Beth.

"Let go."

"No." She bent Beth's wrist back until she winced. "Now, how about you leave me alone instead? Hm? You don't like me. I get it. It used to be that I was human, but as I'm not, it has to be something else and at this point, I don't care what it is. I'm not playing these stupid games with any of you." She looked around and gave Max the *if you stop me I will make your life hell* face. "As it happens, I find this all totally ridiculous and boring. You think you're special because you don't like me? Pffft. Bitch, please, get your ass in line. Lots of people don't like me. All this puffery and proving myself to a bunch of people who have no intention of liking me anyway is just dumb and I don't play." She moved quickly when Beth tried to cuff the side of her head.

Kendra leaned in close. "You have no honor to act this way and endanger your pregnancy this way. You shame your family. Take your meds or start a blog like everyone else. But don't think the baby you're carrying will protect you if you try to hit me again." She pushed Beth away and turned to Max. "I'm out of here."

Imogene smoothly approached and hooked her arm through Kendra's. "Walk with me, Kendra, please?"

She barely held back her annoyed sigh.

"I know this is difficult. It's a time of transition for the jamboree. From old ways to new." Imogene kept her voice down as they moved away from the crowd and into the house. "Have I shown you my sitting room?"

As if she'd agreed, Imogene led Kendra up the stairs and down a long hall lined with photographs.

"Some of these pictures are Renee's work." Kendra paused to look at a shot taken of Cesar and Imogene as they leaned their heads close, with eyes only for the other. It was staggeringly intimate.

"Your sister has great talent for seeing inside people." Imogene closed the door and indicated Kendra sit on the couch.

"She does. I don't want to be rude. I appreciate the welcome you've given me. But I'm not going to take it from Beth like you're going to ask me to. That's not going to happen. Ever. I'm no one's convenient whipping boy. In the future, I won't be at these mixed events for the entertainment of people who should stop gawking and get some manners. Your children included. You can't ask me to prove myself and defend myself and whatever and then add, but not when it's my daughter who's been acting like a monster."

Imogene paused. "It took your sister a few years to get up the nerve to say all this to me."

She shrugged. "She's nicer than I am. She wanted to be loved and accepted for the wonderful person she is. She loves Galen a great deal and wanted to prove herself to his family the

180

same way any other spouse brought into this family has to." Kendra leaned back, crossing her legs.

"And you don't think you should have to?"

"I really like you, Imogene. I respect you and I love your son. So I'm going to be blunt here, because I think it's what I owe you. As a matter of fact, I don't. I don't think *anyone* should have to be treated like crap so your daughter and her bigoted little crew can feel better about themselves.

"I think further isolation and this silly notion that no one is as good as a cat is just absurd. I'm sure if you applied *black,* or *male,* or something like that, people wouldn't tolerate it. And it *shouldn't* be tolerated. I'm all for accepting that you are not human and therefore different rules apply. I understand keeping things in the family to avoid unwanted negative attention. By the way, from humans who are essentially preaching the same thing your daughter is. You simply lose credibility when you act the way those who seek to harm you act."

"The irony of that does not escape me." Imogene sat back with a sigh.

"I accept what Max is. What I am. I'm eager to learn about this entirely new culture. I'm eager to meet the rest of the family and to be part of it. But I'm not going to endure this totally outrageous acting out by your children, simply because that's always how it's been done. It's stupid. I'm not doing it. I did lots of things for a long time to keep from rocking the boat. I won't again. Beth is a problem. She is undisciplined and abusive. Carlos's outburst this evening, right after a possible threat to the jamboree was intolerable and put everyone, especially the children here, at risk."

Imogene's features, which had been inscrutable, relaxed. "And so what do you think should be done?"

"You're their mother, handle it. Spank them. Kick their asses. Put them on a time out. I don't care. More than their mother, you're their alpha. All this acting out has become normal and in my opinion, that's not helpful or conducive to a strong jamboree."

"Are witches so free of drama then?"

Kendra laughed. "God no. Suspicious, bitchy, covetous, fearful. But that doesn't erase the danger I felt tonight. I've been feeling. The danger that almost got my sister killed. That killed my mother. I will not end up dead and forgotten like that. Not without a fight. I aim to drag my brothers and sisters out of the dark ages and into the present. I have a battle on my hands and I really can't say I plan to play silly dominance games with anyone."

Imogene's face brightened as she smiled widely. "Oh he did such a good job with you." She patted Kendra's knee. "You're going to lead my jamboree into the present too, aren't you?"

Ah. That was the reason for this little chat. It'd been to test her and her resolve to lead the jamboree with Max.

"Not without your help and support. Do I have that?"

"Beth is my child. As is Carlos. I don't love them any less than my other children."

"That's none of my concern." She shrugged. "And that's not what I asked."

"You missed your calling. Should have been a lawyer like Max," Imogene said with a laugh.

"No thanks! I'd rather have my classroom with twenty third-graders any day."

"Cesar and I are behind you and Max. We meant what we said earlier. Yes. The cats like Beth need to feel listened to, but they don't have to be tolerated when they cross lines."

"So why do you do it?"

"She's carrying my grandson. She's my baby, even when she's an ill-tempered brat who passed her childhood long ago. But I'll deal with her if you'll allow me. Carlos." She sighed. "Well he's another story. I'd thought he'd calmed down. He seemed to be tolerating Renee, even being civil and respectful. Tonight was disturbing. I'm afraid you're going to have to knock him on his hard head to get him to listen. Cesar will speak with him about it."

"It's not up to me to allow you to do anything. You're this jamboree's alpha. You don't need permission."

"And you're next-in-line. One day soon I will hand my family over to you and Max, if I can't trust you, if I can't speak to you, I wouldn't do that."

"I can't speak for Max. I don't think it's appropriate to be involved in any disciplinary issues with his cats. There are things *he* has to take care of and I respect that. I just don't plan to be coming to any events where I have to deal with all this drama. Max is certainly free to do it, it's his family. But I bent once, so far I lost my way back to myself. And I did it for a man. I let his family take everything from me. I vowed to never go there again. I love Max and I'd die for him, but I'm not giving him my life, if you understand the distinction I'm not making very clear."

Imogene looked at her for some time without speaking until she nodded. "You're making yourself very clear. I respect what you're saying. I do hope you give us all another chance and stay for the rest of the evening, especially as it's supposed to be about you. I think the point has been made, or I hope it has. I really enjoy having you around. My kids, but two of them, certainly seem to like you. You're good for Max. You help him see beyond his job, his duty, you help him understand duty applies to his whole life, not just his role as next-in-line."

Kendra smiled. "All right, thank you. He's good for me too. We've got a lot more getting to know each other to go, but he's worth it. He makes me happy."

They stood and walked out together to where Max paced in the family room even as he looked down at the video game the kids played on a nearby television and gave his input.

Max had been waiting, not so very patiently, but he'd managed not to storm in and demand to know what was happening. While he'd waited, Gibson had come in to let him know they'd swept outside, only to find no one there, but fresh tire tracks at the top of a nearby rise where there was a nice view of the de La Vega house set back from the street.

Gibson had taken Jack with him, the wolves' expertise and input on this was very much appreciated.

Max could see Kendra and his mother had reached some sort of amicable accord. The panicked knot in his belly eased slightly.

"Your lovely Kendra has agreed to give us another chance." Imogene kissed her son's cheeks. "You chose well."

He smiled at his mother. "I agree. Kendra, have you met this motley band of monkeys yet?" Max turned and motioned at the room full of kids.

"Not yet." She moved into the room. "Oh, Mario Cart! I love Mario Cart."

"You wanna play?" One of the older boys handed a controller her way.

"Yeah!"

Chapter Twelve

The drive back to his house, no, their house, was quiet. She and his mother had laid down some sort of law between them in their little conference but neither had given him any details.

After Kendra had so very powerfully owned her new role and told Beth off, she'd left with his mother. Max had then told Beth and her husband to leave. Cesar did not contradict this, though Max did see his father on a long walk with Carlos later.

"I'm sorry," he said as they pulled into the drive, waiting for the garage door to open.

"For what?" As she eased to face him, the slap of heat that lived between them stole his breath.

"Christ. You turn me upside down."

A smile touched her lips. "You're apologizing because I turn you upside down?"

He pulled in and shut the engine off.

The hem of her dress had slid up, exposing the top of her thigh and the flash of bare skin above the hose she wore.

"I'm sorry for that fucked-up scene tonight."

She made her little *pfft* noise at him. "There's a new sheriff in town and they don't like it. Lucky for me, I don't give a rat's ass what Beth or Carlos think. I'm not going back to any such events, you need to know that. I told your mother as well."

"Baby, that's not going to happen. If anyone gets uninvited to jamboree events for behavior issues, it's not you."

She climbed into his seat, straddling his lap.

"Max, I'm a big girl. I can handle myself." She ground her pussy over his cock. There was no room to move the seat back; he had it back all the way. And he needed inside her body right then.

"Fuck me, Max. It's been about six hours and I need you so badly my hands are shaking. My cat is quite slutty apparently."

He laughed, as shaky as she was. "Slutty works for me." He touched every part of her he could reach. But it wasn't enough. "Out. We need out."

She growled, but let him open the door and stumbled out. That's when he pivoted her to face the car. "Hands on the hood. For now. Feet wide."

He pulled her dress hem up, humming at how sexy the stockings looked, loving the rich blue of her barely there panties, which he quickly got rid of.

Leaning in, he took a deep breath, all of her entering his consciousness and driving him wild.

"Hurry," she whispered.

One handed, he got his pants unzipped and freed his cock. A bit more adjusting and a quick slide of his fingers through her pussy to be sure she was ready and he'd positioned himself at her gate and began pushing inside.

Her heels were high, high enough that she was at the perfect height. She pushed back against him, meeting him thrust for thrust. Her hair fell from the pretty updo she had it in, making her look disheveled and ridiculously sexy.

His mouth watered just looking at her, looking at their

reflection in the windshield. Unable not to, he ripped the back of the bodice open, baring the pale skin of her back. She arched on a ragged cry of his name. When he leaned down, he meant to lick and kiss but when his teeth found her skin so warm and pliant, there was nothing else to do but bite.

She gasped as her inner muscles gripped his cock. The taste of her skin was unlike anything else. Magnificent. Salt and spice, uniquely hers and in turn, uniquely his. He let it lie on his tongue like fine wine.

She was close, he felt the change in her body, she slickened, heated to the point where he had to clench his jaw to hold back.

He pulled out, ignoring her growl of frustration as he sat her ass on his hood, went to his knees and, spreading her thighs open, dove in, licking her pussy, delighting in her squeal of pleasure.

Her nails dug into his shoulders, urging him closer.

He found her clit, sucking it into his mouth, pushing her over the edge. He growled his pleasure, always unable to get enough of her, needing more and more, even as he had her.

When he found his way back inside her pussy, she opened her eyes, her hair a sexy mess around her beautiful face. He leaned down, fucking into her body so hard she bounced until she wrapped her legs around him for purchase.

His lips found hers and she opened to him on a sigh, her arms twining around his neck.

Her taste mixed with his until it was all just them.

She broke the kiss as he continued to fuck her, brushing her lips down his neck until he shouted, coming harder than he could ever remember coming when her teeth sank into the skin exposed at the collar of his sweater.

She struggled for breath, the hard, cold hood against her back, a feverishly hot jaguar shifter at her front, his weight against her, his cock still inside her pussy.

"Wow." She licked her lips, hoping the feeling would come back. "I'm going to have to keep you around just for that part."

Wordless, he kissed her chest, over her heart and picked her up. He always held her with such gentleness and care that it brought something out she'd known she was missing but had been unable to quantify.

He cherished her.

"Thank you," she murmured as she stayed wrapped around him like a monkey.

"I just fucked you in the garage on the hood of my car and ripped your dress." Amused, he snorted. "What are you thanking me for?"

"For loving me."

He put her down carefully, kissing her soundly. "Like I could do anything else."

She headed to the bedroom, her dress falling down around her waist. The place he'd bitten stung a little bit, but in the right sort of way. It felt like a secret.

"Good thing I brought clothes over here, huh?"

"Not that you need them for bed." He leered at her and she held her hands out, warding him off.

"Dude, even *you* can't possibly want to have sex again yet."

"There's no yet. It's always."

She tossed the ruined dress on the counter and bent to turn the shower on. "I think I should invest in some of those tear-away dancing clothes with you around. You're murder on my budget."

He kissed her back, where he'd marked her, sending delicious tingles through her body. "I'll make it an item in our household budget. Clothes for Kendra. That way I can rip all I want. That's part of the fun."

Chuckling, he strolled from the room like the hot shit he was.

She laughed, but it snarled in her throat.

Her knees buckled as the first magickal hit slammed into her. On the way down, her head smacked the side of the tub, making her see stars as she scrambled to stand.

The world slowed as Max's cat bounded into the room. He roared so loud it reverberated off the tile, deafening her for long moments.

Using him as balance to stand, she got her legs back and began to focus on whatever it was. In the background she heard other roars, grunts and growls. The guards outside she wagered.

Pushing all that back, leaning into the giant cat who'd placed himself between her and the outside, she opened her othersight and found more than she'd imagined. Sharper, more brilliant and far reaching. Her magick had amped up considerably as she looked for the source of the magickal punch.

It pressed against her, this other magick, unhealthy, not organic so it was more magic than magickal, like a chemical instead of a sunset. But it was powerful and dripping with menace.

"Not my family. Not my house, motherfucker," she mumbled as her hands took flight, fending off, warding and at the very end, as it faded back, tagging it with a little magick of her own.

She slumped, holding her head, her nose now bleeding. Or maybe it had been all along, she couldn't be sure at that point.

189

Max shifted back, his face hard and angry. The scent of his cat still in the air. "What the *fuck* was that? Why do you bleed so damned much? I need to kill him for making you bleed."

She ignored his anger, knew it wasn't at her. "I don't know what it was. An attack of some kind. The wards here held him back, but he got through enough to physically slap at me. The nosebleed happens when I use a lot of magickal energy really fast, without giving myself the time to spool it up correctly. I also might have hit it when I smacked my head on the tub."

"You'll feel better in a minute. Your system will heal very quickly now." He crouched at her feet. "You scared the shit out of me. I felt it so intensely that my cat came without my bidding. That's not happened in a very long time."

Pounding feet ran up the stairs as the guards shouted his name.

"Hold!" He slammed the bathroom door shut. "Do you need to go to the hospital?"

She stood, still shaky but her vision was clear again and her nose had stopped bleeding. "No. I need a shower and then I need to go outside, nearer the edge of the wards so I can see if there's anything else out there."

He blinked at her, opening and closing his mouth like a guppy.

"Go on. The guards are worried."

"You're not going anywhere, Kendra. Wait for me. I'll be back and you can shower while I'm here to be sure you're not going to fall."

She waited for him to leave and turned on the shower.

"Kendra, damn it!" he shouted from the other side of the door. She snorted a laugh as she stepped under the spray.

Within moments he was back in the bathroom. "Didn't I tell

you to wait for me?"

"You did. I needed to shower. I can do that without an escort. I make a lot of allowances for you and this alpha thing. I'll take my own showers, thank you very much."

"You're just being contrary for the hell of it."

"That so? Don't know why I bother thinking at all since you're so happy to do it for me. Like I'm dumb."

"Now you're twisting it."

"Yep, that's me. Twisting my own damned feelings because God knows when the great Max de La Vega speaks he knows everyone's heart and mind better than they do. Don't know why I even bother breathing when you should do it for me."

He stepped into the shower stall with her, groaning when the spray hit his body. "You're bitchy when you're pissed off and scared."

"Keep that in mind, then." She smirked as she turned to watch him, water sluicing down all that muscle.

"I think my father tried to warn me about this," he muttered, a smile on his lips as he tipped his head back.

She got out and began to towel off.

"Don't even think about going outside. Guards are on the door."

"You know what, Max? Fuck you. I told you how I feel about being held someplace I don't want to be. Also, not to sound fourteen or anything, but it seems to have escaped your notice that you are *not* the boss of me." She stormed out of the room, searching through her things to find a pair of underpants and a bra.

Shit. He'd fucked that one up badly. He got out, toweling off quickly and heading out into the bedroom where she stood, strong and feminine, everything he ever imagined needing and more.

Tough. Bitchy. Protective. Compassionate. Intelligent and strong. She had no plans, clearly, to take any guff from him.

She'd been balancing on one foot to get her panties on when he barreled into her, taking her to the bed so she ended up on top.

"I'm sorry about that last part." He looked into her face, genuinely concerned about pushing any buttons her in-laws and ex had put inside her.

"I know you are. Butthead." She leaned down and nipped his lip.

His neck tingled where she'd bitten him. He'd nearly forgotten that part. Smiling, he brushed his fingertips over it. "Never had one of these before. I like it."

"You're just trying to flatter your way out of trouble. I'm still going outside." She kissed him and tried to get up. He held her tighter but she pinched his side and he yelped and she made her escape. "Next time, it'll be your cock if you try to confine me." Pausing, she sent him a raised brow. "Well, outside sex anyway."

He groaned as she pulled jeans on and a sweater over her head.

"You're going to kill me."

"Get over yourself. I'm perfectly capable of going outside and looking around. We have to, Max, it's imperative."

She walked out and the guards, he planned to kill them all later, got out of her way at the sight of the look on her face.

"Gibson, let's talk about the plan to go visit my father and his wife when I come back inside, okay?"

Gibson looked back at Max, who heaved a put-upon sigh and threw his hands up. "Wait. At least let me come out there with you. I need pants or the neighbors will complain."

The corner of her mouth lifted. "Don't be too sure. If I lived next door I wouldn't complain at all."

He put his jeans on, not bothering with shoes as he grabbed a sweatshirt off the banister and followed her down to the front hall.

"Are you sure this is safe? Why not wait a little while?"

"The longer he's gone, the colder his trail goes. You should understand that very well." And with that, she threw the door open and walked out.

Gibson growled, annoyed, leaping in front of her. "Listen here, pretty britches, I'm the guard, I go first. You wait for my signal to go ahead."

She smiled, lowering her gaze in apology. "Of course. I'm sorry, Gib."

"Show me by not using Gib as a nickname." Gibson snorted and her laughter lifted Max's heart.

"What I need to do is walk the perimeter. I won't leave the protection of the wards. I promise," she added to Max over her shoulder. "Give me space, all this testosterone and cat energy is like white noise."

Gibson sent her a dark look, but backed off. Max recognized the hand signals his brother sent to the other guards, placing them around the yard strategically. Max also knew there were others on the roof with sniper rifles if claw and fang didn't do the job.

And yet, the fear clawed at his insides. Fear for her. It was an emotion he'd not experienced much, especially as an adult. He wasn't worried about himself, but she was his to protect. Having her out there under threat brought a cold sweat to his spine.

Lauren Dane

He was not used to being questioned. He knew it and she called him on it. Still didn't mean he had to like it.

"I can feel your cranky mood through our bond," she said quietly as she walked past.

Gibson made no outward appearance of having heard that comment but for a slight tic of his left eye.

"All for you, *querida.*"

She flipped him off before stopping near the high hedges on the southern side of the yard. Going still. Quiet. Her eyes, her cat's eyes lived in her then, and a wave of admiration and love washed over him at the sight. His woman, strong and brave. Damn it, she was something else. Agitating, yes, but he didn't want anyone else. She was the works and he'd take the good and the scary, because it was all her.

He moved closer, but still gave her space. She cocked her head, breathing in deep, her gaze slowly raking over whatever the hell she saw when she used her othersight.

Just as suddenly as she stopped, she turned and headed back into the house.

"That fucking bastard," she grumbled as she rifled through Max's front-entry table to find paper and a pen.

"Is that my new nickname then?" Max paused, taking her hand and kissing it.

She snorted. "Only in my head. Don't you have paper and writing implements somewhere?"

He pulled another drawer open to expose a neat stack of paper and several pens.

"Thank you." She began to write all her impressions down as the men waited patiently. Or they may not have been patient, but outwardly, they held a calm menace.

194

"You want to fill me in on what you found out there?" Max asked her after several minutes.

"It's the same person. The same one who attacked that night." She paused and smiled up at him. "The night you took me to dinner."

His eyes warmed for a moment. "The beginning of this." He brushed his lips against hers and her agitation settled slightly.

"So it's the same person, or group. And to be honest with you, I think that weak attempt tonight *was* a feint. Yes, yes, I was wrong to want to check it out at first. You're right."

He grinned and she rolled her eyes. "I'm always right. If you'd accept that, you'd be so much happier."

"If you're finished gloating? Do you remember when we went over to my father and Susan's place? After they ran off?"

Gibson had organized that and he nodded slowly.

"The signature, energy, whatever, I felt tonight is similar to what I felt there. He's involved somehow. Or she is. They both are. Whatever. He's part of it, and we need to find him and deal."

"I sent out an advance team right before the party at my parents' house. Big fun, huh? Bet you can't wait for more of that." Gibson's smooth, calm delivery only made Kendra laugh harder.

Max wore a sour expression. "Stop it. You're going to make her more hesitant to go back."

Kendra and Gibson ignored Max and went back to their conversation. Gibson indicated the coordinates she'd given earlier. "I had to send out some sweepers first. To keep watch and stake out the area before I could send in a team. They're not that far from here. Just off 93. Somewhere outside Wilmington."

"Why didn't you say? Let's go!" Kendra made to grab her bag.

Gibson said nothing, but kept his arms crossed over his chest. He took a deep breath before speaking again. "Kendra, I would not send you out in a first wave. My people know how to run an operation and that's what we'll do. They'll get all the information and reconnaissance to me and Jack, and I will make a plan of attack. We don't involve you until we have a lot more information. And that's not now."

"I hate to break it to you and all, but I'm more prepared for them than you and your people are. They aren't a physical threat. They're a magickal one. You can't fight that. I can. Also, what if they move?"

"That would indeed be unfortunate. And yet, it doesn't change the fact that I make those choices when it comes to the safety of the leadership of this jamboree."

She looked heavenward, seeking patience. "Fine. Do let me know when I'm allowed to act, then." Before she said anything else, she spun and headed upstairs.

Back in their room, she dug through her bag until she found her phone and called Rosemary.

"All this could be over if we just shot that fucker in the head once and for all. And his bitch of a wife." Gibson leaned against the door and gave his brother a look.

"I don't think so. I mean, at least not right away. We talk to them first. Find out what the hell is going on. What happened with Kendra and Renee's mother. They need the closure and we need the intel. After that, well, accidents happen and you're free to be sure they do." Max punched the speed dial for Galen and filled him in. Galen informed him that Rosemary had shown up moments before and was on a call with Renee and Kendra.

They'd keep Renee inside as much as they could, which wasn't much given that the following day was a Monday and Renee would want to go to work.

Gibson interjected with information as they spoke, beginning to build a plan. Jack added his points, telling them he had his people on it as well.

"Busy girl, your wife." Gibson's mouth might have shaped into a smile very briefly as Max hung up with an annoyed snarl.

"She's not going to let this go and I can't blame her. As much as I want to, I can't. This is about her, about her people, and she has every right to want to deal with it. Her mother needs avenging."

Gibson lifted one shoulder. "Max, it's not going to stop there and you know it. She has a vision for the future of witches. One you and I both realize is totally necessary. This attack thing isn't isolated. Even when we find and eradicate this threat, there'll be more. She has a path. Like *you* have a path. And those will intersect. For instance, when you both drag the jamboree into the twenty-first century. She'll draw fire, but hold you to the course. We all need it."

"She couldn't just be a school teacher. No. She has to be Buffy the Fuckin' Witch Slayer or whatever."

Gibson did laugh at that. "You'd be so bored with a woman who wasn't your equal in the ambition department. But you're both going to fight a lot. She's headstrong, you are too. You're used to total obedience and having everyone simply turn to you for direction. She is not the type to ask permission. It'll make the sex hotter though."

"I draw the line at discussing my sex life with you."

"Must be smokin' hot then." Gibson stood straight. "She won't agree to a driver to work, but if you were smart, you'd take her yourself."

"It would be a lot easier if she just obeyed me."

"Dream on, asshole." Gibson opened the front door. "Gonna be difficult to protect her fully at work. All those kids around, adults are extra watchful of strange men."

"I know. But she won't take any time off. I've asked. Do what you can."

"Always do. Night." With a last wave, Gibson walked out the door, leaving Max alone and agitated in his front hallway.

Chapter Thirteen

"You're going to kick my ass."

Kendra looked up, halfway into a smile for her brother-in-law when he said that. "Gibson de La Vega, what have you done?"

He'd been there, just outside the school, waiting at the driver's side door of his SUV. Where Max had the sleek Jaguar, Gibson had opted for a menacing-looking dark SUV with smoked windows. It suited him.

He opened the passenger door and she hopped in. She didn't feel like arguing over taking the T back home so if they wanted to run out and drive her all over town, so be it. She should make them go shoe shopping or something.

"The place was deserted. Your father's place."

She growled and he huffed an amused snort. "Christ, you two are exactly alike. It doesn't matter if your father was there last night when you decided to run off and stand in the crosshairs. We don't know enough to do anything just yet. Kendra, believe me when I tell you that I want to deliver the justice you so deserve. The justice for what he did to you and Renee, what he did to your mother. But, we need to be smart. Gathering intelligence is smart. I want to know what we're walking into. How many people are there. If they're armed. Even if I don't have magick like you do, I have other skills. You and me, sweetcheeks, we need to work together on this."

She frowned, hating that he was right. "You suck. Who am I just like?"

He made a sort of hissing sound. "Max."

"Did you just hiss at me?"

"Cats hiss when they're annoyed."

"You're going to end up with a woman who is an even bigger pain in the ass than I am. I can't wait." She giggled.

"According to my brothers, pain-in-the-ass women are the best kind." He gave her side eye. "I'm not convinced of that just yet."

"Ha. So what's the next step then?"

"I'm taking you to Max." He drove on, silent and menacing, even though no one could see it but her.

"Are you always so chatty?"

His gruff demeanor eased for a small moment. Amusement danced in his eyes. "Don't tell anyone. They won't believe you anyway."

"Here's my contribution to the whole working-together process. I spoke with the witch who mated with one of Gabe's wolves in Portland. He was very nice, open. But he did not take on a wolf. His magickal energy improved, he said, his focus. I proposed he come out here and learn from Mary and my aunt so he could teach the witches in his neck of the woods. He's thinking about it, going to speak with his wife. He's hesitant. We've all been taught so much fear of learning any other forms of magick. I told him to think it over. Not like I'm going anywhere."

It vexed her. They had all these rules to protect them, she got that part. But when it turned around on them and made them more vulnerable, she wanted to scream. Energy was energy, it could be used for good or ill, it wasn't like she was teaching anyone how to kill the subject to steal their essence. But if those from other traditions could offer some insight and new skills, why not use that? Why not use that to teach those witches their tradition too? She knew some of the loosely created covens would feel threatened at the potential loss of individual power bases, but she'd cross that bridge when she got there. Anyway, if she brought it up, Max would flip his lid and start on her about the danger of this, that and the other thing.

"All right. Thank you. You guys are as complicated as the shifters are, you know that?"

And apparently as murderous. "Meh. Several things. First, what's next with the plan to get my father? Second, I'd rather meet Max at home. I don't want to go to Max's building. Beth is there. I don't have the strength to deal with her."

"Who does, *bebe*, who does? Ignoring her won't make her disappear though."

"I know that. But it saves my blood pressure and short of killing her, it's the best I can do right now. She's pregnant, I'm not going to do anything that would endanger the baby."

"Shall I share something with you about my sister?"

He pulled into his very own spot in the lot beneath Max's building. Totally not listening to her—something else he had in common with his brother—but she wanted to hear the details about Beth, so she let it go. For the moment.

"Beth was really into school. Popular, pretty, had lots of boyfriends. She was a cheerleader, on the debate team, all that jazz. In her senior year she was assaulted after a party. Or I should say someone attempted to assault her and she fought back. She's no one's victim, my sister. But she's the one who got in trouble because by then, people knew about shifters, but

Lauren Dane

like now, they didn't trust us. The boy made it out like she'd seduced him and then flipped out. She lost everything. All her friends, her human ones anyway, she was expelled and my parents sued. Eventually they let her back for the end of the year and graduation, and they publically apologized."

"But she was never the same."

"Nope." Even as he spoke to her, he never took his attention from the immediate area. He was a serious multitasker. "I'm telling you this, not because it excuses what Beth is now, but because it sheds some light on it. You're that way. You want to know. And, since it's just you and me here, I think you might understand what it feels like to have everything you counted on taken from you in an unfair way. You rose above that, you triumphed, and you've found something amazing with Max. She's never shaken it all the way off, and the way our jamboree acts, or has in the past, only made it worse by being so insular."

What could she say to that? It wasn't that it made everything all right, or acceptable at all. But it helped her understand and maybe she could approach it differently. Maybe.

"What's Carlos' story?"

"Him? He's just an asshole. Third-born son in a world where oldest counts most." That barely perceptible shrug again. "Doesn't seem to have held any of the rest of us back, but Carlos's biggest issue, in my opinion is that he's not Galen, much less Max."

She chewed her lip as she thought it all through, or attempted to anyway. "I don't know if it's okay for me to ask you something. I don't know the rules."

He paused. "I am the Bringer. Do you know what that is?"

"A cop of sorts?"

202

"Something like that. I am the bringer of justice. I am the bringer of law and stability. You are next-in-line, but you are also someone I know I can trust. Tell me and I will let you know if you're on the right track."

"Can I say, before you close up again and stop talking in more than one syllable that this is the most you've said since I met you and I really appreciate it?" She knew he would be uncomfortable with the praise so she quickly moved on. "Can you watch Carlos? Max loves you all so much. I think perhaps he might be blind to someone close to him who might wish to harm him for whatever reason." Carlos bothered her a lot. Beth, well Beth was just a spoiled bitch. But Carlos had the light in his eyes. That sort of fervent hate that rarely avoided ending up with violence and pain. She didn't trust him at all.

"It is absolutely acceptable for you to bring any and all concerns for the security of anyone in the jamboree to me. It's your job, and mine. And to answer your question, yes. I have been and I continue to. I also have issued a rule to my guards to not admit Carlos to your home if Max is not present."

Her heart slammed against her ribcage. He'd warned her for her own safety. Had chosen her over his brother. She knew he'd be uncomfortable with any show of overt emotion so she nodded and grabbed her bag.

"Thank you." Nausea writhed through her belly for long moments. If Carlos attempted to harm her or betray him in any way, it would break Max's heart.

"Wait." Gibson got out and walked around, exactly like that brother of his. He opened her door and escorted her through the walkway and into the lobby.

"Yes, yes, it's old school and all. But I'm a gentleman *and* by getting out first I can survey the immediate area and block you as we move into the building." He put a hand on her lower back but kept his gun hand free as they moved. "By the way, Max and I would appreciate it if you'd consider going to the range to learn how to shoot. It's an important skill."

So Max knew then? About Carlos? Or was this about Carlos? Gah!

In any case, he'd phrased it as a request rather than an order. She could get on board with that. "All right, yes. That sounds like a good idea. As long as it's after school or on a weekend I'm in."

Renee waved the two of them over to her small coffee/smoothie bar located in the sun-flooded lobby. "Gibson! Try this." She shoved a tall glass his way.

Suspicious, he sniffed and then drank some of the liquid.

He...purred.

Renee clapped, beaming. "You like it. Yay!" He ducked his head a moment.

"Yes. It's quite good. Thank you."

"Don't let this get out or anything." Renee looked from side to side and leaned toward Gibson. "But Kendra and I are the awesomest sisters ever. Stick with us and you'll have ginger orange juice iced green tea any time you want." She gave him a quick peck on the cheek and he smiled, sweeter than Kendra had ever seen.

Gibson shook his head, but the smile remained a little longer before his normal inscrutable scary-guy face came back.

Kendra hugged her sister. "I want to talk to you, but I expect Max is waiting. So, how about you, Jack and Galen go to dinner with us? You too, Gibson. Max took me to this place, dark, oak paneling, sumptuous banquets and the best steak I've ever eaten. It was our first official date."

"He took you to Amor. He knew it even then." Gibson tipped

his cup. "This is delicious. Thank you, peaches."

Renee blushed.

"Bring a date, Gibson. You're good for the digestion and all, on account of you being so handsome. Renee and I can sneak off to the bathroom and objectify you guys."

He sighed heavily, but she knew he smiled as he pretended to totally focus on his drink.

Before Kendra could take three steps toward the elevator, Max exited, stealing her breath, looking masculine and very handsome in a perfectly tailored three-piece suit.

She sidled up to him, forgetting everyone else but Max. "My goodness, sir, you're the very model of masculine beauty." She fluttered her lashes and he dipped down to kiss her quickly.

"You're one to talk. You know what that school-teacher thing does for me."

She wanted to laugh. She wore blue pants, ballet flats and a deep crimson sweater. Hardly prim, though certainly not sexy. Her hair was loose and she wore a scarf to hide the bite mark he'd given her.

He untied it slowly, revealing the spot where he'd first sunk his teeth into her skin. Her breath came short as she wanted that again.

"Ah, ah, ah. *Cari,* you're going to tempt me to ravish you right here in the lobby and get me arrested and disbarred. Thing is, I want to see you naked but for diamonds dripping over your breasts. Can't afford that if you get me disbarred."

She grabbed his lapels and dragged him closer, tiptoeing up to whisper in his ear. "I want you to mark me again. On the inside of my thigh."

Their energy reverberated, humming, vibrating until she nearly came from it.

"I want to lick you until you say my name. You know how you do it, stuttering, breathless, like a sob. It makes my cock hard. Let's go home right now. I just finished for the day. Was on my way down here to bother Renee and wait for you and Gibson, and look at what I found." He kissed her.

The kiss left her breathless. "We can't." She rested her forehead against his chest. "I invited Gibson, my sister, Galen and Jack to dinner at Amor."

He groaned. "All right. But we don't need to meet them for another hour or two. Let's go home first. Then you can be all relaxed at dinner."

She smiled up at him. "You're naughty and I should feel bad for tempting you off the path of righteousness. But I so don't."

"You know, I don't think I had much whimsy in my life before you. I enjoyed it, but since you hurtled into my life, I've had a lot of fun. You make me laugh. Fill me with happiness." He kissed her forehead. "Not many people are playful with me. You are. That means everything."

She swallowed hard, blinking back tears, pressing herself to him, hugging him as tight as she could.

"Gibson, Kendra and I will go home for a bit and meet you all at the restaurant at seven. Does that work for you, babe?" he asked Renee.

"Totally does. Galen took me there for our anniversary, I love that place."

"We'll see you then. Gibson, thank you for bringing Kendra here."

Gibson bowed with a stiff formality that was more than a run-of-the-mill thank you and you're welcome. That happened at the oddest moments, but Kendra had become sort of charmed by the old-world formality between Max and his family at times.

Kendra darted over, kissed her sister's cheek and rubbed hers along Gibson's. "Thank you for everything. I'm glad to have you in my life, helping me. And I didn't forget that you haven't outlined a plan for what comes next in the search for our father."

Gibson barked a laugh, taking her hands with a huge smile. "Oh I do like you two." He turned, winking at Renee before giving Kendra his attention again. "Tonight at dinner, we'll talk and plan. All right?"

She nodded. "Thank you."

Max loved to watch her get dressed. He stood in the doorway to their bathroom and greedily took in the way she slathered on lotion. They'd most energetically fucked both in the garage and on the stairs up to their bedroom.

Naked, she glistened under the heat lights while he watched her caress every part of her skin she could reach. He'd been banned from helping with this task the last time when he'd coaxed her into three orgasms as he went down on her. All because he'd been helping her get lotion on her back. Really, what was the world coming to when a man got punished for trying to help?

"Get that look off your face, Max." She met his eyes in the mirror, smiling.

"Uh-uh. I have lust in my heart for you, Kendra. I'm busy with that just now."

"We're going to be late if you don't hurry." She narrowed her eyes at him, holding out a hand. "No! If you come in here, you know what will happen."

"That's why I'm trying to get in there."

Trying unsuccessfully to hold her laughter back, she pulled on her panties and bra, and he pouted a moment. "You're so mean to me."

"Go!" She tossed the deodorant at his head and he ducked, grinning. He'd meant it when he told her he hadn't really had much fun in his life before her. She made him laugh. Just by thinking about her, his mood lifted. She pleased him even when she was being a bitchy pain in his ass.

He'd had lunch with his father. His father had spoken to him of how strong and special Kendra was and how much he and Imogene had loved how they fit together.

And then he'd warned Max about the future.

He'd wanted to bounce it off Kendra. She saw things in ways he couldn't. He appreciated her candor and her insights. But they'd been busy with love and who wanted to leave their lover's arms to talk about family politics?

Moments later, she came into the bedroom, her lipstick on, her sweater and skirt hugging every beautiful curve and the highest of heels on her feet.

"I wish we had more time. Damn you look good enough to eat. Again."

She closed her eyes and he took a step forward. Her eyes snapped open and she fake-frowned at him. "No. I want to have dinner with my sister. I want to go out on a date and have a nice time. Keep your penis in your underpants, mister."

"Mean."

He let her go, content to watch her brush her hair back with her fingertips and change earrings.

"You know, watching you get dressed is like being let into a secret club. The way you slather lotion on." He changed lanes and settled back into his seat. "The way you always look back over your shoulder at yourself in the mirror. The way you shake your hair out. It's sensual. Beautiful."

Her lips curved up in her secret smile. "You're so good to me." She took his hand a moment, squeezing before she let go.

She had no idea what she'd done to his life. How she'd filled it when he didn't know how very empty it had been until she was there, vibrant and warm and he'd nearly collapsed at the feel of her in that spot that had been vacant.

"Come on then. Let's go and eat lots of food. This new metabolism thing rocks my world. I need to say that right now."

Amor was safe. When Kendra walked through the doors, everything bad seemed to fall away. She liked that a lot. Liked that this place had been a touchstone for Max and the others in his family, and now it would be hers too. A space like this would have built up its own sort of protective magicks over time. That was a big reason why Renee's place and the de La Vega's house held a ward so well.

"Not to alarm you," she murmured as Max settled in next to her at their large, private table in the back, "but outside, I felt them outside. We're being watched."

"I'm on it." Gibson spoke to Max without him even saying a word. What rhythm they had. "I've known this for a while. Finding their bolt-hole worked quite nicely, helped freshen their scent. They're part of this. He's not out there, neither is she, or I'd be busy." His eyes darkened at the mention of their stepmother. "But they have been, and the people watching you and Renee are with them. Stink of them."

Kendra leaned forward. "And you were going to mention this to me when? You said we would work together. You keeping

209

secrets is *not* together. Just saying."

Max threw himself under the bus. "I asked him not to say anything. I wanted you safe but not worried."

"Max, we've discussed this more than once. I won't have you making these sorts of choices for me. You are not my parent, or even my alpha. You can't hide things this way."

He met her gaze, implacable and unshakable in his conviction. "I'll do what I need to to keep you safe."

"You'll do it alone then. I can't believe we're having this conversation. Again. You either trust me to run this jamboree at your side or you don't. I bet your father doesn't dare hide this sort of thing from your mother. You think I'm less worthy of respect?"

Galen sighed, leaning back, his hand on Renee's. Her sister narrowed her gaze at Jack and then Gibson. "Where is he? My father?"

"You knew too?" Kendra turned to Jack, totally livid.

Jack looked over at Galen, who heaved another sigh and nodded. Damn it, they'd all known.

"Renee, you and your sister knew I was investigating your father's whereabouts. My guards and Gibson's work together so we share a great deal of intelligence. It's been clear for some time that you've been watched, so that's nothing new. And you knew the possible connection here as well. We only learned of the connection, for a certainty, yesterday."

"And yet, you still made the choice for me." She shook her head at Max, totally annoyed he continued to do this. She dismissed that for the time being, needing to stay on task. "Where is our father?"

Gibson blew out a breath. "Truly, I don't know that. We're on it, as I told you, Kendra. But there is a connection, you said so yourself so that's not a surprise to you, is it? What would it have done to tell you? Hm? You know you're being watched. There's a connection. You're aware of all this so why would I hurt you more by reminding you? There will be times when I do my job without informing you of the whole of it. It's how this job works."

"That's not what this is and you know it. And I hate how my face wrinkles up when I get mad so it's totally digging into how cute I'd be looking right now."

Renee laughed and Max did too, but she turned back to him, putting a hand up. "You don't get to laugh. You're in big trouble with me right now. However, we'll table this for the time being because it's vulgar to fight at the dinner table in front of others."

"I didn't do anything wrong. We wanted to be sure, totally sure, before we said anything. I don't want to see that look in your eyes any more often than is necessary." Max took her hand and while she considered punching him, she chose not to. For the moment. Big, dumb butthead was being sweet, even as he was being a pushy, bossy jerk. "They've hurt you both so much. I hate that. And I hate that you have to finish this to get closure. But I know you do and I'm right with you. You can't ask me to not try and spare you more pain. I can't not protect your heart."

She let out a long breath, because she was totally defenseless against him. He cared about her and risked her anger to protect her. Even though she knew it wouldn't do to let him get away with this sort of thing, it still touched her. "Did you practice that in front of the mirror?"

He risked a smile, kissing her knuckles. "It's the truth. I'd die to protect you from the tears I see in your eyes every time the subject comes up."

"You're absurdly good at getting out of trouble," she muttered before kissing him. "No wonder you're a lawyer."

Renee was having her own heated discussion with Jack and Galen so Kendra took Max's jaw in her hand, holding him in place. "No more. I accept that you're nosy and pushy and in my business. I accept that you want to protect me and it means everything. This happened to me. To my mother and my sister. I need to see it end. I need to be part of that. Keeping me away from it doesn't help the way you think it does. It makes me feel out of control and I really need control here. It's the only way I can manage to get through it."

She saw it in his eyes, when he'd understood exactly why he had to share this sort of thing with her. His sorrow that he'd missed it. And his resolution to tell her. Oh, he'd do this sort of thing again, it was who he was. But on this particular issue, he'd share everything. And what more could a girl ask for from an alpha cat?

"All this arguing is ruining my appetite so I think we should eat instead of fight." She looked to Renee. Her sister had come through some rough times and Kendra hated that anything else would mar the happily-ever-after she'd achieved with her two men.

"From now on, you will share with Kendra and me whenever you receive new information about this situation." There was no question in Renee's statement and the men all nodded, agreeing. "Fine. Let's eat."

Gibson filled them in on the investigation. The information about the positive link had truly been the only thing he'd not told her, but it felt better to hear him lay it all out, complete with details about her father's movements. What they'd found, where they'd found it and what it meant. He was careful and methodical, not drawing any conclusions unless the evidence merited it.

"You're telling me our father and his wife are working with the mages to steal magic. Specifically the ones who've targeted Renee and now me." Kendra sipped her coffee and thought.

Gibson nodded slowly. "Yes. And they've been a unit for quite a long time. From what we can put together, your father and Susan have been together, at least working together, since the year Kendra was born. Your mother may have been sure then and that's why she took you to your aunt's. Or she just suspected but couldn't break away herself so she snuck you out."

Kendra tried not to dwell on it just then. She had a job to do. "Mary told me about this magick, concealment and protection magick for one person on behalf of another. If that's what my mother did, it might have been that she stayed in place to make a sacrifice strong enough to keep me hidden and Renee safe. It's just conjecture at this point, but the way everything happened doesn't make a whole lot of sense so it's not that much crazier to think that." And it had felt true when they'd discussed it.

"That may be it." Gibson smiled briefly before continuing. "We managed to uncover their trail. From Gilroy to Santa Fe, where your stepmother read palms and ran crystal-healing seminars."

Kendra growled. "She probably fleeced those who had true power, stealing their energies like a pickpocket."

"We've found an arrest. A group of women filed assault charges against her. Said she'd physically harmed them during a reading. They let her go, but only after a full day in jail. My contacts in Santa Fe tell me there'd been a lot of suspicion toward Susan and your father the whole time you lived there."

"I can't believe I don't remember that. I have had dreams of deserts and mountains, but that's a common dreamscape so who knows." Renee spooned up some of Amor's delicious meatball soup.

"Your memories are beginning to fill in slowly. You'll get it all back, though I wish we could scrub out the bad stuff first." Jack squeezed her hand.

"Then they lived in New Orleans for a year, same sort of story, only this time they were run out of town. I've got investigators down there, seeing if we can't connect up with some of these mages. Perhaps they'd have a reason to give us information if they thought it might hurt your father."

"Be careful, Gibson. I think it's important not to let these mages know how much power you have. I'd prefer it if you'd keep your distance and let humans deal with the mages when you're poking around."

"I take the safety of my people seriously. When you brought up the possible risks, I spoke to them about it to be sure they're using local law enforcement and other shifters to get the info to stay out of the picture the best they can. I agree that it's best to keep how much magick we have on the down low until you figure out how to handle this problem."

Kendra nodded. "Thank you. So after New Orleans?"

"El Paso, Little Rock, and finally Boston where she opened her shop."

"I imagine she's stolen magick and life essence from thousands over the years."

"She's killed for it." Renee spoke, putting her spoon down. "I know this, I saw it in her. Have always seen it in her. Not just our mother, but others."

Galen's cat shone in his eyes a moment. "She wanted to kill you, and there's no reason for us not to believe she wasn't part of selling you out to these other mages. Either way, she'll be dealt with. They can't hide from wolves and cats. Not for long."

"When we find them, we'll deal with them and end this threat."

And then she could truly begin her life. Free of the shadow her father had cast on her life for as long as she could recall.

Chapter Fourteen

"Nice control." Rosemary spoke from the other side of the room as Renee went through her paces in the practice space.

Two weeks had passed since the dinner. Not a whole lot of movement in the investigation. It wasn't stalled so much as garnering small bits of information in the wake of a deluge. Max and Gibson both assured her it was a factor in narrowing down and focusing on the target. Gibson said it was often like this right before he got that final piece that broke an investigation open wide.

In the meantime, she had classes to teach and classes to take and a new life to adjust to on several levels. Max had been incredibly generous with his time and knowledge, answering every question, explaining, giving her the tools she'd need to be part of his family.

She knew she pestered him, knew it agitated him not to just take over and fix things. But he never made her feel guilty, even when she saw the exhaustion and annoyance with internal jamboree politics written all over him.

"Great job to both of you." Rosemary clapped before hugging Renee and then Kendra. "I'm so impressed. You're such a natural."

Renee smiled, blushing, but clearly pleased with the praise.

"This is the coolest thing ever. Each new thing I learn

makes me want to learn more."

Jack grinned at his wife from his perch near the doors. He and Akio were on guard duty, along with Gibson's right-hand man, Saul. Saul, who was also their brother-in-law, married to Diana, the third eldest de La Vega and a glass artist. The de La Vegas liked to keep family business in the family.

Saul was pretty awesome, so hanging with him wasn't an imposition at all. He talked more than Gibson and didn't complain if she wanted to stop for milkshakes on the way home from work.

"We should get over to dinner, Kendra. Max said he'd meet us there."

"Five minutes. Let me change into a dress. It's just in the bathroom so I'll hurry."

Max arrived at his parents' home a little early. He'd wanted to speak with his father but ended up face to face with Beth, who'd wisely been avoiding him.

"Hey." She rubbed her cheek along his and not for the first time, he wondered how it was she could be so good to him, so normal and affectionate with him, and so mean to Kendra and Renee.

"Hey yourself." He let himself into the foyer and hung his coat up. "Why are you here? Is everything all right?"

"Wanted to see Christina while she was around."

Christina was their youngest sister, a history professor at Boston University who was about to leave to spend the next term in Spain with a small group of her students. He smiled. "Ah, good. I didn't know if she'd be here tonight."

"Why?"

"What do you mean, why? She's my sister, I like seeing her.

217

She and Kendra get on well, which is nice for my wife too."

"No. Why a human? Why not Kelly, who you dated and seemed happy with until this bimbo blew into town. There are many beautiful, accomplished shifter females who'd have been better suited to you than Kendra."

"Beth, you don't even know Kendra, so how can you say that? I'm asking you seriously. See your problem, supposedly, is that she's human. Well, Kendra never was, she's a witch. And now she's a shifter too. So what's the real deal here? Why are you so dead set against liking her?"

"I think we have enough problems. We have enough solutions too. We don't need to seek out any outsiders. We're just fine without that. She may have a cat now, but she didn't even get it on purpose. She's rejecting what we are."

He pushed from the wall. "I told Carlos and I'll tell you, don't fuck around with me or Kendra on this. As it happens, I agree we've got enough problems. But unlike you, Kendra is trying to help me solve them. Your bitterness is bad for you. Bad for me. Bad for the jamboree and for that baby you're carrying. Let it go. Just ignore her. I'm not asking you to pretend to like her, though I think you would if you gave her a chance. I'm asking you to act like other families do. You go one way, she goes the other and no one needs to see any drama. There are children around all the time, soon to be yours. Do you want your baby growing up seeing all this antagonism all the time? If you push her, she's going to push you back, and you know, as well as I do, how it'll end."

"I'm second born, Max. How do you know it'll end up with Kendra victorious?"

"I would miss you every day for the rest of my life if something happened to you. I love you, even when you're acting a fool. But my wife is a powerful witch and our bond and taking on a cat has made her even more powerful. She can take you out and she will if you push. You'll end up excised from your family, you'd break *Mami*'s heart and still the result would be the same. Let go of your past hurts. Feel free to dislike my wife all you wish, but shut the fuck up about it already."

He turned his back and went up the stairs where he knew his father waited.

Saul nodded to Gibson, who'd driven out to meet them both. There was some sort of ceremonial thing so Kendra waited patiently for it to conclude before Gibson held the door to the house open. "Come on inside. It's early yet so you have a chance to see the fire pit and enjoy some quiet before the kids arrive."

"Renee will be here shortly, though I expect you know that." Kendra paused, noting a deliberate distance where usually he was more open. "What's wrong?"

Gibson's eyes skirted making full contact with hers. "Nothing. Just busy. I'll be back shortly, I need to get something from my office."

Kendra glanced over at Saul. "He's odd today."

Saul took her coat. "Darlin', he's odd every day. Like clockwork. Go on inside. I hear my wife's voice and you're good to go now that you're here." He rubbed his cheek along hers and ambled off toward Diana's velvety laugh.

Kendra took advantage of not having a guard right on her heels and of the quiet to simply walk through the main part of the house and look at things. She smiled at the pictures on the walls and framed on desks and shelves. So much love in this family, so much respect and understanding, even when they were punching each other in the face.

She snorted a laugh and turned to find herself face to face

with one of Carlos's friends, a far-flung de La Vega cousin, Ramon. He was like one of those sitcom characters who stood behind the bully and said *yeah* a lot. She should have kept walking, but it was important to stand her ground with him. She was higher ranked and he needed to deal with it. He'd made comments the last time they all had dinner and she was just so very done. She'd promised to do her best to keep attending these dinners, and she knew how much it meant to Max that she did. So if that was going to happen, she needed to start acting like them more. Grinding this douchebag into a greasy spot would be a nice first step.

"Yes?" she asked.

"What are you doing to my family?"

"This again? I'm beginning to get so bored with you, Ramon. You don't like me. Point made. What else is there to add that's not clichéd and tedious?"

He growled and she raised a brow his way. It wasn't that she was afraid of him, but that she hated having to do this because she hated harming Max.

"Doesn't it matter to you that this hurts Max? That it hurts your aunt and uncle who're doing their best to lead this jamboree in such troubling times? Do you have no shame?" It bothered her, this sort of thing. Not that she expected everyone to like her, that wouldn't be normal in any family. But this faction in the jamboree didn't seem to care how much damage they did, they didn't even seem to think about the repercussions of what they did. And that was dangerous.

"He'd be better off without you anyway. I'd be doing him a favor."

She didn't bother with her snort of derision at this statement. He needed a spanking, and Max had stressed over and over that she had to give one to make a point. So she spooled up her energy, letting him see it, hoping he'd back off. But he seemed too stupid to get it and fear.

"Don't use your filthy magick here, witch."

This, of course, was the worst possible thing he could say. It pushed many of her buttons and had her fisting her hands to keep from popping him one.

"Some mouth you've got on you. I'll use my magick anywhere I please. I don't need your permission. I outrank *you*. Now back off."

He moved so fast she would have missed it were she not a shifter as well. But she was and she saw the razor sharp claw coming at her face and jerked to the side as she brought a warding hand up, sending her energy through it, enough to lift him from the gorgeous hardwood floor. And enough that when she let go, he clattered down, the breath whooshing from his lips.

It was then Max let his presence be known with a snarled growl. Then he reached down, grabbed his cousin by the scruff of the neck and hauled him up the steps before tossing him out the front door. Kendra watched in awe at how Max moved, as he followed his cousin, getting close enough to own the other man's personal space. "You're barred from jamboree gatherings for sixty days." He hauled off and punched his cousin square in the face. "That's for showing claw to my wife." He punched him again. "And that's for being so stupid you'd do it after you were warned."

It was at that point she noticed they had an audience. She'd knocked Ramon on his ass in front of pretty much his entire family and none of them seemed mad. Not even Beth, who shrugged and walked away.

"Kendra, would you please come up with me?" Max asked, or well, he sounded like he asked, but she knew she needed to speak to the alpha pair about what had happened.

But he didn't take her directly to the office. He hustled her down a long, quiet hallway and into a room that still scented strongly of him.

"This is your old room."

"Are you all right?"

She looked around at the space that, despite several decades of his absence, retained his presence. "I'm fine." She turned, looking up into his face, treasuring it already. "Are you mad?"

She found herself on her back, on his bed, Max looming over her, the light of passion in his eyes and a very ready cock pressing against her mound. Then she smiled. "You're a filthy boy."

"You have no idea what it does to me to see you like that. Tough. In charge. Owning your role." He said it, but the words were nearly a snarl as desire overtook him. He needed her so badly he couldn't see straight.

"Then take me," she whispered and he knew she'd felt the blast of his want through their bond.

And he drowned in her, taking, giving, consuming her, giving over to the near-narcotic effect she had on him, on his cat. Sure in the knowledge as they slid skin to skin, that he'd found home.

"Wow."

She spoke from where she'd burrowed into his side, something else about her he adored. She sought him out, taking comfort from his body. It meant everything.

"Glad you're not mad."

Even without seeing her expression, he knew she teased, a smile on lips that would be kiss swollen.

"I'm mad at him. At the situation. It's a waste of time better spent on other things. But it's not about you."

"This sucks." She paused and started to laugh. "Not this part, this part's pretty awesome. But I think I've had my fill of family acting like they've lost their damned minds. I hate that it hurts you. I'm sorry for that. Sorry I had a part in it. If it would be easier, I can stop coming to these things."

He growled, pinching a cheek of the ass he could write epic poems to. "Not yours to make up for. Now, let's get dressed and set to rights. I was with my father just before you arrived. He says he's got something to tell us."

"Oh great. So everyone's gonna know we came up here and got it on. Icing is that your parents will know." Blushing she headed toward the bathroom. "You ripped my hose."

"Yeah. Well you're going to need to carry around a change of such things. Or I can tuck them in a drawer or my pocket." He leered as she disappeared into the bathroom.

"Or, you could control your lustful impulses."

They both laughed at that.

By the time he'd gotten himself dressed and straightened, she came out looking beautifully unmussed, though it would have been impossible not to see the glow she had about her. "Don't need hose anyway. Your legs are perfect."

She smiled, flattered. "Thank you for saying so. But they're cold. In case you haven't noticed, it's April."

"In case you haven't, your body temperature should be higher. Aren't you warmer since you took on your cat?" He zoomed in, sliding himself against her, covering her in his scent.

"I am now. But we just *had* sex, so back off and let's go deal with your parents." She turned in his arms, straightening his collar and smoothing down the front of his shirt. "Handsome. Is this bad do you think? Is there trouble?"

"I don't know. But given the way things are going, I'd wager there's something up, yes."

"Jeez."

His mother was ending a phone call as they knocked and entered the office. Max scented his father's emotions, could feel the pull of them as they shut the door.

"I'm sorry to pull you two away, but there are some recent developments we need to discuss with you." Cesar sighed heavily. "Thank you, beauty, for setting Ramon to rights. I've heard word about it. Gibson says you handled yourself well. Nicely done to ban him for a time. Perhaps with some cooling off, your cousin can find his head."

"It's wedged up his ass, so don't wait too long, darling." Imogene threw her hands up, totally frustrated. "His mother is the same. Spoiled all those boys so much they think they're smart when actually, they got the short end of the intelligence stick."

"I'm sure you're right." Cesar winked, a little bit of levity lightening the cloud around him. "And yet, I find myself here in possession of information I must speak with you about."

Max looked to his mother, who motioned him to sit. Taking Kendra's arm, he led her to the sofa and sat, her body against his.

"I have spoken to Gibson about this already. I apologize for speaking to him first, but it had to be done. Two years ago, Carlos began to make business decisions that I found myself questioning. Money wasn't adding up."

Max felt himself grow very cold and very still. He realized Kendra was not surprised and wondered why he could be so blind. She pressed into him, enough that he understood it was

224

her way of comforting him without calling too much attention to it.

The cold eased, but not entirely.

"I didn't go to you with my concerns because I didn't want it to be true and I didn't want to involve you in something that could potentially bring a rift to the jamboree, especially without enough evidence. I spoke to Gibson. To have him look into it discreetly. I'll have him get you the file tomorrow, but the story is that your brother began to run with some radical humans."

"Wait. What does this have to do with embezzling money? And why the hell would human radicals want to be with him? He's a shifter."

His father scrubbed his hands over his face. Max noted his mother's body language, the tension in her was anger, not pain.

"If only it was theft. If only it was simply that. At first I limited his ability to get at our resources. Shifted his job responsibilities so he couldn't touch much. All his reimbursements have come straight to me since. I've said no a few times and since then, he's been more careful. At the time, I thought that was it and relaxed a little. Gibson didn't find any gambling debt, no evidence of a drug problem or general levels of high debt." Cesar huffed out a breath.

"But my discomfort didn't alleviate. It rode me all the time and I asked Gibson to keep looking. And then we found the beginnings of what we confirmed totally just this morning. The travel and the people he seemed to be hanging out with suddenly connected. He's got all this hatred of humans but I think he hates himself more. They allow him to hang around because he's their devil. Here's the evil shifter, look at him, he is so dangerous he's telling us how dangerous he is."

Kendra shifted against him, stiffening. "And who's worse than a shifter? A human who'd mate with one. Or who'd become

225

one. Traitors to their own race." Kendra spoke and it hit Max so hard he had to shove his cat back with both hands.

Cesar nodded. "I expect you've heard that a time or two, yes?"

Max looked back and forth between his father and his wife as the horror of it began to settle into his bones.

"My former in-laws were like that. They belong to some anti-shifter group, thinly masquerading as a religion. They said stuff like that all the time. They gave me shots. When they held me to *cure* me. Birth control shots so their son wouldn't have any devil babies. They told me if I just underwent their treatment I'd be cured and able to bear children." She tried to stand and he turned to her.

The ice was back. These people had harmed far too many and they needed to pay for it. "*Querida*, don't let them get to you anymore. You're here with me. That's all in your past. I've already had Gibson looking into it, making sure we know where they are." He had their number and planned to make a call very soon.

"I brought this into your life." She took a deep breath, looking back to his father. "That's how Gibson found out, isn't it? In some freakish convergence of all the things he was looking into, something connected Carlos with the group, or a group like the ones my ex's family was part of."

He sprang from the couch, needing to pace, his cat agitated and vengeful. "Is he high? Has he gone insane? It's the only way to explain this!" Max seethed as his father motioned him to sit back down.

Cesar turned to Kendra. "This isn't about you. Not at all. We knew he was up to something. We just didn't have the final piece until this morning. For nearly three years he's been going on vacations with these people. Letting them use him for

226

propaganda. He's been advocating the wholesale sterilization of any human women who mate with shifters. Gibson is working on it with two teams. I expect we'll know a lot more by tomorrow morning."

"What are you planning to do?" Max wanted to hurt his brother for even thinking of doing what he'd been doing.

"I want you to act as if nothing has changed tonight. I'm sorry, I know it's a lot to ask, especially after I've just told you all this. But I don't want to tip our hand before we know more. I don't want him to get away." Imogene said it, her voice shaking with anger. "That is no longer my son."

She stood and Kendra followed, putting her arm around his mother's waist. "Imogene, I'm so sorry. I wish I could help in some way. I know what it feels like to find out someone who should love you has betrayed you. I'm sorry you have to feel it."

His mother met his eyes a brief moment, hers was an expression filled with emotion, most of it gratitude. Christ, how did this happen?

"Is there any chance at all that this is a mistake?" He knew it was false hope, knew Gibson's skills were unparalleled, but he asked anyway.

His father looked so very sad. "That's why I'm asking you to act as if nothing has happened. There are pictures. Video clips even. Carlos speaking on his infection, on his curse. Hate mail with his face on it. For three years he betrayed us all, whipped up even more anger and hysteria that could have gotten any number of us harmed or killed. He's guilty and I wish it weren't so. You and I will hold on to that sliver of a chance that he's involved in some super secret military operation to bring these hate groups to justice. And when the inevitable comes and there's nothing left but total certainty, we'll know we never totally gave up on him until we had no choice."

"This could destabilize everything you're trying to build. This will only make the anti-human sentiment stronger." Kendra spoke as she squeezed Imogene's hand one last time and returned to Max's side.

"It can, yes, I'm afraid that's true. Max, you and Galen need to work together on ways to move our culture forward in the wake of the devastation this will leave. I expect we'll be challenged for leadership at least twice. I'm old, but not entirely helpless." Cesar turned his gaze on Max and he understood the other shoe was about to drop.

"You want me to take over."

Kendra put her head on his shoulder. Her fear jittered through her system, radiating into his heart.

"There is no one in this jamboree who could best you. You know that." Cesar stood, strolling over to the bank of windows and looking out over the yard where family had begun to gather.

Max wasn't vain, but he knew his strengths as well as his weaknesses. He was alpha and his father was correct. In truth, the chances of receiving a challenge would go down if Max took over. The certainty of losing and losing badly was total. Cats understood how things worked in much the same way humans did. The strong and the cunning ran things, and if they were strong and cunning enough, everyone lived well and safely.

The potential threat to his cats, to his family, had filled his system with adrenaline and Kendra spoke softly. "You need to calm or they'll feel you and wonder what's going on. If you're going to take over, do it right. Do it decisively."

Imogene's face registered surprise and then pleasure. Max felt that approval from the toughest judge he had ever known, and it humbled him.

"You're right, *querida*. Are you on board for this? If I run the jamboree, you do too. It'd be a huge commitment and there'd be cats at our house all the time. Meetings. You'd have to run a lot of meetings."

"There already are cats at our house all the time. You have guards. Gibson practically lives with you. Um, us. This is the future. You may not have planned it this way, but it's here and now you have to do what you're supposed to do. I'm happy to help in whatever way I can. I only ask the space to find my father and deal with him."

He kissed her forehead. "I'm behind you totally on that. I expect since Gibson will be so busy on this situation, we can have Jack's people help more. I'll make sure you get the help you need on this."

"Akio has been keeping me updated on everything. I'll speak with him and Jack, explaining everything. Or, well, what I can anyway. Are you all sure I should be doing this? There will be so much upheaval when Carlos is exposed for what he's done, should we add a former human witch to the mix?"

His mother waved a hand at that. "I've been alive along enough to see a great many things. Coming out to humans was the biggest and we survived it. My son's cat chose you, your own cat chose you. You are meant to be here and meant to help Max and your cats through this. I know it."

Kendra shrugged. "All right then. I expect I'll need help so get ready for all my phone calls."

His mother smiled. "Of course."

They spent another twenty minutes discussing the transition. Max wanted his father to continue on with the day-to-day running of the jamboree. He'd done it for thirty years and had done it well, the continuity would help.

He hated this moment, hated knowing his brother was capable of such hatred against his own people, hated knowing people said these things to his wife.

But he had no room for it just then because he had to pretend everything was fine and smile as his father handed over the reins.

Chapter Fifteen

"I'm sorry you had to find out this way," Gibson murmured as they all came downstairs. Kendra was shocked and off balance, even as she sought that calm place to pretend everything was hunky dory.

"I understand the why, but from now on, you'll report to me." Max stood tall, regal, she realized, owning his role completely.

Gibson nodded solemnly. "Of course. Congratulations and I mean that."

"Let's grab some food. I'm starving." Kendra figured if they all ate, things would be less tense. Hungry shifters were a very agitated bunch.

Max grinned, taking her hand. "As always, very forward thinking."

"Don't get used to it, but why don't I make you a plate? It'll give you a chance to sit and visit, and I can mill around. I know there are already rumors about Ramon so why not just be upfront and in their faces?"

When he leaned down to kiss her, she whispered in his ear instead. "I believe in you and all your limitless potential, Max. You can do this."

He took her hands and slipped a ring on her finger,

catching her totally off guard. "I've had this for a few weeks. I wanted to give it to you at the right time. Since we're about to start an even wilder ride than marriage, I realized this might be it."

She looked at it, at the band filled with diamonds, and knew he got her more than anyone else ever could. It was a simple ring. Not flashy, though certainly filled with plenty of awe-inspiring sparkle. He knew her and that filled her with so much pleasure she nearly made a very girly squee sound. Instead she grinned up at him, not caring who saw it, throwing her arms around him for a big hug as she thanked him before nuzzling his neck.

"I take it you like the ring?" His pleasure rolled through their bond.

"I love it. You're the best thing that's ever happened to me. You know that right?"

His smile softened. "I never knew what it meant to be in love before you. Making you smile has become one of my to-do list items every day. Now, go get me some food, woman, before I grow breasts and turn into a girl with all this talk."

She laughed, swatting his very fine behind and ambling off toward the big buffet table.

Max watched her through the evening. Watched as she charmed those members of his family who may have been on the fence. Watched as they assessed her now that they knew she'd tossed Ramon on his ass.

She didn't really get it, not yet, but that bit of viciousness from her had taken her light years forward in the eyes of his cats. Of their cats. When his father made the announcement, which would be any moment now as he was just finishing his ramble about some upcoming family stuff, the other cats would understand that Kendra was more than capable of running the jamboree and protecting them from threats.

He still wanted to kill Ramon for daring to move against his wife though. Oh and his stupid, fuckall brother who'd lost his damned mind.

Renee shifted, leaning closer to Kendra. The sisters had created a bond he admired and knew would serve them both well. Renee was very well respected after years of struggle to make her place in the jamboree, and Kendra openly credited that with her own success. They were unified and strong, and it pleased him inordinately to see it.

"Lastly this evening, I wanted to let you all know I'm turning the jamboree over to my next-in-line and his wife as of right now. It's not much of a surprise as Max has been the declared next-in-line for nine years now. Imogene and I have discussed it amongst ourselves and then with Max and Kendra, and we have every confidence they will lead this jamboree into a new era blessed by even more success and happiness." Cesar delivered the lines and smiled at the assembled group like he hadn't just tossed a bomb into their midst.

Kendra looked to him, showing him her heart on her face. He'd needed that just then and sent her a grin back as he hauled her to her feet, bracing an arm around her waist to hold her there.

"I know we haven't had a transition here in over thirty years, so I wanted to encourage everyone to remember my door is always open if you have a concern or question. Kendra and I really look forward to this new phase. I'll shut up now so we can get to dessert."

Galen stood, bowing his head. Gibson followed. Diana, Christina and Armando and, much to Max's surprise, Beth.

Nearly the entire rest of those assembled followed. It wasn't fake, the rush of fidelity and trust swelled through the bond his father had handed him. He held them all inside, and instead of fear, he realized how monumentally awesome it was to experience.

Kendra, while touched by the show of support by nearly everyone in the room, wasn't impressed by those who didn't show it. Carlos sat sullenly as far from them as he could and still be in the room. A few like him dotted the space, and she wanted to knock some sense into them.

She kept her eyes on him, waiting for the moment when he peeked up from his pout, and when he did, she sent him a look that told him just what she thought of his behavior. It might have been small to be pleased by the way he flinched, but so be it.

She had no doubts at all that he was guilty of what Gibson alleged. She knew Gibson well enough, had seen him at work often enough to know he didn't play around when it came to investigation and building a case. If he took it to Cesar, he could back it up. And given what a disgusting, cowardly piece-of-crap Carlos was, it wasn't as hard for Kendra to believe it as she thought it might be for those who loved him, like Max.

She narrowed her eyes at Carlos as he dared to glance at her again. This time he actually tried to hold her gaze in challenge, and she simply stared, unblinking, letting him see every ounce of loathing she had for him.

Max squeezed her as they sat back down. "What's going on?"

"Pffft. Just letting Carlos know what I think of his not standing up."

Gibson barked a laugh and patted her hand. "Aw, *bebe*, you're going to do just fine. Do you have a few minutes later on? At your house? We can talk about the other work I'm doing."

Jack leaned around Galen, stealing a stuffed mushroom from his plate as he did. "I'd like to be in on that one. I have some new information as well."

"Why don't we head over there after dinner then?" Max slid a thumb along the inside of her wrist as he spoke, sending a slow pulse of pleasure through her system, fogging her brain.

Leaning in close, she nuzzled his neck before speaking quietly to him. "You're making me all loopy with that. Stop."

His grin in response told her he knew exactly what he was doing.

Her phone rang. Normally she'd have ignored it, but as she saw her uncle's number on the screen, she had a feeling, a very strong feeling, she should answer.

"'Scuse me." She got up and found a reasonably quiet corner to answer.

Max felt it through their bond, saw the sag in her spine and was at her side in moments.

"What is it?"

"That was my uncle. My ex contacted him, fished for details about me. He knows I'm here in Boston."

His cat surged to the fore and she noted it, placing her palms on his chest. "Shh. It's okay. I have you. I have several giant shifter males all quite happy to hurt anyone on my behalf. I'm nervous, but not in the same way I would have been even six months ago." Right before he'd met her and his entire world had upended and changed for the better.

"Let's head home anyway. We can talk to Gibson and Jack about this newest development." And he could let his guard down a little at home surrounded by those he trusted implicitly.

"Stop. Stop the car!"

235

Max jerked the car to a halt with a squeal of tires barely in time to stop his foolhardy wife from falling out the door she attempted to fling open, even as the car still moved.

"What the fuck." He slammed the locks on. "Damn it, Kendra, you're going to get killed."

"Turn! Turn here. Now, now!"

The cars that had been following screeched to make the turn he did. His phone began to ring and he thrust it at Kendra. "You have to tell them whatever you're doing."

"Just follow us. I feel him. At the end of the thread I connected to him." She disconnected and if he hadn't been trying not to kill them both, he'd have laughed at the expression he knew had to be on Gibson's face.

Her head fell back against the seat and he began to slow. Her hand reached out, grabbing his wrist and digging in. "He's out there. Don't stop until I say. Keep heading...get on...get on 93, north, yes, north. Go, Max!"

He barely made the onramp, but he sped north on her orders. His cell rang again and this time, he flipped on the stereo to answer it that way. "De La Vega."

"Mind telling me where we're going?" Galen's voice sounded. Kendra had her eyes closed, lines of concentration on her face so he didn't want to disturb that.

"She's taking us to her father I think. Call Rosemary and let her know what's going on. Get Gibson on it too. You may as well stay on the line and listen so you know where we're going."

Renee spoke in the background, making the calls and Max smiled for a moment. The sisters worked together.

"Off!" She sat bolt upright, pointing at an off-ramp.

He bit off an annoyed comment and took the ramp, keeping it slow, listening to her and letting her lead.

They hit dead-ends a few times, and he'd have to stop and let her listen to whatever inner map she had until they could find a way around it.

It was incredible that the two cars following had kept with them the whole time. Gibson would never let him hear the end of this.

She opened her door, having used her magick to override the locks he'd thrown back near his parents' house. At first she just stood there, listening, cocking her head. And then she was off like a shot, down a long block.

Cursing a blue streak, he managed to get the jag parked, grab the keys and follow, only barely resisting his urge to yell her name.

Up ahead of him, she ran, graceful and full of fury. Her legs were long as she ate up the pavement but his were longer, he'd catch up to her soon enough. Gibson was craftier as he reached Kendra first, obviously having taken a shortcut through a nearby alley.

Her rage pulsated not only through their bond, but in the air all around her. Her sorrow and confusion too. She tried to maintain a hard-assed stance, but he knew this had to hurt her. How could it not? His cat clawed his insides, trying to get to her to fix whatever was wrong.

Kendra saw them, standing not too far away. She wondered at Max's ability to not scream her name as she'd taken off, but thank goodness he'd kept quiet so she could get the drop on them.

She'd spooled up her power as she ran, letting her cat keep focus on her quarry as she got her magick ready to go. When she skidded to a halt, she sent out a blast of energy strong enough to knock her father on his ass.

Susan turned, seeing her and sneering. She sent a blast

Kendra's way, but now an entire jamboree of jaguars lived in her, there was water nearby, trees, grass, apartment buildings and houses. So much energy, she drew a small wisp of it, pulled it into herself and rebounded that blast back at Susan.

Because the magic Susan had tossed was so vile and toxic, it stuck to the other woman like shit. Apt.

But she wasn't totally out. Susan hit her again twice more and her father aided that bitch, amping her power up.

Dimly in the back of her mind she felt Max through their bond. Max barreling down the block getting closer and closer.

It burned, blacking her vision out for a long moment before she grabbed more of the energy around her and brought it into herself. She allowed herself to tap into her cats, just a small bit and blasted back at them both so hard, Susan ended up with her husband, on her ass, on the ground.

The pounding of Max's approach vibrated through her shoes, up her legs. The wash of his energy, of his fury boiled over, shoving everything from his way. He was a badass freight train of pissed-off protective alpha male.

"Hey, guess what? I got married. That sound is my husband coming."

"What the fuck do you think you're doing?" her father asked, his voice thready and freaked. He understood who she was. There was no way around it. She knew how much she looked like her mother and Renee.

That he could be so nasty, even after what he'd done, made her crazy. It felt as if her cat actually paced inside her body. "What, no tearful reunion? I might have to go to therapy now."

He tried to move, but found himself stuck to the spot. She felt him try to draw on her and shocked him, slamming him out so violently he stepped back, holding the hand he'd been working the spell with. She'd pay for that later. A nosebleed had started, but the nice thing about this shifter business was that it stopped nearly immediately.

She stood back as the blur moved to the side, grabbing her father by the scruff of his neck and slamming him against the side of a nearby car setting off the alarm.

"I got that," Renee said quietly as they arrived, using her energy to short the alarm out.

Kendra realized how exposed and in the open they were. But Max was barely holding on to his human skin as his protective instincts raged within him. She'd need Gibson's help to get the situation under control.

"Let's get this away from the noise," Gibson said carefully to Max, staying in Max's line of sight, urging calm. His hands were loose and at his sides, his gaze averted from Max's eyes, accepting the other man's dominance.

Max seemed to relax a tiny bit as Jack spoke up from just to the side where he'd been waiting with Renee. "We're out here in the street where anyone can see."

"Over here." Rosemary approached with Mary, they stood at the entrance to a nearby park.

"You made it fast," Max murmured to them as they hustled Andrew and Susan over, cats and wolves fanning out to set a perimeter.

"Mary sat up at dinner and told me to get in the car. We were driving to your place when we got the call. Renee talked us here." Rosemary shrugged before turning her gaze back to where Susan and her father were. "You are to move carefully to that park and sit on the bench you're told to. If you don't, I'll drain you until you can't move on your own."

Kendra had never seen her aunt so vicious, but it was clear she meant it and they both seemed to understand she was serious, even if Susan had a look on her face so obnoxious,

Lauren Dane

Kendra wanted to slap it off.

"Yes, let's!" She leaned in close as they walked, keeping an eye on them. Max growled, putting himself back between them again.

Mary did something and the sounds around them dampened. That was so cool, Kendra planned to ask her about it later. "This will give us some privacy for a time."

For now she had other concerns. She motioned to Max, who had his arm around her waist, his lips pulled back in a snarl as he looked toward Susan and her dad. "Now here's the thing. He's a protective alpha jaguar shifter. They don't come in other flavors. And he's really mad. At you. Which, well, I guess that means it sucks to be you."

Mary flanked the bench on one side, Rosemary on the other. "We've got it handled for now."

They needed to move this along or get inside. The nearest safe place was fifteen miles behind them, though, so it was time to improvise.

"Now back to me for a moment, I'm a witch too. Surprise! But you knew that, didn't you, you naughty boy. So you should also know that if you try to use any magic on anyone here I'll suck you dry and not feel a thing. If not me, Mary will, or even Aunt Rosemary. I'm sure she's got a lot of anger with you over that murder thing. You know the thing, where you and your bitch killed our mother. Oh that was quite out of bounds. So you need to understand this." She focused on Susan, who was far more powerful than her father. "You're some piece of work, aren't you? I should throw you to these very unhappy boys to deal with."

It was Galen who growled that time, and satisfaction bloomed through her belly at the way Susan flinched.

"So to wrap up, these people are my family. I will kill you to

240

save them. And I can. I've learned a bunch of nifty new spellcraft. It would be self-defense. So keep your shit together, don't cause a scene and you might just end up walking away alive at the end."

"Would it be easier to take care of this piece of shit if I make him bleed?" Max's voice would have scared the hell out of her if she hadn't known him.

"Thank you, baby, but I think we're okay for now." If blood were spilled, it could be a lot harder to keep Max and the other shifters calm.

Max leaned down, getting right in her father's face. "You have harmed my woman and my sister. You seek to harm them still. Why should you be allowed to live?"

"That's a good question," Jack added.

"Not that I'm opposed to killing him or anything. But how about we get some answers first? Like say what they're doing here? Where his compatriots are? Who these contacts that have been routinely attacking our women are? Those little details." Gibson slowly, making sure Max saw it and didn't react negatively, put himself in between the two men, taking over.

Max reluctantly moved back, shifting to stand in between Kendra and her father.

"I need to see him," she murmured, sliding her hand up and down his arm. She'd never seen him so close to the edge. That such a controlled man would be on the verge of shifting because of a perceived threat to his mate. No one had ever reacted to protect her the way he did.

"He wants to hurt you."

She nodded. "He does. But he can't right here."

He brushed his lips against hers. "I'm not going to let him hurt you again."

She nodded again. "I know. Thank you, Max."

He seemed to be satisfied with that. Sort of. "If he tries anything, Gibson, anything at all, break his fuckin' neck. Not enough to kill, just you know, paralyze him. He can still talk with a broken spine."

Kendra took Renee's hand and they cautiously moved closer, far more concerned about the enraged and protective males than with their father.

She bent, taking her shoes off, immediately getting a boost to her energy. The cold woke her up, sharpened her focus. "That's better. So you know, they're not joking about the broken-neck thing. So let's just quit any ideas of trying to get away without giving us answers. If we can do this right, you might live. Maybe."

Renee waved at Andrew. "Hi there, Dad. I wish I could say it was nice to see you. But since you murdered Mom and have been cooperating with people who tried to kill me, I have to say I'm feeling far less fond of you these days."

He tried to come off as upset and rude, but his fear stank. It didn't stop him from using yet another chance to lash out at his youngest daughter. "Renee, what are you doing with these people? I thought you knew better than to consort with thugs and idiots. Look at them! Not even human. Shifters. For God's sake, they're lesser beings and you give your body to them. And that trash who says she's your sister, how do you know that for sure?"

Kendra snorted. "Thank goodness I got my intelligence from Mom's side of the family. I think the question is, what do *you* think you're doing?"

"I don't have to tell you anything. You're no one to me."

Gibson punched him in the face.

"Thank you, Gibson. I feel much better now." Kendra

turned back to her father. "Now, shall we do this again? Why don't we start with why you killed our mother?"

"You can't win. We're stronger."

Mary snorted. "Please. Andrew, you have no real concept of your power and how little you have." She touched him and Susan sprang to try and keep them separate. Rosemary grabbed a hank of Susan's hair and yanked her back into place.

"Don't move again, bitch."

Kendra sighed. "You're so silly. You're not here by choice, are you? Your nose isn't bleeding because you were so strong you could hold a shifter back when he wanted to punch you. I don't have a dick to measure against yours so let's just not play this game."

He sent a bolt of energy toward her, knocking her sideways. Max made a choking sort of roar that freaked her father out so much, making him so pale, Kendra wondered if he'd pass out. If this didn't move forward soon, Max would shift and eat him or just flay him alive. Or whatever.

"Oh, now that was ill-advised." She dusted her hands off while Gibson increased the pressure of his grip on Andrew's throat. "Dumb of both of us. I shouldn't have let my guard down and you shouldn't have thought you'd be successful. The only reason you're not dinner for my husband right now is me. You got that?"

"Use my energy, Kendra. I know you're holding back and I'm gonna kick your ass if you don't do what you need to take care of this," Max spoke quietly in her ear. She wanted to speak with him in private, but she didn't want to take her attention away from Susan. The hit had tasted like her magic, not his. Her muddy, disgusting magic fueled most likely by the bloody nose they'd caused. She squeezed Max's hand.

"Gibson, can you stand back a moment?" Mary asked.

Mary did something, Kendra thought she altered the molecules around her father's body, starving him of oxygen for just a short burst. Kendra was already skirting the line by using magick to hold him in place, though she told herself it was self-defense. Mary had a different view of her magick and how she could use it. The cost would be between her and the universe, and it was one she willingly and knowingly took on. Kendra was not so vain that she'd tell the other woman what to do in this situation.

He looked to her, his eyes wide as he wheezed until she let go, watching him choke for air.

"You only have yourself to blame. Just be glad he didn't break your neck instead." Kendra shrugged.

"*Bebe*, I may have to start bringing you along when I go out on jobs." Gibson grinned back at her, his grip on her father's throat again.

And with that three more mages entered the park. Kendra knew this because she felt the swell of their intent, the beginnings of something dark and unwholesome.

"Get down!" She screamed as she, Mary, Rosemary and Renee stood in a line, keeping Susan and their father behind them. "Don't you let these assholes get away." She motioned back at her father and Susan.

That's when Jack popped Susan one first, and then while Andrew was still shocked, Max growled and punched her father.

"They're out and you better watch your pretty ass," Jack called as Max materialized behind her. Wolves and cats fanned out, flanking the three mages who'd entered the park.

"Don't get too close. Max, if you get yourself hurt I'm going to hurt you even more."

He snorted in her ear, standing right behind her, his arm around her waist. "And if you don't draw energy from me, I'll
244

hurt you."

Tough guy. If they lived through this, she might go for some old-fashioned punishment. Heh.

"You are not welcome here," Rosemary called out, and they hit her so hard she lost her footing, falling back.

Slices into her skin.

The coppery tang of blood in the air, in her nose.

Max pushed around her and ran toward the man who'd made her bleed. One moment he wore his human skin, the next he was his cat, black and sleek with razor sharp teeth and claws that gleamed in the yellowy light of the street lamps.

He hit one of them, taking them down with a scream, a garbled scream and crunch.

She lost focus for a moment and that cost her dearly as she took a hit from one of the remaining mages.

It hurt. So much she could barely hold on to her magick, but she did and she yanked it back from the mage trying to steal it from her. Instead she took his, drawing it from him with a snap that took him to his knees.

Renee, damn, her sister kicked butt as she sent energy to Kendra, healing energy that began to soothe immediately.

"Draw on him. You know it's what you have to do, Kendra. Take his weapon against you or he will win!" Rosemary screamed as she fought. Sigils sparked in the air between the two groups as magick met stolen magic.

But the stolen magic felt different than her own magick. It didn't belong to the mage throwing it her way. She'd need to think on that later. If she survived.

But right then she grabbed it and pulled, pulled hard as she drew the magic from the mage nearest to them. It filled her, dark and roiling, but it powered the spell she was working, made her stronger even as her system registered it as an intrusion.

Things were a blur as she worried for Max and her cats, worried for her sister, Mary and Rosemary, worried for the wolves.

In the midst of her worry, she still had a job to do so she did it. She let her magick take over, let that part that intuited her use of power take over. Lights flashed, lights no one outside the park could see.

Her energy waned, but she knew the mages were worse off because she'd drained one. He'd fallen to his knees, disappearing under the weight of a shiny black wolf. Akio she'd have guessed.

One still stood.

She stumbled forward, feeling Max through the bond but not seeing him. Renee had moved to Rosemary's side, and Mary stood alone in the middle of the grass, locked in a magical battle with the last mage.

They seemed to be well matched, though she worried for Mary and everyone else. Things happened so fast all around her, shouts, lights, the stench of burning flesh and blood. Her cat pushed forward, relishing the sights and sounds of battle.

And then something hard and heavy struck the back of her head, the world exploding in vibrant color for moments until things faded, and she hit the cold, wet ground.

Chapter Sixteen

She knew she was alive because she hurt too much to be otherwise. She got to her knees in time to see Max running toward her at full speed. He blurred a moment and caught her up into his arms as he shifted back to his human form.

"Are you all right?" One handed, he felt around and she found enough energy to be amused. Just a tiny bit.

"Put me down. This isn't over."

Mary came over. "It is for now, sweetheart. Susan got away, I'm sorry to say. She's the one who hit you. But we still have your father and the clan witches just arrived."

Max set her gently back on her feet as two very businesslike witches approached. Mary indicated the newcomers. "Kendra and Max, these are the hunters I spoke of, from the Rodas Clan down in Providence."

She reeled at the news of her stepmother escaping, but had to keep her shit together yet one more time. Max squeezed an arm around her.

A tall, broad witch with pale blond hair blowing around his face stood forward. "I'm Callahan Peters. You can call me Cal. And this is Miles Dolan." He pointed to the man next to him, this one with close-shaven dark hair and wary brown eyes.

"I'm Kendra de La Vega and this is my husband Max.

Thank you for coming to help."

"I'm sorry Susan Tolliver got away. We've been looking for her for years, and I can't believe she was here in Boston all this time. But we have her accomplice. Your father, I hear?"

Another man approached. This one hummed with power and Kendra knew he was far more powerful than the other two.

"I am Arel Haas, the Hunter of the Rodas Clan." He shook Max's hand first, the two men never taking their eyes from the other. Some sort of dominance crap, she assumed, waiting not so patiently for it to be over. Finally he turned to Kendra and shook her hand, speaking to both of them. "Please accept our apologies for not arriving sooner. With your permission, we'll take your father and the two remaining mages to see what we can find out."

"Take them where?" Her voice sounded rusty, but she was regaining feeling in her fingers and the cuts all began to heal. They were magical wounds and would take longer to heal, even with her shifter boost, than a normal injury would.

Max held her closer. "My wife is bleeding. Her aunt has an arm that may be broken and my people have been injured. We're standing in the middle of a public park out in the open, so perhaps now might be a time for you to tell us where you're taking this trash and why we should let you."

Arel raised an eyebrow but nodded before he spoke again. "We have facilities where we can hold them without a chance of escape. And if they won't cooperate, we have...techniques to extract information if they fail to be forthcoming. You're not equipped to handle this here. You must know that. But we do and we're happy to share what we find. I know these people murdered your mother, and we've been told they attempted to drain one of you and have been attacking other witches in the area. This makes them an enemy to all witchkind and my job to deal with."

Mary had joined them and spoke up. "He's telling the truth. I've spoken with Sadira Rodas and I've followed her career over the years. She runs a tight ship in Providence and I believe they are far better able to handle this than we are. We can't hold them, Kendra. Not without keeping them so drugged we'd be unable to get any information from them."

"Sadira would like me to let you know how much she'd enjoy meeting you and working with you in the future. I give you our word to share everything we gain from these people. You are free to come down now if you'd like to watch us work. Or come tomorrow. Whichever you prefer." With a flourish, Arel handed business cards to them.

Kendra nodded. "All right then. Yes."

Arel motioned to Cal and Miles, and the remaining mages, including her unconscious father, were whisked away and into a van parked just outside the park entrance.

"She's not coming tonight. She needs rest." Mary looked her over and shook her head.

Max hummed his agreement. Jack and Galen were busy fussing over Renee, who allowed it. Kendra didn't blame her sister, heaven knew how much she wanted to simply let Max drive her home so she could throw up a few times and pass out.

Cal returned to them. "You'll feel ill for some time from drawing the magic into yourself. But your body knows what to do and you'll expel it within a few hours."

"That sounds pleasant."

Cal laughed. "Well, I've done it a few hundred times by this point. It's not what I'd call fun, but I'm not a shifter either. Your ability to heal yourself should be greater because of that."

"I will be in contact with you first thing." Arel bowed

slightly toward them. "Sadira would very much like to meet you and speak about this mess. The situation is fluid, changing very quickly and not always for the best."

"All right. We'll speak to you then. I'm getting Kendra home. I'd take her to the hospital but she'd refuse to get out of the car. But I know for damned sure I don't want her standing out here another moment. If you're lying, I'll find you. You have my word on that, witch." Max narrowed his eyes at Arel.

A glimmer of a smile caught Arel's lips for a moment and skirted away. "I'd expect nothing less."

And with that he was gone.

Max picked her up and she didn't complain as he marched to his car. His car that had appeared at the park, already running, her seat heater was even on. Galen assisted Mary while Gibson helped Rosemary load into their car. Renee would see to it that their aunt was taken care of, so Kendra let go of that particular worry.

"Have someone drive their aunt and Mary home, Gibson. Make sure they have what they need. And I want a guard on each of them."

Gibson rubbed his face along her jaw and the scent of her cats soothed her belly. "You did great out here tonight. I'll get guards on them right away. Akio has assigned some of Jack's wolves too. Don't worry about them, they'll be safe. Now you go home and get yourself better. I'm going to check on you first thing."

Max hugged his brother briefly before relaying more instructions. Finally he slid into the seat beside her and without another word, shot off toward home.

Max winced as the sounds of his wife throwing up, yet again, reached him. He paced, forcing himself to not go to her. She'd warned him the last time that she'd kill him if he didn't leave her the hell alone while she vomited. From the look in her eyes, he believed that threat.

His cat was agitated. The scent of the wrong magic she'd drawn into herself hung in the air, acrid and stale.

She stumbled from the bathroom and back into bed where he'd tucked her after a hot shower.

"I think I'm done." She burrowed down beneath her blankets and he settled in behind her, his arms around her body, giving her warmth and, he hoped, comfort. God knew he needed some of his own after the day they'd had.

His brother was a traitor and a group of witches had tried to kill his wife. He'd been there when bloody strips were torn into her skin. Had been there when magic had sent her to her knees.

He'd killed that night. It wasn't the first time, but it was close. Killing was rare for their people. He didn't feel guilty. In fact, he wished he'd killed them all for daring to harm Kendra.

Yes, tooth and claw had worked just fine, though he did concede Kendra's point about it really being a magickal war. This was not a good sign, and he didn't think they'd seen the last of this mage situation. He'd just have to be ready when they came back at his family.

He wished her father had at least faked being sorry. If for no other reason than to spare Kendra and Renee any more pain. Barring that, he was very sorry he hadn't killed Andrew and his bitch of a wife. He hated that she had gotten away. Felt as if he'd failed his woman on that.

"You should have taken more energy from me tonight." He kissed her shoulder and she snuggled back into him. "I hate

251

that you're so sick. And I'm sorry Susan got away. I'm sorry your father is what he is."

"Max, I love you so much." Her words were drowsy, but the love pouring through their bond was clear and let him know she was on the mend. Earlier, the sickness she'd had to rid herself of had done something to their bond, had narrowed the stream of information and emotion back and forth. That had alarmed him nearly as much as the bloody welts.

"I needed to do it my way. I know how hard it was for you to allow that and I thank you for it. She got away because her people came to her rescue. He's not important and so they abandoned him. She hit me in the back of my head, and before this is over, I'm going to get some of my own back for that and what she did to my sister and my mother. Using the jamboree and you to get energy to kill without it having been self-defense would have tainted my magick. I did draw from you, from the cats, from the air, the grass, the water, all the people around. But it was me siphoning off their magic that weakened them the most. I need to talk with Mary about it, about how easily their magic came to me. I think it's because it wasn't theirs to start with. It made me hella sick, but it weakened them and made me stronger. This is good to know for next time."

"Next time? Oh, hell no. Kendra." He broke off into a streak of curse-laced Spanish at how dangerous his wife's life might be if she hared off on some freaking warpath with these mages. "No next time. You're mine and I do not give you permission to throw your pretty ass in harm's way again."

He caught sight of her quick grin. Her eyes were closed and she lay totally relaxed against him. "God you undo me. You know that? Here I am with a bunch of shape shifters, some witches and my asshole father and two bad-guy witches are in some clan high-security prison of some sort, probably being interrogated at this very moment. It reads like a play, doesn't it?

Or maybe a Tim Burton movie. I won't do anything that would endanger my cats. And they're my cats, Max. On top of that scene in the park, we took on your jamboree. It's my responsibility to protect them. My duty. And I will. I'd never forgive myself if I did something to purposely harm the cats. Even Beth is mine to protect."

He smiled against her hair. "And *you're* mine to protect too."

"I know. Thank you for that. I'm sorry you had to kill. I'd never want that for you."

"Don't be sorry. It's one less threat to you and he deserved it. It was self-defense and I'd do it again."

"I don't think it's a coincidence that my ex-in-laws called my uncle looking for me on the same night that we find my father."

Max's stomach churned. "I spoke briefly with Gibson about this while you were in the shower and refusing to let me help." He paused.

"Carlos?"

"Gibson has had Carlos's call log from his phone forwarded to his own. There were three quick calls to cell phones. One with an 857 area code, one with 617 and a last with 408."

"Are you kidding me? What is he doing calling Gilroy?"

"Gibson is on it." He sighed heavily. If his brother was involved in this, it would be considered treason, and there was only one sentence for treason in jamboree law.

"Gibson is paying Carlos a visit tonight to see what we can find out. Gibson has been in contact with the Hunter and his people from the clan too. They're getting answers already. Those hunters are hardcore. I like that."

"Better than putting our heads in the sand and pretending

everything is just fine. They're organized, or they seem so. Powerful without a doubt, which is comforting. I didn't sense any lies from them. But my senses were messed up from the magic I'd taken in."

"Arel was telling the truth. Cleanly. I didn't sense even the tiniest bit of evasion from him at all. He's strong. My cat was impressed. I don't like that you might get dragged into something because of them though."

She turned to face him. "I'm sorry." She kissed his chest over his heart. "I'm sorry about Carlos. But you know I can't ignore this. And you don't want me to. Not really. I promise to leave the expert stuff to the experts, but this is about the survival of my people. Both of them now. I expect my fears about the mages knowing the power of the shifters is moot because of the involvement of your brother. If he's involved, I should say."

He sighed. "Carlos is involved. I can feel it to my bones."

"He has exposed us all. Not just witches, but damn it, if these mages truly understand shifter magicks, they will want to steal it."

He groaned. "I knew you'd been trying to protect me without me knowing it. Damn it, Kendra. You can't do this."

She made that little *pffft* sound at him, and he found himself caught between annoyance and amusement. He loved that she wanted to protect him. Loved that she'd thought of their cats earlier, had protected them and understood her duty so well. But he didn't love how fragile she was and how easily harmed.

"I can so."

"Go to sleep. We have a big day tomorrow and we're both going to need rest. Gibson will call if there's an emergency. He wanted me to repeat that to you so you'd rest knowing he'd let us know if anything big developed."

He didn't say, but Carlos was with Gibson now. Their father had gone to supervise, urging Max to stay with Kendra. The distance between Max and whatever was going on between his father and brothers would most likely help Max in the future. Father to son, Cesar had asked to be the one to mete out any punishment, should it come to that.

So he let himself go, once her breathing had changed, let himself sleep with her at his side. Safe and his.

Chapter Seventeen

Kendra woke up, sore and feeling a little hungover. Must have been that huge infusion of outside magickal energy and the stuff she'd pulled from the mage. But the cuts in her arms had faded to red lines and her power was back, humming in the pit of her stomach, stoked like a fire, warming her and keeping her focused.

"Why are you getting out of bed?" Max spoke sleepily and she didn't resist the urge to turn back and take a look at him. Naked, warm and staring at her like he was going to eat her up.

The good way.

"Well, aren't you delicious?"

"Come over here and taste, just to see." He slid the sheet back and she saw how ready he was for that.

"Why, hello there, sailor." She moved back to him, unbuttoning and sliding out of the oversize shirt he'd helped her into the night before.

Touching him brought her back to herself in ways she'd probably never be able to adequately describe. His skin against her lips, against her cheek, the warm, solid muscle against her bare skin, it brought her home every single time.

I didn't matter that they'd most likely hear terribly sad details about his brother, about her father and that mess, what mattered right then was that he was everything to her.

His taste brought a soft moan from her lips, her hips jutted forward, seeking more contact.

Usually in charge, he let her take over, looking up at her as she rolled on top of him and kissed her way across scratchy cheeks, over jawbone, down his neck, pausing to breathe him in. Her cat stilled, curling up within, even as the woman felt the stir of his cat in response.

"I love to look at you." She kissed the hollow of his throat, arching back as he slid his palms up her thighs, the tips of his fingers brushed, quite deliberately, against her labia when he cupped her ass.

"Look your fill. I'm all yours."

She smiled, sitting up. "Forever."

"And then some, yes."

A breath and he was inside her, where he belonged.

The scent of her magick and his built between them as she rose and fell over him, as she took him into her body over and over, building the heat between them until, with his hands all over her, playing the ring and her clit, tugging, squeezing ever so gently, she came.

Moments later, he pressed up, holding her down on him as he followed.

Trying to catch her breath, she used him as her pillow, his cock still inside her while she rested.

"I could have lost you last night," he said very quietly. "When you were hit, when the mage slammed that bolt into you, my cat took over. Logically I agree with your statement about magick being the best defense against magic. But logic was nowhere near my heart when you stumbled, when the scent of your blood filled the air, and I felt, damn it, I felt you weaken. I would die to save you, you know that. But I'd kill to achieve that too."

His voice rumbled through his chest, where she rested her head. The beat of his heart was steady and strong.

"I know." She did. She hadn't been insulted or angry the night before, she'd understood why he'd done it. "I love you and I love that you'd do anything to protect me. I just wish I hadn't come into your life when all this drama did. I hate that I'm part of this mess."

He sat up and she let him move her body however he wanted to. He carried her into the bathroom and began to run the shower.

"Get your ass in there." He wore his grumpy face, which for some unknown, inexplicable reason delighted her.

"Only if yours is right after mine or I'm going to think you're mad at me."

He got in, his body taking up nearly as much space in the stall as his presence did inside her.

"I am mad. Mad that you'd blame yourself for this fuckery. You know it's not about you at all."

"Bullshit." He snorted and she ducked under the spray. "It's totally about me. My ex and his family, this whole thing with the mages, Carlos. It's all about me."

He sighed and soaped her hair, kneading her scalp with strong, talented fingers. "Not so. It's connected to you, but that doesn't make it your fault, or even about you in the sense you think it is. Carlos…"

She felt part of his pain over it and turned to hug him tight. "I'm so sorry for that. I know that's not my fault and all, but I wish I could make it not happen. I wish he wasn't doing this. I hate that you're hurting from it."

"Aw, babe, you're everything. I wish it wasn't happening too. But it is and I have to face it. Today."

She got out, handing him a towel when he followed.

"I suppose one bright side is that it's Spring Break at school and I have the day off. It's not quite five, sorry I woke you up so early."

He kissed her so thoroughly she got revved up all over again. "Damn, you're good with that mouth."

His grin made her knees rubbery. "I am and you taste so good too." He moved toward her and she leaned against the counter, watching.

His phone rang, breaking the taut silence between them. "Damn."

She groaned. "There goes my phone. Let's get this show on the road."

Naked but for the towel low-slung around his hips, he grabbed the phone and sent her a look over his shoulder. "I will be eating your pussy later. We have a date."

She laughed for a second until she saw the caller info on her phone.

"This is Kendra."

Rosemary, calling from the Clan building in Providence, sounded exhausted. "Why don't you go ahead and come down here? I've sent the directions to Gibson. We've found out a great deal since last night."

"Have you been home at all? Is your arm all right? You sound terrible."

Her aunt gave a bone-deep sigh. "Arm is fine now. Renee and Mary did something to me. I'm sore, but I can move it. I slept over at Mary's. She and I drove down about an hour ago because we couldn't sleep."

"It's bad."

"Yes. It's terrible and I hate that you have to hear it."

"But I do. I'll get Renee too."

She dressed quickly, grabbing up her things as she phoned Renee. An apology for waking her so early was on her lips until her sister answered, clearly awake.

"Is it bad?"

Kendra swallowed, deciding to hold back details until she was face to face with her sister. "I'll be by to grab you shortly."

Max interrupted. "*We* will be by to grab her shortly. I'm having Gibson bring the SUV. He and I need to talk about Carlos on the way."

She looked to Max, seeing the stress lines around his eyes. Knowing he hurt. "Did you hear that?" He nodded.

Renee spoke again. "Galen just came in and told me the same gruff bit about all of us going. I'll bring coffee."

"You rock. Love you." She hung up.

"Tell me." She grabbed her coat and Max helped her into it, pausing to breathe her in, letting her scent settle him even just a small amount.

That she cared so much, especially after some of his family had been so unwelcoming to her, meant a lot. Sometimes it blew him away that the joy of holding this woman against his body was something he'd never imagined at this time the year before. Life was fucking odd sometimes.

Max opened the door. "Gibson's outside. Let's go and he'll brief us. Since we're in charge and everything."

She made a face and shook her head. "I keep forgetting that part."

The drive wasn't long, and in the predawn hours, it wasn't too crowded either. Max gave the order to Gibson to brief Galen and Jack on the Carlos situation as well.

Kendra sat curled into his side, warm and soft, their connection wrapping around him and easing some of his anxiety. Some.

Jack drove while Gibson spoke.

"Carlos tipped them off last night. He gave them not only your home address, Max, but Mom and Dad's address."

Kendra tensed and a growl trickled from her lips. His cat responded until Max wrestled his control back into place.

"It gets worse."

"How the fuck can it get worse than my brother hanging my wife and family out to dry? He set us up. Set my wife up to be killed!" Galen pulled Renee closer and Kendra squeezed his hand briefly before settling back into Max's arms.

"What else?" Max asked.

"He's the one who told them...the mages...about Renee."

Jack nearly got them into an accident at that.

"Get your fucking mind on the road or don't drive the car." Kendra sat up straighter, and right before Max's eyes, she owned her alphaness totally. "I know you're pissed off. I am too. But what will it solve to have a cowardly, self-loathing prick like Carlos cause you to kill us all? You're an alpha wolf, Jack. Revenge will be yours."

He sighed but the sound was precariously close to a growl. Renee kissed his cheek and rolled her eyes at Kendra. "Be nice. He was just shocked."

Gibson began to speak again after a bracing sip of coffee. "It was Jack. Or rather, it was when she mated with Jack and Galen. It pushed Carlos over the edge he'd been walking for years."

Kendra's voice was clipped, businesslike. "What part did my ex-in-laws play?"

"He met them at some gathering. They're quite active in the anti-shifter movement and were talking about you, about how they'd held you in their basement. Chained." Gibson paused, his jaw clenched as Max saw spots of rage. "They chained you, *bebe*?"

Kendra blinked back tears. "Yes. What else did he say?"

Renee turned to her sister, tears in her eyes. Max saw it and shook his head to stay her. The last thing Kendra needed just then was to have them all upset on her behalf. She was barely holding on as it was.

Gibson met Max's gaze for long enough that they agreed to take care of this little problem very soon.

"He didn't know it was you they were talking about. Not until you came into Max's life. I did a background check on you and your aunt when you first got to town. He overheard me reporting to my father and Galen. He knew it was you when I said your ex-husband's name. He got back in contact with his friends in *the movement* as he called them and eventually they hooked up and he led them straight to you. Well, first to Renee, with the help of Susan and your father, Ren. I'm sorry, but they were part of all this from the start.

"I had his place swept, took all the electronics, all his files, cleaned out his car, his desk at work, his everything. Part of this started a week ago. As Max knows, we've suspected Carlos for a while. Just...not this. He told us everything anyway. We have names and numbers. Jack, you and I need to decide to share or not with Arel. The anti-paranormal groups are working together now with self-titled bounty hunters of all sorts. These mages painted themselves as humans out to drain witches of their demon-possessed magic. There are those who hunt shifters and those who poison vampire blood supplies with holy water."

"The witches need to know." Kendra seemed to come out of a dream. Her entire world had been torn from around her, but she had to get over it and lead. "They have to know. The shifters need to know. The vampires, fuck me, there are vampires." She shook her head. "They need to know too, because we have to fight back."

Gibson's gaze went to Max, and she snarled, putting herself between them. "I am alpha too. I gave an order and I won't have you patting me on the head and waiting for my husband to give you permission to obey me or not. I'm either in charge, or I'm not."

Max's brows flew up, but he shrugged. "She's right."

"I won't give orders on things I don't understand and I won't be a despot, but *I* am a witch and this is genocide. I won't sit by and let my people, jaguars, withhold information that could save us all."

Gibson nodded. "You're right."

"*Papi* was there you said? How is he?"

Gibson looked at his brother. "How do you think he is? He's angry. He's grieving. He's worried about Kendra and Renee. He hates that this happened and feels responsible. He had to carry out the sentence, which tore him apart. But he told me it was his duty. He expects you both to be around later today. They've called an all-jamboree meeting and you'll need to tell everyone."

Kendra didn't want to ask what carrying out the sentence meant. She had a feeling she knew and she didn't want to think about it.

"I think we should send your parents on a trip. Send them to Kingston or Seville. Just let them grieve and heal but out of the glare of attention." She spoke softly to Max, who took in a deep breath and then sighed.

"Good idea. I'll get my assistant on it. You're going to need an assistant too. Running the jamboree will take a lot of your time and you'll need the help."

She nodded, numb.

The clan building in Providence was as pretty as the ones around it. It looked like any other office building, but when they got to the doors, Miles was there to let them in. Silently they rode an elevator up several floors to a reception area where Rosemary and Mary were waiting.

The rest was sort of a blur. They were ushered into a conference room where some food and coffee had been laid out. A sleek, beautiful woman in her early thirties stood and moved to them.

"I'm Sadira Rodas, leader of Clan Rodas. Please be welcome." She shook hands, her gaze lingering on Arel for just a few seconds longer than everyone else. Not that Kendra could blame her, the Hunter was in fact a very fine-looking man.

"I'm afraid we have some distressing news. Please sit down and have some coffee or juice. There are bagels and other things. Mary reminded me about shifters needing protein so the covered platters have eggs and bacon."

Rosemary sat, holding Renee's hand on one side and Kendra's on the other. "I'll do most of the talking. It's easier this way. Carlos de La Vega has been selling information about you and the shifters to these radicals."

When no one looked surprised Rosemary sighed. "You knew?"

Kendra nodded. "We only just found out. I've advised

Gibson to cooperate and share information with Arel and the other clans. We're being targeted. We need to protect ourselves."

Sadira nodded. "Yes. Thank you."

Rosemary began again. "Andrew was a bit player. In this anyway. He didn't really know much. The other two did. As we discovered last night, Andrew had been working with the mages for some time. His memories were spotty and it appears they'd messed with him too. In the plus column, I think Mary and I have the key to unlocking Renee's memories totally. Though we might want to continue doing this slowly because I worry about the emotional and mental trauma that may come from a rush of bad memories."

Renee leaned into Jack. "Good grief."

"Yeah."

"Your mother had always been suspicious so she got you out of there. She went back to protect your whereabouts, Kendra, but eventually she ended up pregnant. This part is garbled, but it may not have been consensual. She had you, Renee, and Susan became a far more dominant force in his life. They stole magick from your mother and sold it to these other mages. Susan appears to have used the magick herself, your father learning how later."

"He got stuck." Stuck was magickal slang for an addict.

"Indeed. He's rather eaten up inside from it. That's how I could get in so easily."

"Why would they let him of all people come out here then? If he's so fucked up and all, why let him come instead of someone who was stronger?" Galen sat next to Renee, his arm around her.

"He's expendable." Mary spoke from the other end of the table. "It could be that they underestimated your strength. They don't know you're taking lessons from me. I've kept a low profile in Boston and they certainly haven't paid me much attention."

"They killed our mother."

Mary sighed sadly. "They did. She'd erected a great many personal wards and over time Susan couldn't get anything out of her. Killing her was the way to free everything left over. I doubt your mother would have imagined they'd actually kill her. She was smart, your mother. Smart enough to ward Renee with her own blood, the wards she has are bone deep, which is what kept her alive I'd wager. But even just a decade or two ago this sort of targeting for theft of magic, *killing* for it, wouldn't have been commonplace. These thieves' numbers have only recently begun to rise."

"And unfortunately, Carlos de La Vega has given them enough information that they've leapt years ahead in intelligence gathering." Arel spoke, looking at Max, "I'm sorry about this. I'm sorry to have to reveal this to you. No one should have to deal with the betrayal of family."

"No, they shouldn't. But that's all on Carlos and he won't be a threat to anyone again."

Max and Arel shared a moment of understanding. Kendra leaned her head on Max's shoulder for a moment and his cat eased back a little.

Rosemary looked to Renee. "They killed your mother, found they couldn't kill you and instead took you along, stealing your energy slowly over time. Just a year ago, they hooked up with the group of mages who attacked you. It wasn't until Carlos, until you mated with Jack and Carlos apparently got crazy angry and told these thugs all about you. They've got quite a racket, stealing magic, using the anti-paranormal movement to get their information on the whereabouts of witches ripe for their victimization. Worse, one of them became obsessed with you. Instead of slowly siphoning—and this is what happened each time you had one of your mental breakdowns, it was your body's way of shutting down and trying to protect itself from them—he went rogue and decided that killing you would be his way of not only taking your power, but possessing you in the bargain."

Mary turned those pale green eyes to Kendra. "And you they didn't bargain for at all. Not until, again, Carlos. When Renee confronted Andrew and Susan about you, they panicked and bolted. They're in trouble with their so-called friends who want you badly."

"They want us all." Arel sat forward. "Question is, how do we handle them?"

Kendra looked to Max, who gave her a narrowed glare but broke off with a sigh. "We fight. You have our jamboree behind you. After all, we're threatened too and Kendra is our alpha now as well."

Jack nodded. "And the wolves. I spoke briefly with Cade Warden, the National Pack alpha and he's given me the green light to cooperate with you."

Gibson sat back in his chair and eyed them all. "Well then, let's get this show started, shall we? Kendra and Max have to attend a meeting tonight where they must inform our cats one of their own has betrayed them. My parents will need some time away and yet, time is of the essence."

"Step one is getting witches on board and training them all." Sadira looked to Kendra. "You know you're going to stir a lot of anger and fear. There'll be success, too. But also estrangement and accusations. Witches love drama. Some will embrace that instead of the harsh realities we offer."

Kendra shrugged. "Fuck 'em. We have to be strong or become meat. I have no intention of becoming meat for anyone."

Max took her hand, kissing it. "We'll fight and we'll win."

267

About the Author

To learn more about Lauren Dane, please visit www.laurendane.com. Send an email to Lauren at laurendane@laurendane.com or stop by her messageboard to join in the fun with other readers as well. www.laurendane.com/messageboard.